AUTOPSY OF A FAIRYTALE

AUTOPSY
OF A
FAIRYTALE

NICOLE SCARANO

Paperback ISBN: 979-8-9871935-3-2
Hardcover ISBN: 979-8-9871935-4-9

Cover by Fay Lane
Character Art & Crime Scene Sketches by Mary Begletsova
(@marybegletsova)
Interior Formatting by Nicole Scarano Formatting & Design

Contents

For China.
Cerberus exists because of my love for you.

Author's Note

This book was previously published as a Kindle Vella, but it has been reformatted to be read as a book and includes never before seen crime scene sketches! Each book/season will be a new crime, but the overarching story of Bel, Eamon, & Cerberus will weave through the series and end on slight cliffhangers. If you would like to read along, you may read the next book on Kindle Vella, or you can wait for the book and the fun bonus art.

This is a darker crime series, so I would like to take this opportunity to say that some of the crimes will be violent and weird. Rest assured, I do not write about SA, but this is not a cozy mystery. There will be romance of course! (How can you do Beauty & the Beast without a love story). The romance will be a sexy PG13 (think Vampire Diaries, Grey's Anatomy, etc.) - I also want to point out that while I did do research into crime scene investigation, I will be speeding up some of the processes. I also set this story in a fictional town (Bajka means Fairy-tale/Fable/Story in Polish) so that I can take liberties with some of the procedures and police structures. Plus with the fairytale elements, I wanted the freedom to bend the rules of nature.

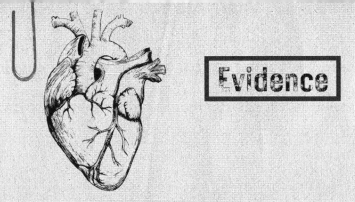

Chapter One

TEETH. IT WAS ALWAYS THE TEETH THAT WOKE HER. THE WAY they scraped. The way she bled. The nightmare of that memory haunted her. Forced her to suffer through every painful second of that night. Every broken bone. Every tear in her flesh until the teeth scored her skin. Then, and only then, would she wake, paralyzed by fear, the sting still coating her throat.

A heavy weight shifted at the bottom of the mattress, and all seventy pounds of furry muscles heaved onto her chest like a living, weighted blanket. Only once his soft head nuzzled her neck did she relax. She was safe in her bed, not bleeding out on the street, and her arms wrapped around her pitbull. He was her best boy, always sensing her panic and driving it away before replacing it with pure adoration. She breathed in his scent, letting the mix of fur and shampoo ground her, but it wasn't until his tongue licked the tears from her cheeks that she realized she was crying. The nightmares came less and less since adopting Cerberus, but when the memory hit, it struck with a vicious malice that left her crippled. After the attack, sleep had been nearly impossible. The stench of blood filled her nostrils. The crack of her bones rang in her ears, and the paralyzing fear that settled like chains on her limbs would pin her to the bed long after she woke. They said she was lucky. She had survived, but *fortunate* was not one of the words she used to describe herself. Her words, the ones that plagued her darkest hours, were ugly. Cruel. Unforgiving.

Until she met Cerberus, the seventy-pound black pitbull with cropped ears that the shelter claimed was friendly but unadoptable because of his harsh appearance. His face captured her attention the instant she wandered into the kennel. She was alone and single, and one Saturday, still limping and in pain, she saw a flyer for a local adoption event. Fate dragged her to his cage, and while the other prospective dog parents avoided him like he was diseased, his gravity drew her to his door. She was helpless against his pull, and one look into his soft brown eyes was all it took to convince her. He was her dog. Her best friend. Her good boy. She was well acquainted with evil. She had stared it in its rotten soul and survived. This animal was pure goodness, and she adopted him on the spot. He was named Cerberus after the three-headed hellhound of Hades, and that name felt prophetic. The Cerberus of myth guarded the Underworld, and the black pitbull guarded her darkness. Her furry beast with a beautiful soul.

Isobel Emerson pushed Cerberus off her chest with a kiss on his meaty head and escaped the confines of her sweaty sheets. Months had passed since the assault that haunted her sleep. Most of her peace was thanks to the bed hog currently digging at her pillows, but the transfer to Bajka reduced how often she looked over her shoulder. Bel—her father had given her the affectionate nickname, and it stuck with her all these years later—had been a fearless cop in her twenties, but making detective at thirty-one in New York City corrupted something deep inside of her. She had seen humanity's underbelly. Its darkest, cruelest self, but it wasn't until the attack that the fear she kept chained down in her soul broke free. She remembered little of that night. She had answered a call that led her and six other police officers to an abandoned warehouse, but the chaos that exploded upon their arrival separated her from the group. The doctors blamed her memory loss on the lingering trauma from the ordeal, but Bel never believed their explanation. Something happened that night that left her alone in the darkness, a fruit ripe for plunder. The assault was vicious; the attacker driven by bloodlust. Bel had never experienced such excruciating pain, and as she fought and failed to escape the powerful assailant, she knew that was how she would end. A homicide victim the likes of which she swore to protect.

But despite the holes in her recollection, one thing she always remembered was the teeth. Sharp and filled with dread, they dragged across her skin, cutting like a surgeon's blade. They carved up her flesh as if they were a sculpture's chisel and she the marble. The ripping had started at her throat before plunging down her chest to her belly, and then, as suddenly as it began, the teeth abandoned her shredded body. No one could explain the attacker's actions. Every fractured part of her pointed to his intentions. He didn't crave her fear. He wanted her death, but moments before he finally claimed her for the darkness, he fled. She was alive, scarred but alive because a predator had inexplicably discarded his prey.

Bel found it impossible to remain in the city after the doctors cleared her to return to work. Every building, every siren, every alley held a threat. Something in her broke, and she seized the first escape she could find. Bajka—a quaint and relatively crimeless town—needed a detective, and she had a moving truck packed before the ink was dry on her contract. Beast of a dog in tow, she rented a small cabin on the outskirts of the town a few hours south of the city and fled New York.

Bel shuffled into her rustic kitchen and pulled a pitcher from the fridge before filling a glass. The nightmare had ripped sleep from her body, flinging it out of reach, and she leaned against the sink as she drank the cold water. The cabin was a single, large room, her bed only feet away from where she stood, and she savored the cool liquid calming her dry throat as she watched Cerberus snore. At least one of them was enjoying the king-sized mattress that dominated half of her home.

The clock on the microwave read 4:00 a.m. in angry red letters, and Bel glared at it as she shoved the pitcher back into the fridge. A light outside caught her attention as she put her cup in the sink, and she peered out the picture frame window, watching Vera move around her cabin. The elderly woman was Bel's first friend in Bajka. She owned the cabin on the opposite side of the grassy yard, and Bel watched her grey curls bob in and out of view. From her movements, it looked like Vera was cleaning her kitchen, and Bel smirked before snagging her book off the table. Ships passing in the night, both women were unable to sleep. One due to her age, and the other to her demons.

Cerberus had stretched out over both pillows, and Bel surrendered any hope of shoving him out of her way. She settled below him, head resting on his snore-rumbling ribs, and she cracked open the novel, her eyes drowning in the written words that always brought her peace. Suddenly she was no longer Detective Isobel Emerson plagued by anxiety but Louise the pirate, running from the only man who loved—

The ringing phone jarred her awake, her forgotten book slipping off her chest as she rolled toward the bedside table.

"Emerson," she groaned into her cell, eyes too blurry to decipher the name on the screen.

"Bel?" Hesitation edged her partner's voice, and she sat up, his tone a warning to brace for what was coming. "I'm sorry to bother you on your day off, but you need to see this."

THE CLOCK on the microwave read 8:30 a.m., and with a swipe of annoyance coated in apprehension, Bel turned the coffee pot on as she shoved her legs into her black jeans, tripping as she struggled to do too many things at once. She'd been grateful that her nightmare had the decency to arrive on her day off, and she had switched off her alarm, hoping the extra sleep would atone for the lost midnight hours, but the urgency in her partner's voice killed any lingering exhaustion. She had not received a call filled with such dread since New York, and the knot of fear that this quiet town had finally loosened, coiled with a vengeance in her gut. The timing of her dream made sense. It was an omen. A warning. A threat.

"Outside?" She gripped the door handle and looked pointedly at Cerberus, but the pitbull made no move to get off the bed. She had promised to take him hiking in the woods that backed up to her cabin, and while she knew the dog didn't understand ninety-five percent of the ramblings she directed at him, the accusation in his brown eyes seemed to call her a liar today.

"I'm sorry," Bel coaxed. "If you won't do it for me, how about for a cookie?"

Cerberus slid off the bed with an agile thunk and padded to the door, strolling outside as Bel rolled her eyes. If only all of life's problems could be solved by cookies.

The pitbull roamed the yard as she pulled on a shirt, thankful she had opted to shower before bed instead of waiting for morning, and poured the coffee into a travel mug. She scooped Cerberus' food into his bowl, topping it with the promised dog treats. A moth drawn to the flame, the furry beast raced inside at the sound of the bowl clinking against the floor, and Bel kissed his meaty head before locking the cabin behind her. As she passed the kitchen window, she peeked in at him as he licked his dish clean, and her heart longed to turn back, grab all seventy pounds of his comfort, and take him with her. She feared she would need his calm support today, yet she had to leave him home. A crime scene was no place for an untrained animal, regardless of his sharp instincts and protective nature. As if he sensed her watching him, Cerberus jerked his gaze to hers and wagged his tail. The little whip was so powerful, she heard it thwack the cabinet drawers, and she smiled, waving at him before walking to her car.

Twenty minutes later, Bel pulled up at the address her partner had given her, surprised by the chaos swarming the building. *Lumen's Customs*, owned by Brett Lumen, was home to both his workshop and showroom. Bel had wandered inside once when she first arrived in Bajka, but the prices of his custom furniture drove her back outside and across town to the thrift store. The man was an artist of unmatched skill, his craftsman-ship crossing all mediums. People came from all over the country to purchase or commission his one-of-a-kind pieces, and as Bel approached the deputy monitoring the perimeter entrance, she wondered what exorbitantly expensive piece of furniture had been stolen.

"Morning, Detective," the deputy said as she flashed her badge and passed through the police barrier. The yellow tape encased the entire building, blocking off even the parking lot from the onlookers and media, and Bel's heart constricted. *Why was there this much tape?*

"Bel," a smooth voice interrupted her concern, and her part-ner, Garrett Cassidy, jogged over to her. "Thanks for coming. I know it's your day off, but…" he trailed off.

"What happened?" The pit in her stomach gaped ruthlessly wide at his hesitation, at the unnerving edge in his voice. At six foot one with curly brown hair and hazelnut eyes, thirty-five-year-old Garrett was storybook handsome, strong and soft and sweet around the edges, which was why the tension in his face terrified her. It didn't belong there, not on features so gentle.

"Emerson," Sheriff Griffin interrupted, and Bel watched as the man strode toward them. In his early fifties, with specks of grey gracing his beard, the Sheriff was kind and intelligent, remarkably fit for his age, and he made an excellent boss. "Thanks for coming. I asked Cassidy to call you because I want you to run lead on this. We'll need your experience."

Bel froze, her feet growing roots to anchor her where she stood. Her experience? She was a homicide detective. This wasn't a case of stolen furniture, and her nightmare flooded her consciousness. *Teeth, always the teeth.* She should have known they heralded a dark foreboding.

"What happened?" She wasn't ready to plunge headfirst back into the fray.

"I think it's best if you see for yourself... so you can form your own opinions." The Sheriff handed her protective gear, and she slipped the sterilized covers over her shoes before snapping on a pair of gloves.

Once all three of them were covered, Garrett led the way into Lumen's Customs, but he lingered in the entrance to allow her to enter alone, her view unobstructed.

Bel sucked in a fortifying breath, forcing her professional shell to assume control before she stepped into the showroom. Looming windows lit the impeccable space, the high ceilings offering a sense of grandeur, but she hardly noticed them. All her sight registered was what hovered in the center of the room, its grotesque form both magnificent and disturbing, and her breath caught painfully in her throat. She couldn't breathe at the vision, at the beauty, at the terror. Her lungs constricted. Her heart thundered.

"Oh my god." Her voice broke free from her lips, the tremble of those three small words insufficient to convey the depths of her shock.

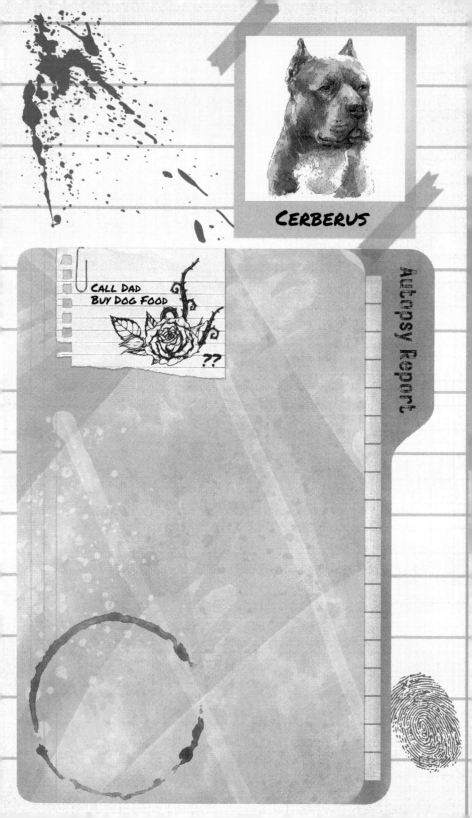

CERBERUS

CALL DAD
BUY DOG FOOD

??

Autopsy Report

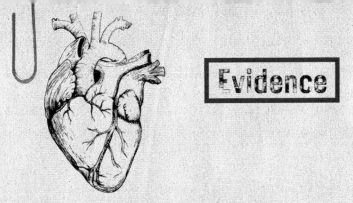

Chapter Two

"THE VICTIM IS BRETT LUMEN, THE FORTY-EIGHT-YEAR-OLD owner of Lumen's Customs." Garrett's voice broke through the shock engulfing Bel's brain, ripping her from her tortured memories and depositing her harshly in the present. "His assistant Violet Lennon discovered him at approximately 8 a.m. this morning when she arrived for work."

"Medical examiner?" Bel heard her question as if it came from someone else's mouth, pushing through thick waves of fog to reach her ears.

"Should be here any minute," Garrett answered.

"Has anyone touched the body?" Bel fiddled with the elastic of her gloves. She had transferred to Bajka to escape death, to hide from torture, yet in all her years on the force, nothing compared to what stared down mockingly at her for attempting to outrun life's horrors.

"No, not since we arrived," Garrett confirmed. "Violet said she took one look at this and dialed 911. Didn't even enter the showroom."

"Has anyone collected any evidence?" Bel was stalling, and she hoped Garrett was oblivious to it. No amount of time could prepare her to step closer, but the lie of '*just a few more minutes*' steadied her.

"No," Garrett said. "Sheriff Griffin wanted you to take the lead, start to finish. You are the only one with…" he trailed off as if afraid to voice the truth.

"Homicide experience," she finished for him, and his muscles flinched slightly at her words. He seemed as disturbed as she was, and with a deep breath and the resolve of a thirty-four-year-old New York City detective, Bel squared her shoulders. A brutal attack had not destroyed her. Neither would this horror, and judging by the uncertainty circulating the room, every tech and deputy needed someone to look to for direction. The brutality that had reared its ugly head this morning demanded a performance unlike any in this room had ever given, and if Bel expected the officers to rise to the occasion, she would have to discard the demons clutching at her ankles. To lead the investigation into the torment before them.

"He wants everything done right," Garrett continued. "Bajka has seen nothing like this."

"I don't think anyone has seen anything like this," Bel said, meeting her partner's disbelieving eyes, and she gripped his forearm for comfort. Hers or his? She wasn't sure.

"I'm going to take a look before the M.E. handles the body." She thanked God her voice didn't falter as she addressed the crowd. "Then we search and photograph every inch of this room. Make sure you get every angle—wide, medium, and close. Everyone needs to wear protective gear. This didn't happen by accident. This was not a spur-of-the-moment decision. We need to document everything. No mistakes. No oversights."

The few techs and deputies present nodded their understanding, and then Bel stepped into the showroom. The closer she walked, the more the oppressive darkness pushed against her skin, filled her lungs, muddled her brain. There was no mistaking the evil defiling the air. Mankind harbored some of the world's most savage monsters, and as she drifted closer, Bel knew one such terror had entered her town.

Lumen's showroom was clean and spacious, the tall windows offering gorgeous natural light. Normally displaying his high-end furniture, the room currently stood bare save for one work of exquisitely terrifying art positioned at the center of the floor. Rising taller than Garrett, beautifully sculpted wood and twisted metal rose from the ground on a sturdy base before it branched out into a nest of multiple curved candlesticks, radiating out from all sides of the body. Wax dripped down from the puddled remains of thick, white candles, and a wide candlestick protruded from the center to complete the structure. A Chandelier. And while most light fixtures of this design hung from the ceiling, this carving rested atop a broad, floor-standing foundation. Towering over even Garrett's six-foot frame, Bel did not have to step closer to understand why the constructed piece was so large or why it was carved so securely. Its reason was as plain as the pooled wax, as the claw foot base, as the metal coiled and welded tight around the wood to ensure its form held. For built into the light fixture to serve as its skeleton was Brett Lumen.

His head made the centermost candlestick. The melting wax dripped over his eyes and mouth, giving his skin a pallid, synthetic appearance. Both of his arms curved skywards in a 'U' shape around his skull, forming two of the chandelier's branches. Ornately chiseled wood buckled in place by metal rings supported them, forcing his palms to face heavenward to serve as holds for the once burning candles. The multitude of surrounding candlesticks held no flesh in their thinner curves, and they bloomed around his shoulders in exquisite uniformity as if designed for the entrance of a castle instead of a wooden death shroud.

The melting wax had singed some of the skin closest to the candles, and Bel clenched her fists as she slowly circled the body. Lumen's legs and hips were entombed within the structure's base, his lower half hidden by the sculpture. His stomach and back stood naked, thick screws drilled into his flesh to hold the more delicate carvings to his corpse. His torso was bare besides the wax and wood, and Bel guessed he was naked from head to toe. Clothing would mar this macabre masterpiece of art, and whoever did this had taken great pains to perfect every curve, every screw, every position.

"There's no blood." Bel leaned closer to one of the screws drilled into Lumen's shoulder blade. Each smooth arch of wood was pristine, each screw and metal ring shining. The killer took pride in his work. He wouldn't have wanted stains marring his art. "The M.E. will confirm, but I suspect Brett was killed first, cleaned, and then assembled."

"How?" Garrett cleared his throat. "How does someone do this?"

"It was clearly premeditated," Bel said, squatting to examine the claw foot base. The designs looked like the feet of a beast, the claws sharp and curved, ready to rip flesh free from bones. "Someone planned this for a long time. They tailored every inch of this to Lumen's body." She stood up, gesturing to a slender coil of wood that wrapped around the pale ribs. "The killer knew how tall, how heavy and wide Lumen was. They also encased him in some of the most beautiful furniture I have ever seen, a piece Brett Lumen himself would strive to produce. A furniture designer entombed in the works he loved most."

"It's disgusting," Garrett blurted, and Bel quirked an eyebrow at him. "Sorry, I don't mean to be disrespectful, but someone killed Brett and turned him into furniture. And as if that wasn't enough, they peeled open his chest."

Bel finished her circle of the body and settled beside her partner, staring at the gaping hole in Lumen's ribs. She had noticed that gruesome wound instantly, but she had needed a minute to fortify herself for the gore, choosing to examine the craftsmanship first to ground her emotions.

"I can understand the chandelier's inspiration," Garrett said, gesturing to the monstrosity before them. "Lumen was well known for his work. People from all over the country paid thousands to own his pieces. His furniture was unique. He refused to create duplicates, so entombing him in a one-of-a-kind piece is almost sickly poetic. But why carve open his chest to show his heart?"

Bel leaned forward, careful not to touch the body, and examined the gaping wound. The flesh and bones above Lumen's heart had been ripped apart, the missing pieces absent from the crime scene. The wound had not been carved with any recognizable blade, but instead, gave off the impression that a massive clawed hand had reached into his chest and tore it free. The claw foot base flashed through her mind, and Bel shoved down the foreboding flickering to life in her gut. Her first thought upon seeing the design had been this exact act. Claws tearing flesh.

"Everything about this scene is making a statement," Bel said, careful to avoid the carved claws inches away from her shoes. "The body encased in furniture. The wound mimicking the—"

She froze mid-sentence, her voice lodging painfully in her throat. She leaned forward again, this time focusing on the cavity and not the torn skin. She had been too busy comparing the mangled and missing flesh to the carvings, but staring at it now, she wasn't sure how she missed it.

With rapid steps, she lunged backward to get the full view. The base of the structure was composed of bestial clawed feet, but the coiling wood and metal that wrapped around the body formed intricately carved branches and vines. Delicate leaves and thorns decorated the sculpture, the melted wax gifting it with an otherworldly glow, and she understood.

"It's a rosebush," Bel said, and Garrett looked at her with raised eyebrows. "The statue is a rosebush, and that's not his heart. Those are rose petals."

13

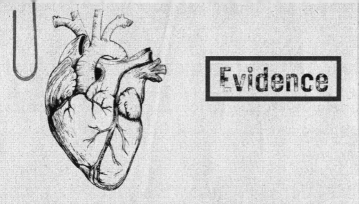

Chapter Three

MEDICAL EXAMINER, LINA THUM, ARRIVED WITH SOME WARNING of what to expect—unlike Bel who had entered the scene blind—since she had the unfortunate job of transporting Lumen's entombed body to the morgue, but even knowing what awaited her in the showroom did not prepare her for the monstrous reality of a man encased in a human-sized light fixture. Her straightforward approach to life was one reason she was so good at her job. She never beat around the bush or sugar-coated her words, but even her no-nonsense attitude experienced a temporary shutdown and reboot at the beautifully crafted heart of petals blooming in Brett's chest.

"This entire piece won't fit in my van," Lina said after she examined Lumen and made her declaration of death. Her professional mannerisms were fully in control, but Bel still heard the threads of unnerved awe woven into her words. "The killer assembled the statue around the body, so let's attempt to remove parts of the base and the arms for transport, but everything screwed into flesh remains until I get him to the morgue."

"Do you have any idea when he was killed?" Bel asked as

Lina began directing deputies on how to dismantle the furniture without disrupting evidence.

"Because rigor mortis is still present, I estimate some time yesterday," she answered. "I'll know more once I complete the autopsy, but that makes the most sense since his showroom was closed every Sunday. Almost everyone in this town knows this building is abandoned, save for Brett, from Saturday night until Monday morning. Killing him and then assembling this piece would have taken hours, and yesterday was the only uninterrupted opportunity available. Did you notice the lack of blood?" Lina pointed to a screw protruding from Brett's ribs, and Bel stepped closer despite having already studied the pale skin.

"There is no blood at the drill sites," Lina continued. "Combined with the very little lividity, I believe he was drained and washed before this was assembled. At least he was dead before they mutilated his body." The group fell silent for a moment, the gravity of her statement sinking achingly deep within their chests. This had been a man, a human being. No one deserved this level of disgrace, even if their spirit had already vacated their flesh.

"We've found no traces of blood," Garrett said as Thum resumed her careful disassembly. "We'll keep looking, but someone cleaned the room well... too well."

"Or he wasn't killed here," Lina added.

"You said anyone friendly with Brett would know the showroom was closed on Sundays?" Bel asked, sidestepping a deputy as he peeled back a curve of wood. "This chandelier was tailored to fit his body, which leads me to believe his killer had been studying him. Knowing he would be alone here aligns with that theory."

"My sister came to visit last year, and her husband had read an article about Lumen's Customs," Lina said. "He wanted a tour, but it was a Sunday, so he never got the chance. Lumen was a relatively quiet guy. In all the years I've lived here, I rarely saw him, but from what I understand, he didn't break his routine."

Bel exchanged a look with Garrett. "I don't think he was killed somewhere else. The showroom's size offered the perfect workspace, and the attached workshop is stocked with tools. Even if he brought his own, which I believe he did based on the premeditation this required, he would have had access to tools he might not have foreseen needing."

"He?" Garrett asked. "Are you using the term in a general sense, or do you think the killer is male?"

"My guess is he is male," Bel answered. "I'm having a hard time visualizing a woman possessing the strength to pull this off. Honestly, I am having a hard time picturing anyone doing this, but Lumen wasn't small, and this piece is extensive. I could be wrong, of course, and I'm hesitant to profile our killer until we learn more, but I think we're looking for a man. A powerful one at that."

As if to reinforce her point, Lina stumbled, trying to remove one of the bigger carvings from the body, but a deputy caught her before she fell hard on her tailbone. Bel quirked her eyebrows at Garrett, and he nodded as he stared at his partner. Bel was fit, her job and her love of hiking with Cerberus strengthening her muscles, but he still couldn't picture her pulling this off. He wasn't even sure he could handle a task of this enormity alone.

"We could be looking at more than one killer," Garrett said as Lina and three deputies wrestled the body into a black back. "This took extraordinary skill and strength. Something or someone had to hold him in place as they constructed the surrounding chandelier."

"It's entirely possible." Bel watched them wheel Lumen out of the showroom, hoping something in this chaos would speak to her. Experience told her to never deal in absolutes without evidence, but the way this homicide settled in her bones warned her that nothing about this case would resolve as expected. That, for all their speculation, it would defy their logical explanations.

Garrett nodded, and the crime scene, finally vacant the body, flurried to life. Cameras flashed. Voices murmured, and every inch of the floor was searched in a grid pattern. The sun rose higher as the morning blurred to afternoon. Stomachs rumbled in spite of death's stench, and by the time they had scoured the showroom, Bel's stomach had tied itself into an uncomfortable knot. Her eyes burned, bloodshot and dry, and she desperately needed another cup of coffee to face the last half of this cruelly bizarre day. They had found nothing. No abnormalities stood out of place. No blood hid in any crevasses. Fingerprints didn't stain any surfaces, despite Brett having touched them on a daily basis. Lumen's Customs was spotless, cleaner than the day it was built.

"There are no signs of forced entry," Garrett said as he settled beside Bel in the rear workshop. It too had been scrubbed, not even a speck of sawdust waiting to be unearthed. It was clean, too clean, and Bel's stomach twisted from uneasy to painful as if a phantom hand had coiled her organs into a loop and yanked them tight. Lumen's Customs was the type of estab-lishment that survived in a constant pristine state due to the owner's habits, but this absence of all but sunshine and air? The abnormal sterileness set her teeth on edge. She felt like she had walked onto a stage, a freshly designed workshop meant to mimic reality without ever experiencing the filth of the living. The perfection was as unnatural as the body's pose. It nagged at Bel's gut, taunting her with a meaning that hovered beyond her grasp. How had someone killed and positioned Brett Lumen and cleaned all traces of human life from the building? In her experi-ence, there was always something that led to the guilty party's downfall. No one could achieve this level of sterilization, yet there she stood without so much as a pile of dust tarnishing the floors.

"No signs of robbery from what we can see," Garrett continued. "Brett either knew his killer and let them in, or they had a key. There is a safe upstairs in his apartment, but it appears untouched, as are his other pieces of furniture, which are all worth thousands."

"You don't kill someone like that to steal from them," Bel said, not meeting her partner's eyes as she stared at the back of the workshop. "Was the apartment cleaned too?"

"No," Garrett followed her line of sight. "It is organized. Brett seemed to enjoy structure and cleanliness, but there are signs of life upstairs. Fingerprints on handles, garbage in the cans, hairs on the pillow. My guess is Lumen let his killer in and never made it back upstairs... Bel, what are you staring at?"

"The security footage." She gestured to the rear of the room, and Garrett finally noticed the dark monitors sitting on the desk against the wall. "It's been disabled."

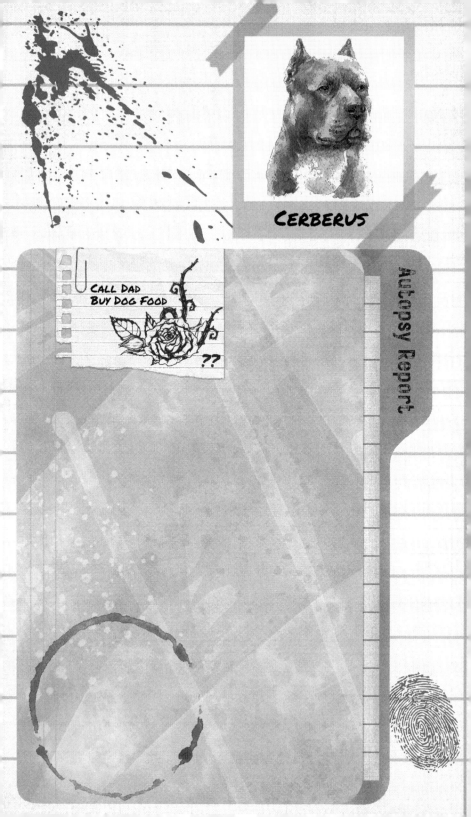

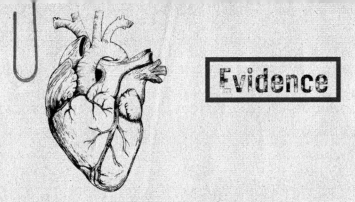

Chapter Four

A DEPUTY RETURNED FROM A COFFEE RUN, AND BEL GUZZLED the cup of lukewarm liquid in the time it took Garrett to call Lumen's security company. She desperately needed something to eat, but the knot in her stomach twisted tighter with each passing hour, and the idea of food made her go as pale as Lumen's bloodless body.

"They store their client's footage, but their contracts have strict privacy clauses," Garrett said as he snagged a cup of coffee and downed it almost as fast as she had. "If we get a warrant, they'll gladly turn over all of Brett's stored footage, though, which I don't think we'll have a problem getting. The killer may have disabled the cameras, but if he was watching Lumen, maybe he was caught on tape."

"Hmm," Bel grunted in agreement before nodding at a woman in her mid-twenties standing outside the perimeter. Bel had used drinking her coffee as a shield to study those congregated, hoping someone would stand out. Killers, especially those prone to theatrics, often lingered to watch the police, but it seemed half of Bajka had gathered along the road. Even Vera stood in the crowd, comforting onlookers with her warm smiles, and for a solid thirty seconds, Bel contemplated asking her neighbor if she had brought any of the baked goods she constantly was making. She really needed to eat something.

Bel's gaze returned to the girl. Her visage was the only one that snagged the detective's attention. The young woman had long, straight black hair with cute fringe bangs, and she wore black-rimmed glasses, a black pencil skirt ensemble, and black stilettos that Bel would have had to work for a year just to afford. "Who is that?" she asked her partner

"Violet Lennon," Garrett answered after he followed her line of sight. "Brett's assistant. She found the body."

"Did you get her statement?"

"A deputy did, yes."

"And she's still here?" Bel's feet were uncomfortable in her sensible shoes, and she reflexively stretched her back, her vertebra popping in protest. She couldn't imagine how the girl still looked regal all these hours later as she towered over everyone in her designer heels.

"Wouldn't you if it were Griffin?" Garrett asked, and Bel nodded, choosing not to point out that if the Sheriff had been murdered, it would be her job to stay. Her eyes flicked to her partner, studying his pinched eyebrows and ruffled hair. Normally so classically distinguished, he looked frazzled and uneasy, and she had to remind herself that he was not accustomed to violence the same way she was. A murder as unfathomable as this would both capture and immobilize this town. Death was a cruel and intoxicating master, enslaving not only its victims but also the living caught in its wake. It was a difficult task to resist its pull. Even fleeing hundreds of miles could not save her from its hold. Death had followed Bel, reminding her she was bound to it, a servant to it, and her neck stung at the memory of sharpened teeth. Violet Lennon had felt the grip of darkness when she discovered her boss, the scene's gravity denying her an escape. It made sense she still hovered on the outskirts, unless… Bel shot Garrett a look. Killers often lingered to watch their masterpieces unfold.

"I want to talk to her." Bel stalked off toward Violet, and Garrett hurried after her. As they closed in on the refined girl with her immaculately manicured purple nails, Bel doubted she had more than a superficial role in this morning's events. Based on the lack of wrinkles in her skirt, the perfection of her straightened hair, and the impeccable blend of makeup on her face, this model of a woman clearly had spent her morning before a mirror, not cleaning up the lingering gore from ripping a man's heart free from his chest. Bel unconsciously tucked her own brunette waves behind her ear. She was a natural beauty with big blue eyes, soft curls, and dark eyebrows defined enough without makeup, but the flawless grace in front of her would have made even the most gorgeous of women insecure.

Violet smiled nervously as the detectives approached, and the shudder of intimidation Bel had felt vanished. The girl wore kindness in her eyes. No hint of superiority graced her aura, and as they settled before her, Bel noted the woman's size. She towered above Bel, only because of the dangerously spiked stilettos. If both women were barefoot, Bel would have been significantly taller and stronger. Violet was thin and delicate, and Bel was all toned limbs and lean muscles. Power coiled in the detective's body, a strength of both will and muscle, but not even she could have handled mounting Lumen's corpse like a macabre trophy. If her strength would have failed her, the chandelier would have crushed the assistant.

"Violet Lennon, I'm Detective Isobel Emerson, and this is my partner, Detective Garrett Cassidy. Do you mind if we ask you some questions?" Bel asked as the young woman stood to attention.

"Of course not." Violet's voice was as kind as her eyes, a sharp contrast to her black ensemble.

"You found the body, correct?" Bel asked, and Violet

flinched before nodding. "I am sorry for your loss and that you had to be the one to find him," Bel continued, sensing the girl needed an offering of comfort. Up close, she could tell Violet's eyes were red and swollen, and her makeup was smudged where she had attempted to reapply it after her tears dried.

"Thank you." Violet nodded, her gaze snagging on Garrett for a second too long before returning to Bel.

"Can you walk us through this morning?" Bel asked, wondering if Garrett's handsome features would loosen the girl's tongue or cause a distraction.

"Yes, um…" Violet paused as if to fortify herself. "The shop opens at 9:00 a.m. Monday through Friday. Saturdays are by appointment only unless Mr. Lumen is hosting an event. I usually arrive at 8:00 a.m., and Mr. Lumen is always awake and in his workshop by then. His schedule is rigid. He goes to bed early and wakes up at 5:00 a.m. every morning, no matter what. He makes a big pot of coffee first thing, which he drinks black, but he keeps hazelnut creamer in his fridge because he knows it's my favorite. We always drink a cup together before we open. He was nice, even if he was eccentric." Violet swiped a tear from her cheek. "I'm sorry." She hiccupped as she fought the sobs.

"It's okay. Take your time." Garrett patted her arm reassuringly, and Violet leaned into the contact, his soothing voice seeming to center her. Bel would have rolled her eyes, except she understood Garrett's pull. Classically handsome and sweet, he was a storybook prince come to life, and she often wondered why he chose such a violent line of work.

"Thank you." Violet smiled as she dug in her purse, withdrawing a tissue. "This morning, I unlocked the shop like usual, but the minute I stepped inside, I knew something was off. It smelled like bleach and caustic cleaners, not coffee. Mr. Lumen was a particular man. He liked everything organized and clean, so the smell, while overpowering, wasn't unusual, but the lack of coffee was. He hired me right after I graduated college, and ever since, he has had a pot of Emily's dark roast waiting for me when I arrive. It's the only kind he drank, and he had me order it in bulk every few weeks."

Emily Kaffe owned The Espresso Shot, and her coffee shop was a local legend. The woman was magic with her brews, and most of the locals either got their morning fix from her shop or brewed her grinds at home. Even Bel's long-finished to-go thermos she prepped that morning had been filled with Emily's famous French Vanilla.

"What happened after you unlocked the shop?" Bel asked, suddenly craving a latte despite having just downed a cup of tepid caffeine. Of all the days to barely sleep.

"I didn't find him in his workshop, so I checked his apartment upstairs. I thought maybe he was sick, but it was empty. We had no appointments scheduled, but I figured I should check the showroom in case. That's when I found him."

"Did you, by chance, touch the body?" Bel asked.

"Never." Violet looked like the question might make her vomit. "I took one look at him and dialed 911. Then I waited outside. I've been here ever since."

"You did the right thing," Garrett encouraged.

"Can you think of anyone who wanted to hurt Lumen?" Bel asked before Violet got lost in Garrett's eyes. "Did he have any enemies? Unhappy clients?"

"No one is ever an unhappy client." Violet pinned Bel with an aggressive stare. "That man was a genius. He might have been peculiar and lacking in social skills, but he was nice. Really nice. I mean, he hated creamer but kept his fridge stocked with hazelnut just for me. He paid me well and trusted me to run his day-to-day schedule and handle all the paperwork. He barely slept while working on a piece, and when his clients saw the finished furniture, half of them would cry. Mr. Lumen may have liked his life structured and predictable, but no one hated him. I don't know how anyone could be so barbaric to such a decent man?"

Bel didn't know how to answer that question. She believed herself to be a good person, yet someone had beaten her within an inch of her life, only to abandon her in a pool of her own blood. Sometimes life was cruel for cruelty's sake.

"We will do everything we can to catch who did this." Garrett slid seamlessly into the conversation, sensing Bel's hesitation. They had only been partners for a few months, but their vastly different puzzle pieces clicked together to form a whole. She was all darkness, and he was her light. She dwelled among the demons, but his smile was a gift from the angels. They complemented each other, and Bel was thankful he found his voice when she couldn't. She had shared little about her attack with him, but he knew enough to understand when she needed him to step in. Just as he understood this case was wildly beyond his capabilities and had handed her the reins.

"I need to ask, Violet, but where were you yesterday?" Bel forced her face to remain neutral.

"Running errands." To her relief, the girl answered without hesitation. "I got coffee and a bagel at The Espresso Shot for breakfast, and then I bought groceries, did laundry—the works. I went to dinner with some of my friends. I can give you their numbers for you to confirm, but then I went home and was in bed by 11:00 p.m. since I had to be up early for work."

"Thanks, a deputy will collect those from you," Garrett said. "What restaurant did you go to?"

"La Signora, the new Italian place."

"Was it good?" Garrett flashed an art-worthy smile, and some of the heaviness lifted from Violet's chest as she blushed a pale pink.

"It's great, you should go."

"I just might." He winked at her before his eyes drifted to

Bel, as if there was a meaning behind his statement she was supposed to understand.

"Thank you, Violet. We'll be in touch if we have any more questions." Bel handed the girl her card before turning to leave. The look on Garrett's face at the mention of the restaurant clenched her already knotted stomach, and she needed to escape this conversation before it took a turn she was wholly unprepared for.

"Thanks, Detective." Violet tucked the card into her purse.

"Actually, I do have one more question." Bel turned back to the pretty woman in black. "Was Lumen currently working with a client?"

"Yes..." Violet dug out her phone and tapped the screen with her delicate manicure. "Here it is," she said after a minute of scrolling. "A Mr. Eamon Stone is... was Mr. Lumen's last client, but I never met the man. He preferred all of his consultations to be in private."

Bel and Garrett exchanged a quick glance while the girl was preoccupied with her phone.

"He bought the old Reale Mansion. He plans to restore it, and he commissioned Mr. Lumen to design the furniture," Violet added.

"Someone bought that place?" Garrett asked with disbelief, and when Violet nodded, he let out an incredulous whistle.

"What's the Reale Mansion?" Bel sensed she was missing an unspoken importance.

"The Reale family founded Bajka," Garrett answered. "They owned most of the town and the surrounding forests, but decades ago, the family suffered bankruptcy. The last living heir died alone in that house, a widower without children, and it took two weeks before anyone found his remains. The mansion has been abandoned ever since. It's a massive estate, and in its day, I'm told it was magnificent, but now it looks like something out of a horror movie." Garrett turned his attention to Violet. "Even in disrepair, that estate is worth millions."

"Mr. Stone commissioned multiple pieces, but Mr. Lumen was currently only working on one," Violet said, nodding to confirm that Garrett's assumption was correct. The mysterious client was a man of exceeding wealth, and yet no one was aware of his presence in town besides the victim and his assistant.

"What piece was that?" Bel asked, trying to recall the unfinished furniture in the workshop, but all she could picture was Lumen's pale and contorted body.

"Let me check." Violet glanced back at her phone, nails clicking as she searched. "Here it is. The first piece Mr. Stone commissioned was a custom chandelier for his foyer."

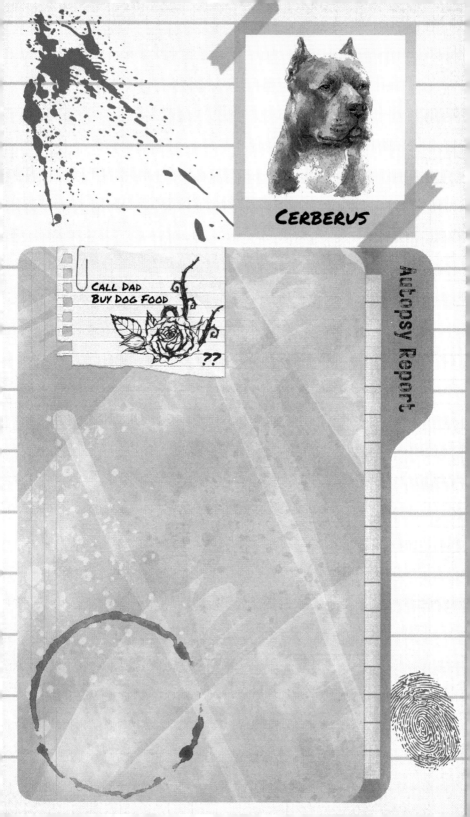

CERBERUS

Autopsy Report

CALL DAD
BUY DOG FOOD
??

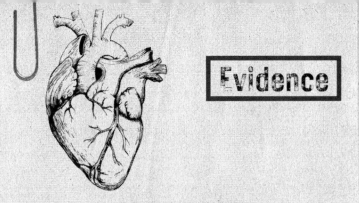

Chapter Five

VINEGAR DRIPPED DOWN BEL'S CHIN, BUT SHE COULDN'T BRING herself to care. The turkey and cheese layered with tomatoes and a dressed salad sandwiched between crispy bread was heaven, and she ignored the mess as she leaned against the hood of her car outside the deli. She hadn't eaten all day, and even though her stomach roiled in pain at the day's events, she couldn't stop eating.

"You got…" Garrett gestured at her chin and then smirked as he realized she both noticed the dressing dripping over her jaw and didn't care. With a gentle wipe, he lifted his napkin and cleaned her skin, his paper-clad touch lingering a fraction longer than it needed to. Bel's eyes snapped to his, and he read the wariness hidden in her gaze. He pulled his hand back and returned to his own sandwich, eyes staring ahead at the quaint street as he attempted to ignore the look she gave him. He tried even harder to ignore the scar on her throat. She rarely talked about why she moved from New York to a town that looked as if a picture book spat it out, but she didn't need to for him to recognize that something horrible had happened to the gorgeous brunette. The scars on her neck trailed low beneath her shirt, and he often found himself wondering just how far the angry flesh descended. No matter how often he thought about it, though, he learned quickly not to stare. It made her uncomfortable, and that was the last thing he wanted.

Bel bit off an unladylike bite, hoping it would mask the flush his fingers bloomed on her skin. She wasn't blind. Her partner was handsome. Like the brushstrokes of a sunset painting, he was bright and fresh and captivating. He was kind and intelligent, and she often felt his gaze when he thought she wasn't looking. She noticed how he found excuses to touch her; the contact always delivered innocently with reverent respect. If she had been any other woman, she would have lost herself in his warm brown eyes long ago, but every time she considered letting someone in, the sting of teeth savaged her neck, and her emotions shut down. She hadn't dated since the attack, her flesh still pink and angry with scars. Deep down, she knew they would mean nothing to a man who truly cared. She shouldn't be ashamed, but she was afraid to let someone see how far down her torso they descended. By the way Garrett sometimes studied the visible ones, she guessed they wouldn't faze him if she let him in, but she was apprehensive. The notion of anyone besides Cerberus touching her made her skin clammy. Not because a man had assaulted her in that way, but because the last hands to grip her body had fractured her bones, had begged to murder her. With a rough swallow, Bel forced both her bite and her anxiety down.

"Lumen has no next of kin to notify," she said, desperate to change the unspoken subject.

"Griffin notified his lawyer, who is the executor of his will." Garrett graciously humored her, not fighting the conversation's new direction. "It should give us someone to notify."

"On one hand, I'm relieved that we don't have to go knock on someone's door and ruin their day by telling them they lost a family member, but it also makes me sad he had no one. I don't know what I would do without my family."

"You have a big one?"

"Yeah." Bel picked a tomato slice off the sandwich and shoved it into her mouth. "My mom passed away years ago, but I'm the youngest of six sisters."

"Six girls? God bless your dad."

Bel nudged him in mock disapproval. "He loved having daughters. We all turned out differently, though. I'm the only one who followed in his footsteps. He was the chief of police before he retired."

"He must be proud of you."

Bel shrugged. She had been afraid moving to Bajka would disappoint her father. Her sisters lived within a few miles of their childhood home, but New York was no longer the same. She couldn't remain in the same city that her monster dwelled in. Her father's disappointment was all in her head, though. He under-stood better than most what happened to a person when confronted with their own mortality. Her oldest sister practically threw a fit when Bel accepted the position here, but her dad silently helped her pack her apartment and sent her off with a kiss and a promise to always be a phone call away.

"I am going to the autopsy in the morning to collect the evidence," Bel said, finishing her sandwich. "If I don't get off my feet, I may fall over on you, so see you then?" The familiar turn their conversation had taken filled her chest with anxiety, and she steered it back towards work.

"Of course. See you tomorrow." Garrett wiped his hands on his napkin before gathering their trash and throwing it into the garbage bin. "And thanks, Bel. Today was…" He gave up, unable to find the words to describe the hours he never expected he would have to endure.

"You're welcome."

"Hey." He stopped halfway to his own vehicle. "Have you ever seen anything like that?"

"Never."

"We see crime here, but nothing like this." He ran his fingers through his hair, the brown strands sticking up on end. "Don't tell anyone, but I'm afraid of what this means."

"You don't have to worry." Bel stepped forward, awkwardly patting his biceps before crossing her arms over her chest. "I feel the same, and I think we need to pay Eamon Stone a visit."

"Agreed." Garrett fished out his keys and sat in the driver's seat, hanging out so he could hold her gaze. "Get some sleep, Bel. You look like you need it."

"Thanks." Bel rolled her eyes good-naturedly. "Good night, Garrett."

"Night, partner." He sped off, and Bel turned her car toward her cabin on the outskirts of town. Her mind replayed the day as she drove, and by the time she pulled into the driveway, her stomach cramped uncomfortably. Thankfully, Cerberus was feet away, waiting to ease her stress with sloppy kisses and aggressive cuddles.

"Hi, baby beasty," she crooned as she opened the door, and seventy pounds of muscle barreled across the floor to collide with her shins. He had taken her out a few times when she first adopted him, his sheer size and power embarrassing her at the park the first time he chased a squirrel when she wasn't paying attention. She had been standing one second, and on her stomach the next, and when she had gotten home, she found grass stuck in her underwear. She still blushed when she remembered the expressions on the onlookers' faces as she ate dirt, but she was now accustomed to his exuberance. Her legs braced for impact, and she caught his thick chest as he slammed into her.

"I missed you," she murmured into his neck. "I wish you were with me today. I needed this." He bumped her face with his muscled head, his toes tap dancing across the wood floor as he tried to get closer.

"Did you miss me?" Cerberus' tail whipped through the air, a menace to anything in its way. "I love you too. Do you want to go outside?"

The dog almost knocked her to her tailbone as he shoved toward the door, and she barely hooked his leash on his collar before he flew out into the yard. He made a beeline for the woods, and, exhausted as she was, Bel let him force her into a walk.

Twenty minutes later, she had to bribe Cerberus with extra cookies to get him to agree to go home, and as they closed in on her cabin, a figure emerged from the trees. Bel squinted at the form until Vera's curly grey hair came into view.

"Vera," Bel called, and the older lady turned with an exuberant smile.

"Hi, sweetheart." She waved. "I haven't seen you all day. I thought you were off?"

"I was supposed to be." Bel remembered seeing Vera at the crime scene, but the woman must have been too busy with her comforting gossip to notice which officers were present. Bel moved around the trees to get closer to her friend, but the minute Cerberus caught sight of Vera, all hell broke loose.

He lunged and growled, jaws snapping at her neighbor, and Vera shrieked in terror. Her fear did nothing to deter the pitbull, and not wanting to face his aggression, the elderly woman launched into an unsteady run. Bel yelped at his sudden vicious-ness, digging her heels into the dirt to keep the dog at her side.

"I'm sorry," Bel yelled over the violence. "He is a rescue. I don't know what got into him."

Vera ignored her as she raced for her cabin, waving her wrin-kled hand behind her as she escaped, but the moment she disap-peared, Cerberus calmed. Gone was the demon-possessed animal, and Bel stared at him in disbelief. Cerberus looked tough, but he was the biggest softy she knew. He had not met Vera, but he interacted with other strangers regularly without reacting. She had never heard that low snarl escape his fangs before.

"Cerberus, what just happened?" she asked, but the dog simply wagged his tail as if nothing was wrong.

THE NEXT MORNING, Bel walked Cerberus down the street instead of on the forest trails that flanked her cabin, but after passing two jogging mothers pushing strollers, an elderly gentleman checking his mailbox, and a man dressed in a crisp suit getting into his car, some of the tension bled from her muscles. Cerberus barely glanced at the businessman. He let the elderly man scratch his ears, and he attempted to keep up with the mothers for two blocks before a squirrel captured his focus. Not once did he act out. His voice remained firmly in his throat until he saw the squirrel, and even then, the loud barks were playful as he stood under the tree. By the time Bel pushed him through her front door, attempting to feed him while changing out of her workout gear, she decided the incident with Vera was a fluke. The dog hadn't realized she was there, and she startled him. That was the only explanation for his bizarre behavior.

"Love you, little beast," she called as she locked the cabin behind her, his thumping tail thwacking the floor in response from where he sprawled across the cool wood, drooling as he panted. She had purposely left early, craving a latte from The Espresso Shot before the autopsy this morning. Once she walked inside that morgue, she knew the smell would turn her off to anything digestible for hours, and she desperately craved caffeine. Cerberus' reaction to Vera had set her nerves on edge, and every time she closed her eyes to sleep, all she saw were teeth and wax and clawed feet. A cup of home-brewed coffee would never do the trick, and she wondered how many espresso shots she could add to her latte before Emily banned her from the shop.

"Morning, Detective." Emily Kaffe smiled as Bel stepped up to the counter. The air swarmed with the aroma of freshly ground coffee beans and toasted pastries, and Bel reveled in the sugary warmth. Within the hour, she would have to trade this enticing scent for that of decay and evil.

"Large vanilla latte with an extra shot," Bel said.

"Will that be all? I made chocolate croissants today and have two left." Emily waggled her eyebrows enticingly. The blonde woman in her forties was magic with coffee and a sorceress with baking. Bel didn't believe in the supernatural, but this shop sometimes had her rethinking her stance. The pure decadents Emily could create with flour and sugar and foamed milk could convince even the toughest skeptics.

"Fine," Bel sighed helplessly with fake exasperation. "I'll take one." Emily smiled wide, well aware of how skillfully she manipulated her patrons into indulging, and she placed the pastry into a bag.

"Actually," Bel interrupted, staring at the forlorn croissant abandoned in the case. "Give me both, and then can I also grab an Americano?" If she was going to enjoy chocolate for breakfast, she might as well not eat alone.

"An Americano?" Emily raised her eyebrows conspiratorially as she proceeded to make the drinks. Bel stared at her in confusion until the blonde returned to the register.

"Your latte and pastries." She placed them on the counter. "And your Americano," she added with a wink, and her meaning hit Bel like the stench of the dreaded morgue. This was the one aspect of small-town living she wasn't sure her New York blood would ever acclimate to. Everyone knew everyone's business, and as an introvert who preferred a book and her dog, Bel hated how one simple look, one innocent wipe of the napkin, possessed the power to turn her life into a story she didn't realize she was living.

"Thanks, Emily. Have a good day." She exchanged cash for the breakfast and fled for her car. Denying the insinuation would only somehow prove her guilt, so she ignored the comment. Emily was harmless, a woman who mothered everyone, and maybe if Bel had more years with her mom, she would have relished the opportunity to talk about men. But her mother was gone, and her sisters were older, living their own lives by the time she reached her teens, and so Bel felt nothing but awkwardness at Emily's romantic insinuations.

"Oh my god, I could hug you," Garrett said when she arrived at the station six minutes later, coffee and pastries in tow, and Bel stiffened at his phrase. Her partner seemed to register his words and quickly added, "I am exhausted. This is a lifesaver." He took a sip of the Americano as he checked his watch, and seeing they had a few minutes before they had to leave for the morgue, he peeled back the parchment paper. "Emily made chocolate croissants?"

"I got the last two." She sat across from him, letting the flaky sweetness melt on her tongue.

"Thanks for this." He smiled at her, the expression genuine despite the fatigue in his eyes. "I couldn't sleep…" he trailed off as if embarrassed.

"Me neither," Bel offered, and his gaze dipped to the scar on her neck for a fraction of a second.

"I keep seeing him strung up." Garrett pretended he hadn't just stared at her scars, and Bel pretended for his sake that she hadn't noticed. "I didn't know him well, but I grew up in this town, with these people. I cannot fathom how someone could desecrate his body like that." He paused, drinking half of his Americano down. "And then every time I tried to sleep, I kept smelling bleach. It was stuck in my nostrils, and it got me thinking. Bleach can clean DNA, but nothing is foolproof. How do you rip out someone's heart, drain him of blood, and then drill him into furniture without making a mess? I don't see how it is possible to clean the scene so effectively that not even trace evidence exists."

"That's been nagging me, too." Bel downed the last of her latte and threw their packaging in the trash. "It's almost as if a biohazard crew scrubbed the place."

"My car?" Garrett interrupted as he led the way out of the station.

"Sure." Bel followed him to his parking spot. "There is the possibility they killed him elsewhere, but I don't like that theory. Lumen was an introvert who liked routine. His shop was closed every weekend between Saturday nights and Monday mornings. I'm willing to consider any explanation, but my gut is asking me why drag a man away from the perfect killing grounds only to return him?"

"I agree." Garrett eased into traffic. "The timeframe. The disabled security cameras. The open space, and the thorough cleaning. His shop makes the most sense, but something doesn't sit right."

"None of this sits right."

Garrett grunted his agreement. "Hopefully Lina will find something helpful."

It took them less than ten minutes to reach the morgue, and by the time they had donned the protective gear, Lina Thum was ready to start.

"Will you stay for the autopsy, or are you only here to collect the evidence?" She asked, but when Garrett's face paled, she turned her attention to Bel.

"I might stay," Bel answered, "unless something else comes up. The lack of evidence at the scene bothers me."

"Everything about yesterday bothers me," Lina humphed before securing her mask and goggles in place.

Thum spent the next half hour photographing and x-raying

the body and aiding the detectives as they collected and bagged all the remaining pieces of furniture drilled into Brett's corpse. Without the carvings encasing him, the gaping wound appeared even more gruesome, and as Lina pulled the petals from his chest cavity, she cursed.

"It's a heart." She held it forward for Garrett and Bel to examine. "They created a beautiful heart of roses to replace his organ."

"You didn't find his actual heart inside the furniture's base, did you?" Bel asked, the realization that they were still missing an organ dawning on her.

"No," Lina answered, carefully bagging the petals. "We did not locate it."

"Do you think the killer took it?" Garrett asked, and even though Bel couldn't see his lips below his mask, she knew they were grimacing.

"It's possible—" Bel started, but a shrill ring interrupted her train of thought.

"Be right back." Garrett left the exam room, the ringing phone in tow, and Bel turned back to the autopsy.

"Why take the heart?" Lina asked Bel, her voice laced with horror. "Why leave roses in its place? Lumen never struck me as the flower type, so what do they mean?"

"I don't know." The knot in Bel's stomach returned with a vengeance. "I—"

"Bel?" Garrett's head popped through the door. "The security company received the warrant for Lumen's Customs' stored footage. They just sent it over for us to examine."

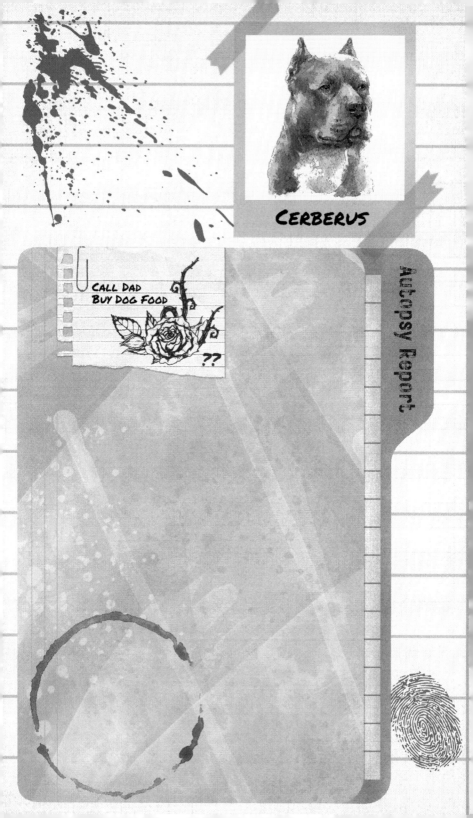

CERBERUS

CALL DAD
BUY DOG FOOD
??

Autopsy Report

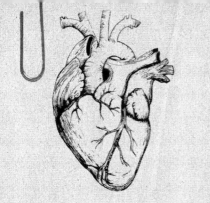

Chapter Six

"LUMEN DISABLED THE CAMERAS HIMSELF?" GARRETT REPLAYED the last few minutes of the security footage, but the images didn't change. 11:00 a.m. on Saturday, Brett Lumen walked downstairs into his workshop and turned off his security system. It was the final entry stored before Violet found his body on Monday.

"He didn't receive any phone calls Saturday morning," Garrett continued, "so it doesn't appear he was threatened into turning them off. No one shows up on the exterior cameras, either."

"He doesn't display signs of duress," Bel agreed. "That doesn't mean he wasn't coerced, but based on his movements, he seems at ease."

"Lina estimated the time of death to be sometime on Sunday, and this confirms he was still alive Saturday morning. We should check if he had a showing scheduled after he shut off the cameras. If he met someone, it could give us the last person who saw him alive. I assumed the killer disabled the security, but it appears Lumen didn't want a record of who he was meeting."

"Or it could have been a date." Bel shrugged, and Garrett glanced at her as if she had just admitted she believed in bigfoot.

"All I meant was there are other reasons someone might turn off the cameras in their private home and business," she explained. "We can't assume either event is connected, even if the coincidence is convenient."

Garrett conceded with a nod and started scrolling back through the footage, but the only anomaly was Lumen turning off the surveillance himself. Days rewound into weeks, and each ticking second followed a predictable timeline. Lumen was a creature of habit, making him an easy target to track. Violet appeared often, her presence the only other consistency besides Brett's. Her outfits varied in design but never color, and her bubbly personality sharply contrasted with the ever-present black. The footage seemed to confirm her statement. Brett Lumen was particular, but the two appeared to work in genuine harmony.

"I recognize some of the people," Garrett said after an hour of constant scanning. Bel's eyes burned from staring at the screen, and she welcomed the break as she glanced at her partner. "His sales records should confirm his clients' names and dates so we can match them to the footage, but tourists and casual viewers will be harder to identify."

"None of the strangers have shown up more than twice, though," Bel pointed out. "The regulars are either locals or clients, and as much as it sickens me to say this, I suspect our killer is local. Bajka isn't the smallest town, but word travels fast." She had to fight to keep her face straight as Emily's insinuations about her and Garrett played in her memory. "The residents would notice a stranger staying beyond their welcome. Whoever did this studied Brett, and no one was the wiser. This crime was painfully specific, and I'm having a hard time picturing an outsider with this intense of a motive."

Garrett cursed softly and opened his mouth to reply, but Sheriff Griffin strode up behind them, silencing his comment.

"I just got off the phone with Lumen's lawyer and executor of his will," the Sheriff said by way of greeting. "He has no next of kin. Both his parents and grandparents passed away. He was unmarried and an only child. We hoped his will would point us to any remaining family, but it didn't. It did reveal something interesting, though. Brett left everything to his assistant, Violet."

"Everything?" the partners asked in unison.

"His business, his money, his building, and his car. All of it," Sheriff Griffin answered. "Seems she was the closest thing he had to family."

"Inheriting a fortune like that is a powerful motive," Bel said, her gaze shifting quickly to Garrett. "She also had the perfect opportunity to observe Brett without raising suspicion."

"There is no way Violet posed him, though," Garrett argued. "You and Lina possess ten times her muscle mass, and you both struggled to dismantle the chandelier."

"She could have had help," Sheriff Griffin added, voicing the possibility they had discussed yesterday. "Possibly even hired someone."

"According to her statement, Lumen paid her well. The designer shoes she had on yesterday confirm that. It is plausible she possessed the funds to hire the killer," Bel said. "Did anyone check her alibi?"

"Yes, while you were at the morgue," Griffin answered. "Most of her day checks out, but there are still gaps in the timeline."

"If she had help, she could have left the technicalities to a professional, therefore ensuring she had an alibi," Garrett added. "Lumen's Customs is worth a lot. She could have promised someone a large payout if they helped rid her of her boss."

"Go talk to her," Griffin said. "I'll get a deputy to comb through the rest of the footage."

A half-hour later, Garrett knocked on Violet's apartment door. Bel hung back, remembering the way the young woman's gaze had raked over her handsome partner. She hoped Violet might confess more in the face of charm and sex appeal.

"Detective Cassidy?" Violet said as she answered his knock, her puffy red eyes a disheveled contrast to her expertly tailored black jeans and the peter pan collar blouse. "Detective Emerson," she added quickly when she noticed Bel's shorter frame behind her partner, and while her features didn't light up like they did when she greeted Garrett, she offered Bel an equally warm smile.

"Good afternoon, Violet," Garrett said with a professional tone and a charismatic grin. "Do you mind if we ask you a few questions?"

"Oh…" she paused and looked uncomfortably behind her, but when she caught Bel's curious stare at her hesitance, she blurted, "Of course. Just ignore the mess. I can't stop crying."

"No worries," Garrett soothed, and the young woman stepped aside to let them in.

The apartment was small but adorably cozy. Unlike her dark apparel, her home was eclectic and earthy, filled with plants and custom furniture supplied by her boss. Three lazy, black cats adorned the sofa cushions, and Bel had to fight the impulse to roll her eyes, for '*the mess*' was a pizza box and a few crumpled tissues on the coffee table.

"Can I get you something to drink?" Violet asked as she scooped one of the midnight cats off the couch and hugged him against her chest before collapsing onto the opposite loveseat.

"No, thank you." Garrett sat, leaning comfortably back on the cushions as Bel settled beside him.

"Are you here about the will?" Violet blurted before either detective had the chance to part their lips. "I only just heard this morning. Since there is no next of kin, Mr. Lumen's lawyer called me in for a meeting. I was shocked when I found out."

Her eyes went wide as the puzzle pieces clicked into place, and sensing Bel was the one to convince, she leaned for her with aggressively graceful desperation.

"Oh my god, you think the will is motive," she blurted, hugging the cat so tight, Bel had the urge to pry the poor thing from her grip. "I know it looks odd, but I promise you, I had no idea about it until this morning. I knew Mr. Lumen didn't have any living family, but I never guessed he would leave his business to me... although, he started giving me more responsibilities lately. I assumed it was because he was busy and tired of handling the paperwork."

"Money is often a motive in homicides," Bel said, forcing the woman to hold her unwavering gaze as she leaned forward, but Violet's earnestness didn't falter.

"Mr. Lumen was my friend. He gave me a great job, and despite his idiosyncrasies, he made sure I was comfortable at work. He was never inappropriate. It was more of an awkward older brother friendship, and I would never hurt him. I would never hurt anyone... I'm a vegetarian." She gestured to the takeout box. "Veggie pizza. And I can't help but rescue every black cat I see. These are just the social ones. There are another two in my bedroom. They are elderly, so they stay in there, especially when I have company." She set the cat she was clutching down on her lap, and Bel breathed easier knowing the creature was no longer being crushed, even if the animal seemed to enjoy the embrace.

"You have five black cats?" Garrett asked.

"Yes, I know it's a little cliché, but I can't help it. I love animals, and won't even hurt spiders in the house. I try to take them outside unless the cats get them first,"

"I understand loving pets," Bel said, relaxing a bit as the girl's conviction bubbled over. She was younger than the detectives, still in her twenties, but if they cleared her of all suspicion, Bel could see them getting along. "I have a black pitbull."

"Oh my gosh, I've seen you walk him," Violet gushed. "I didn't want you to think I was crazy since we hadn't met, so I never approached, but every time I see his beefy face, I want to hug him."

"He would enjoy that," Bel said, and Violet grinned as if she had been given the world.

"I know you might not believe me, but I didn't kill Mr. Lumen," Violet continued. "I have no idea who did, and I can't stop crying. I woke up this morning and almost got ready for work before I remembered."

"Do you mind if we look around, then?" Garrett asked, studying her for any hesitation.

"No, of course not. Just don't judge the mess."

Bel stood up before the young woman caught her smirk. Bel wasn't a messy person, but her job made it hard to maintain perfection. Ever since the accident, she struggled to perform normal tasks. Panic attacks often hit when her mind was empty, and cleaning was the perfect activity for a wandering memory. Thankfully, Cerberus' companionship kept the darkness at bay. Her life was slowly normalizing, but his constant shedding also added to the mess. Perhaps she should ask Violet to organize her cabin.

Garrett and Bel wandered the small apartment, but they found nothing of interest other than two senior cats and an over-stuffed closet of black designer clothes. Violet walked them through all the pieces of furniture Brett had crafted for her over the years as Christmas and birthday gifts, and within fifteen minutes, Bel was convinced they wouldn't find anything. She had survived evil. She knew what it looked like, the dark taste it left coating your tongue. This girl, in all black, was pure sunshine.

"Thank you, Violet," Garrett said as they drifted toward the door, and the woman blushed slightly.

"Of course, Detective Cassidy. Anything I can do to help."

"Try to have a good day," he smiled as he exited the apartment. "We'll be in touch if something comes up."

"Call me anytime," Violet answered, and Bel knew she intended it to sound helpful, but the undertones of her words were meant for Garrett's ears alone. Surprisingly, Garrett, while all smiles and charm, seemed unaffected by her beauty. A fact that made Bel nervous.

"Goodbye." She shoved the thought away as she followed her partner. "This past Saturday?" She paused, turning back to Violet. "Did Lumen meet privately with a client, by any chance?"

"Yes, he did." Violet nodded. "He didn't need me present, though, so he gave me the day off."

"Would you know who he was meeting?"

"It was that new guy in town he was building the chandelier for. Eamon Stone."

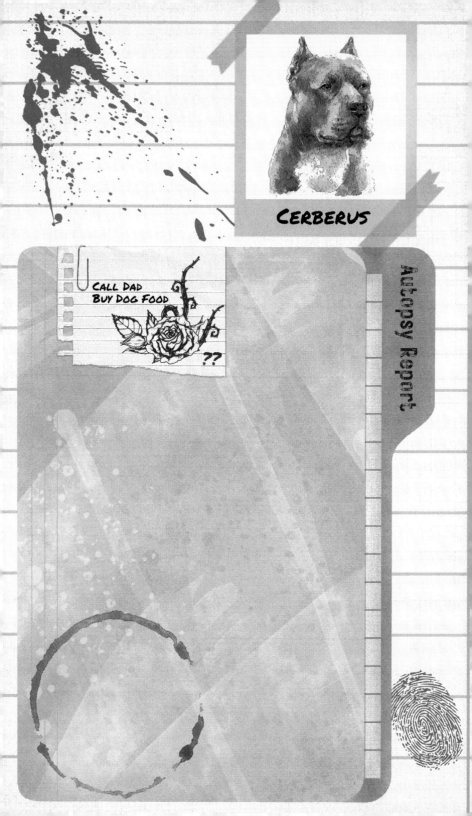

CERBERUS

CALL DAD
BUY DOG FOOD
??

Autopsy Report

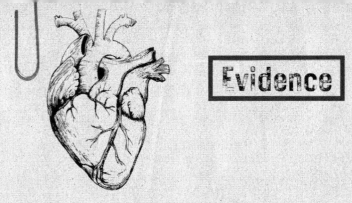

Chapter Seven

THE DETECTIVES WORDLESSLY SLID INTO THE CAR. AN exchanged look was all the conversation the partners needed as Garrett eased out of the parking spot and into traffic. Silence accompanied them as they drove through the town, the houses and shops giving way to a winding, tree-lined road. Bel had never ventured in this direction, the drive serene as they plunged deeper into the woods. No sign of humanity lingered along the lonely two-lane highway, leaving them abandoned in the quiet, and Bel hoped they didn't lose cell reception this far into the forest. A foreboding deep in her gut gnawed at her with razor-sharp teeth, and the minute the Reale Mansion came into view, its darkness captured her breath.

The decaying monstrosity before them was a haunted castle, its disrepair hinting at the ghosts within. Life was not welcome here, and as the tires crunched against the gravel driveway, evil seeped in through the car's cracks to suffocate Bel's soul.

"Someone lives here?" She glanced at Garrett's equally horrified face, the thick dread in the air stinging the scar on her throat. She hadn't experienced this threatening oppression in a long time. Not since that night.

"It's worse than I remember," Garrett said, not making any move to exit the car as if the carved gargoyles perched on the towers might swoop down and attack, their faces etched in eternal agony. "We used to sneak beer out here as teens, but that was almost twenty years ago. This…" He trailed off as if he couldn't find the words to convey the doom this mansion's shadows inspired.

"Should we return with backup?" he asked.

Bel adjusted the gun on her hip as she opened the car door. "It's just a house."

Garrett stared at her, neither of them convinced by her statement, but he followed her lead, pulling his taller body ahead of hers as they strode across the driveway.

"Bajka Police Department." His knuckles rapped forcefully on the ornately carved front door, and the latch popped free, swinging open slightly on silent hinges. "Police Department, is anyone home?" he called for a second time when no one answered. The partners glanced at each other in a wordless conversation before Bel tentatively nudged the door with her toe. Neither of them stepped inside as it swung wide, the once grand foyer coming into view.

Tarps and construction supplies littered the floor, and a ladder stood below the looming ceiling where electrical wires hung out. Bel lightly elbowed Garrett and jerked her head upwards towards the electric work intended to connect to Lumen's commissioned chandelier.

"Police. Is anyone—"

"Hello, detectives," a whiskey smooth menace drifted from the shadows, interrupting Garrett. Bel's eyes snapped to the darkness, but all that emerged was the rich voice. It was death and sex. A threat and a caress. A sound enticing enough to pull you down into the depths and drown you, and gooseflesh pricked her skin.

"I apologize for the delay. I didn't hear you arrive," the voice

Nicole Scarano

came again, as deep and rough as the tires crushing the gravel on their approach. A graceful movement captured Bel's eyes, and she squinted at the dark hallway. For a moment, nothing happened, and then a looming shape emerged from the shadows.

Bel's breath caught in her throat, her heart ceasing to beat as the figure stepped into the light. He was a man, a sculpted statue, a god. A perfect body carved from stone and transformed into flesh. He was tall, too tall, towering over Garrett's six-foot, one-inch frame. The rippling muscles etched into his pale skin matched his intimidating height, and Bel barely came to his chest. He was pure strength and dominance. He was grace and silence as he slipped through the shadows, and when the sunlight kissed his face, Bel's stomach dropped. She had never witnessed such perfection. She had never stared at such evil. He was beauty. He was a beast, and every inch of him oozed darkness and power.

His hair was a dirty blond. Not dark. Not light. It hovered in the grey, like his aura, equally good and evil. Both saint and sinner. It gave him the air of royalty, a king who was both your savior and your executioner, and the perfectly groomed undercut hairstyle contrasted the short, neat facial hair gracing his razor-sharp jaw. He was all angles and lines, sharp enough to slice through skin, too perfect to be real, and his eyes? Black as death. This stranger was perfection. He was the devil, and Bel had no doubt that he possessed the strength to hoist Lumen up and drill him into furniture. Judging by the array of tools plaguing the foyer, this man also had the know-how to accompany his power.

"I am detective Garrett Cassidy, and this is my partner, Isobel Emerson," Garrett said, not moving from the doorway. "We are looking for an Eamon Stone."

"I am he," the dark stranger soothed with a faint growl echoing his words, and his sight drifted to Bel as he stepped further into the light.

His eyes froze her in place, rooting her feet to the floor as he drank her in. He was shirtless and covered in dirt, his hands gripping a work rag as his gaze ate her alive. Bel struggled to swallow under the weight of his observation. It was predatory and hungry, so intense she almost felt it brush against her skin, and the scar on her neck burned. She wanted to revolt against his hold over her. She wanted to flee and never return. She wanted him to capture her and never let go.

"Do you mind if we ask you a few questions?" Garrett shifted uncomfortably, and Bel wasn't sure if it was because of the fear Eamon Stone inspired or because a single look from this god-like stranger had them questioning their beliefs.

"Of course not," Eamon answered Garrett, but his eyes remained on Bel, searing her skin as if it longed to slice her open and see what lived within. He smiled as he beckoned them inside, the expression unbearably beautiful and terrifying. Both detectives hesitated at his invitation, worried if they obeyed, they might never leave the confines of this mansion.

"Do be careful, though," Eamon rumbled, his words rattling Bel's chest. "I have only just begun the renovations. I would not venture further into the estate at the moment. Don't want anyone getting hurt." The look in his predatory stare said otherwise.

"We are here to ask you a few questions about Brett Lumen," Garrett started as the detectives crossed the threshold.

"Yes, what a shame. Such a talented man. Pity he won't be able to help me complete the renovations. His work was exquisite." Eamon stepped forward; his height exaggerated in the close quarters.

"You heard what happened?" Bel asked in surprise. She knew how gossip traveled, but she had never seen him in town. His intoxicating presence would be impossible to ignore, and even her introverted tendencies would have heard tales of his bone structure.

"Yes." He pinned her with his stare, holding her in place as if with chains. "Horrible what happened."

"You had business with Lumen's Customs?" Garrett resumed control of the conversation, shifting slightly in an almost protectively territorial stance before Bel. "According to his records, you were the last client he worked with."

"I was." Eamon finally tore his stare from Bel, leveling his sights on Garrett, who, to his credit, did not back down. "We had multiple projects planned for the next few months as I restore this estate, and the chandelier was first." He nodded to the ceiling, where the wires hung loose, and crossed his arms over his chest. The muscles curled like stone beneath his skin, and Bel studied his profile. He looked to be in his early forties, a man in his prime and distinguished with maturity, but his skin was perfectly smooth, giving him the appearance of someone in their twenties. He was neither old nor young, every angle, every curve, every line tailored so that one's eyes might trace his danger.

"His assistant reported you met with him on the Saturday before his death," Garrett continued.

"I did."

"What was the meeting about?" Garrett bristled at the man's short answers.

"Brett had completed the chandelier. I made the final payment and picked up the piece. If you had arrived later, you would have seen it hanging in its glory. The electricity was the first repair I worked on when I bought the estate. Can't have this house burn down around me."

"Did you know Lumen disabled the security cameras at his shop before your meeting?" Bel asked, and Eamon's head tilted down at her.

"Yes. It was at my request."

"Why?"

"Because I am a private person, Detective Emerson." He said her name like a threat. He spoke her name like honey. "I am aware of this estate's dark history, and I am well versed in small-town gossip. I purchased this mansion to remain far from the public eye, intending to restore it in peace. These grounds are to become my sanctuary to escape the demands of my business."

"Hiding something?" Garrett asked.

"Aren't we all, Detective Cassidy?" Eamon's eyes slid to Bel's scar as he answered her partner, and her pulse stumbled.

"Were you aware that Brett's body was found encased in a piece of furniture resembling a chandelier?" Bel asked.

"I am." He smiled, setting her teeth on edge. "Coincidence, is it not?"

"Are you handling the renovations yourself?" she asked.

"Yes, I am." He angled his towering form toward her, completely ignoring the other detective in the room.

"A man has been murdered, his corpse displayed like the very furniture you ordered from him, and you are clearly knowledgeable in the art of restorations and construction. I would say that is not a coincidence."

Eamon's eyes glared at her, but his mouth twitched into a grin as if he enjoyed the bite of her words. "So, you have decided I am guilty, Detective?"

"I am merely making an observation. I do not speak in absolutes until I have all the evidence." She met his gaze with a strength of her own despite her pounding heart, and Eamon leaned forward as she asked, "where were you on Sunday?"

"Here." He took a deep breath before leaning back, and Bel swore he was smelling her. She recoiled slightly, but his eyes caught her movement, and he smirked. "Working."

"Can anyone confirm your alibi?"

"No." Eamon uncurled his arms and returned to the shadows, signaling the conversation was over. "I am quite busy, Detectives, if that is all?"

"For now, yes," Garett said. "But do not—"

"Leave town?" Eamon finished for him. "I wouldn't dream of it." His eyes landed pointedly on Bel as if to reinforce his statement, and the weight of his predatory gaze had her unconsciously stepping backward toward the front door.

"We'll be in touch if we have any further questions," she said.

"Please do," Eamon purred. "I hope you find who did this, Detective. We certainly don't want someone that dangerous running around our little town."

"Have a good day, Mr. Stone." She ignored his comment and left the foyer, gasping at the freedom the fresh air brought. She hated her body's reaction to him. Hated how, despite the lack of concrete evidence, she knew he was the very monster he warned against.

"Goodbye, Detective Emerson." He did not address Garrett as the partners escaped for the car, and Bel felt the heat of his stare digging into her spine as they moved. She gripped the door handle in relief, pulling it open, but her gaze slipped to the mansion. Eamon had emerged from the shadows, his hulking frame filling the doorframe as he watched her without blinking. His black eyes collided with her crystal blues, and Bel had the overwhelming sensation that Eamon Stone wanted to kill her.

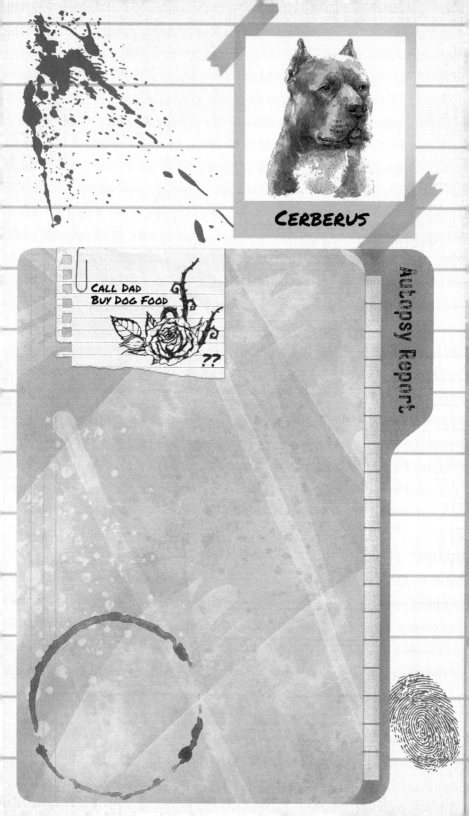

CERBERUS

CALL DAD
BUY DOG FOOD

??

Autopsy Report

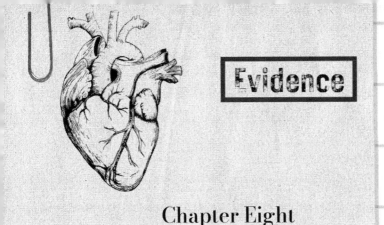

Chapter Eight

EAMON STONE WATCHED DETECTIVE ISOBEL EMERSON GET INTO the car and drive off down the tree-studded road, and his hand curled into a fist because she had not come alone. He knew the police would question him. He had been biding his time, waiting, hoping, craving their attention, but the sight of her prince charming partner made his teeth ache. Eamon wanted Isobel Emerson to himself.

He had seen beautiful women in his life. Knew their scent, their taste, their sounds, but none of them compared to the detective, whose fragrance still hovered in the air. He detected the faint hint of decay wafting off her skin, soap and perfume attempting to cover it up. He realized they must have come from the morgue, but not even the stench of death dampened her gravity dragging him close. Those big blue eyes. That glorious brunette hair, the kind his fingers ached to curl into, to thread into until she could not escape. He wanted to fist those gorgeous chestnut locks, to pull her head back so that she could stare defiantly up at him through her thick lashes, her full lips challenging him as she scowled. He longed to watch her throat dip as she swallowed in fear, to study how that pink scar moved when he tilted her head. That marred flesh. He wanted to drag his nose down it, to see how far it descended.

She would struggle, refusing to submit. She had fight in her, her muscles well defined and strong, and he reveled in the fantasy of forcing her to surrender to his will, knowing she would defy him every step of the way. His chest warred with the desire to grab her wrists and pin her against the wall, to make her fear him and love him. He wasn't sure what he would do if he trapped such pretty prey. Would he feel the thundering of her heart and spill the crimson blood pulsing in her veins, or would he claim her mouth, making her gasp against his lips?

Eamon groaned as he retreated into the darkness of his house. That detective was dangerous. She was too smart. Too determined. She would pin his hide to the wall as her trophy, and part of him liked that idea. She was too beautiful for her own good. He should leave this town. Leave her, but he knew he wouldn't. He had only just begun. He could not abandon her now. Not when her intoxicating scent wrapped him in her beauty, enchanting him.

Eamon cursed, throwing the dirty rag and snagging his tool belt from where he left it. He should get to work before he followed her home. Before he caved to every dark desire burning his blood.

JEALOUSY PULSED off Garret in such thick waves, it coated Bel's skin as they parked in the station's lot. She had a suspicion her partner harbored feelings beyond friendship for her, but nothing had ever pushed him this far before. She hardly blamed him, though. The hunger in Eamon Stone's gaze had rattled her, sweat soaking her shirt at the memory of the murder in his eyes and the desire coiling his muscles. Garrett had sensed it, and his protective nature reared its head. They both sat, unable to move, unable to leave the car, and Bel anticipated what was coming. She didn't want him to say it. She hoped he did.

"Do you think he did it?" Garrett interrupted the silence with his question.

"He has the strength and the skill," Bel answered, refusing to look at her partner. "He is currently the last person we know of to see Lumen alive, and he lacks a provable alibi."

"What do we do?"

"We have no proof." Bel finally turned her gaze to meet his, his brown hair framing his face like a portrait. He was the exact opposite of Eamon Stone: pure goodness and joy. "There is no obvious motive, either. Doesn't mean he didn't do it, but why? Why buy a house in a relatively unknown town and hire a designer to help renovate only to kill him? It makes no sense."

"We'll find something."

Bel sighed, rubbing her eyes. She hated this off-kilter sensation, hated feeling out of control. The last time she experienced this, someone had tried to rip her open and leave her for dead, and Eamon Stone incited the same emotion from her.

"It's late," she said, searching for an excuse to escape the tension in the car. "Cerberus is probably cursing me for forgetting his dinner."

"Poor pup," Garrett said, his response on autopilot as something else consumed his thoughts.

"Good night." Bel reached for the door.

"Wait." Garrett leaned across her and closed his hand over hers, trapping her against the seat. "I may never get the nerve again, so I'm just going to say it. We're partners, and I realize you have things in your past that you don't talk about, that keep you guarded. I respect that. I respect the hell out of you, Bel, but I also like you. You're a great partner and a good friend." He lifted his gaze to hers. "But I don't want to be your friend."

Bel opened her mouth, but then clamped it shut. He had

finally said it, and she wasn't sure how she should feel. Relieved? Terrified? Excited?

"I realize this is a lot to spring on you," he continued before she could turn him down. "It's probably the worst time to ask with this case, but then again, maybe not. Life is short. It is beautiful and fragile." His gaze drifted to her scars before snapping back to her eyes. "If I don't tell you how I feel, I'll regret it. Bel, I like you. I understand it would require work, and it might complicate our jobs, but all I'm asking for is one date."

"Garrett…"

"Just think about it, okay? Don't decide now. Go home. Walk your dog. Sleep on it. Take the whole week if you need to. If you say no, that's fine. It won't change how I act around you. I won't be mad, and I'll remain the best partner you've had. I just want one chance. Can you do that for me? Can you at least consider it?"

Bel stared at Garrett, studying the warmth in his eyes, the soft curl of his hair, the strong jaw, and his pleasant voice. Her first reaction was to refuse him. To run home and hide with a book, and she had to fight the urge to touch her scar. He was kind, and she liked him. Was her desire to turn him down simply based on her fear of letting anyone close enough to hurt her? Garrett would never judge her imperfections. He wouldn't hold her trauma over her.

"Okay… I'll think about it."

CERBERUS BLEW past Bel as she unlocked the cabin door, squatting the instant his paws hit the grass. Bel snagged his leash off its hook and snapped it to his collar before he could escape. She rarely let him roam off lead, and not because he misbehaved, but because she understood what could happen in the blink of an eye. She wasn't sure she would survive if something happened to him, if someone took him from her. Her attachment to the dog grew with each passing day, and some might call her codependent, but no one loved her like that beast except for her father... and maybe her sisters.

Cerberus finally finished relieving himself, and a wave of guilt washed over Bel. Before yesterday, Bajka's crimes were regulated to troublemaking kids, town drunks, and the occasional theft, ensuring she was usually home on time to take care of her dog, but this homicide was something she had never encountered. Not even her assault had been this disgraceful and confusing. She didn't want to admit it, but she knew this wouldn't resolve quickly. She should get someone to visit the pitbull. If they cleared Violet of suspicion, she should ask her if she would dog sit.

Movement caught her attention, and Vera's grey hair popped up from behind a bush. Unlike Bel's basic cabin and plain curb appeal, Vera prided herself on her garden. Half vegetables and half flowers, her elderly neighbor sometimes gifted Bel tomatoes and cucumbers. It was one thing she loved about living in a town like this. Hardly anyone had a garden in the city, and if they did, most of her neighbors didn't care that she existed. Vera, on the other hand, spoiled her with baked goods and fresh produce at least once a week, and guilt pricked Bel's conscience that she offered nothing in return.

Cerberus twisted his neck and caught sight of Vera, and a low menace escaped his throat. He lowered his stance, his growl rumbling his ribs, and Bel tightened her hold on his leash, shoving him back into the house before her neighbor noticed the dog's aggression.

"What is going on with you?" she hissed as she pushed him into the kitchen.

"Isobel?" Vera interrupted before she could close the door, and Bel wedged herself in the doorway so Cerberus couldn't escape through her legs.

"Hi, Vera." She waved awkwardly, hoping her dog wouldn't react to the woman's voice. She didn't understand his visceral reaction to the woman. Perhaps Vera's scent reminded him of something harmful in his past. The shelter had little information about his history, and while he was young, trauma could affect any creature of any age.

"I baked cookies," Vera called over her bushes. "Come help me get rid of some."

Bel glanced longingly back at Cerberus, who stood expectantly before his bowl. All she wanted was to curl up next to him and listen to him snore as she read.

"Just a quick cup of tea," Vera urged. "I go to bed early, anyway."

"Let me feed the dog," Bel sighed, caving to the pressure. After her day, cookies and normal conversation might lift the tension from her chest.

Five minutes, a bowl of food, two guilt-induced treats, and a ton of kisses to the dog's meaty head, and Bel crossed the lawn to Vera's cabin. Everything about her neighbor's home was welcoming. It was warm and cozy, constantly smelling of baked goods and lemon cleaner, and Bel allowed herself to imagine that this was what it might be like to have her mother back.

"Have you had dinner?" Vera surveyed Bel as she walked through the front door as if she could read the detective's day on her face.

"Not yet." Bel took the offered seat as the teapot sang on the stove.

"I already ate," Vera said, pouring the boiling water over the peppermint tea bags. She set both mugs on the table where the still warm chocolate chip cookies sat in an enticing pile. Bel didn't know how the woman managed it, but her baked goods were almost as magical as Emily's.

"I could make you a sandwich," her neighbor continued as she drifted toward the fridge.

"I don't want to impose."

"Nonsense, child. My grandkids don't live close, so I like to pretend you are one of them. It gives me someone to spoil." She pulled turkey and cheese from the meat drawer and then grabbed an heirloom tomato that she had just picked from her garden. "Besides, you can't eat cookies for dinner. It would be unforgivable of me to let you chase a murderer without a proper meal in you."

Bel wrapped her fingers around the steaming mug. Arguing with Vera was pointless. The woman was aggressively friendly, and she had adopted the detective as one of her surrogate grandchildren.

"How is the case going?" her neighbor asked as she sliced the tomato before layering it on the bread.

"You know I can't talk about it."

"You look tired. Are you sleeping?"

Bel smirked behind the woman's back. Vera lived for the questions and not the answers. "I'm fine."

"You don't look fine." The woman placed the sandwich before Bel and took a seat, snatching a cookie as she settled in for her affectionate interrogation. "All alone over there, working such a dangerous job. I worry about you. You need to eat more; you are too skinny."

"If you keep baking, I won't be."

"Nonsense." She swatted Bel's wrists. "You are such a pretty girl. You should be married. Having lots of babies for me to spoil."

"One day." Bel knew not to argue, and as Vera opened her mouth to continue her barrage, Garret's question rang through Bel's memory. Her mother had died before she began noticing boys. Her father raised her and her sisters himself, and she had become too much like him. Her job was her life and breath. Perhaps Vera was someone she could finally talk to about something other than autopsies and motive.

"Actually…" Bel started, but then paused, reconsidering. She didn't want rumors of her romantic entanglements—or lack thereof—spreading like a wildfire throughout town. "Never mind."

"Oh honey, don't be shy." Vera plucked up another cookie. "You can tell me. Your secrets are safe." She mimicked locking her lips and tossing out the key.

"Someone asked me out," Bel admitted with a soft laugh at her neighbor's excitement for gossip.

"Was it that gorgeous partner of yours?" Vera leaned forward conspiratorially, and when Bel raised an eyebrow, the woman swatted the air as if Garret's name was written in neon lights above the detective's head. "Oh honey, anyone with eyes can see that boy is crazy about you. Has been since the minute you landed in town. Honestly, I'm surprised it took him this long to ask."

"We work together." Bel popped the last bite of sandwich into her mouth. Garrett was a year older than her at thirty-five, but every time her neighbor referred to him as a boy, she felt like a teenager being humored. She half expected Vera to give her a curfew while awkwardly attempting to explain the birds and the bees.

"Oh, that means nothing when it comes to love."

Bel stiffened at the comment. She liked Garrett. If she allowed herself to be honest, she also liked the idea of them being more than friends, but love? She wasn't sure it was in the cards for her. Her father had worshipped the ground her mom had walked on, and losing her had almost destroyed him. Bel wasn't sure she wanted to open herself up to that brand of heartbreak.

"Is that your only reservation?" Vera asked, oblivious to Bel's stiff shoulders.

"No. I…" Bel paused. "There is a reason I moved to Bajka. My life? It's complicated."

"And you're afraid to let anyone in?" Vera finished for her, and Bel took a bite of a sinfully rich chocolate chip cookie to avoid answering.

"Love is scary. Life is scary," her neighbor continued. "Don't let your past keep you from a good thing. Garrett is a sweet boy. Handsome too." She waggled her eyebrows. "Give him a shot. I hate seeing you so lonely over there."

"I'm not lonely," Bel argued. "I have my dog."

"Dogs are nice, but you need a husband."

Bel choked on the cookie crumbs and grabbed her mug, gulping the tea despite its heat. "Husband? I haven't even gone on a date with him."

"Details," Vera humphed. "Go out with the boy. It will be good for you. Don't miss out on an adventure because you're scared."

"Sometimes it's easier dealing with the dead," Bel whispered.

"I know, sweetheart." Vera placed a wrinkled palm over hers. "But you aren't dead, and you need to live like it."

"Thanks for dinner." Bel smiled at her friend, suddenly needing this conversation to be over. Between the raw sex appeal of Eamon's terror and Garrett's heartfelt confession, she needed the safety of the one man in her life that didn't fuel her anxiety.

"Anytime, dear." Vera stood up and grabbed a Tupperware stuffed full of chocolate chip cookies off the counter. "Here, take these. You're too skinny."

They were back at that again. Bel silently accepted the container, knowing she would have to bring these to work. They would make her sick if she tried to eat that many before they went stale. "Thanks." She wrapped the older woman in a quick hug.

"You know I love baking for you. Have a good night, dear. Get some sleep. You have bags under your eyes."

Bel forced her eyes not to roll as she left Vera's comfortable kitchen. Anyone else and the onslaught would have offended her, but she knew her neighbor meant well. She liked the woman even though her dog didn't, and normally she trusted Cerberus' instincts, but maybe he was more like her than she realized. Maybe his past, his pain, had changed him so mercilessly that his soul was forever scarred.

"Hi baby," she called as she opened the door to her cabin, and Cerberus rolled onto his back. His tail whipped the mattress, and she toed off her boots, stripping on her way to the bed. She should shower. She should open her laptop and do some work, but instead, she pulled on the baggy tee shirt crumpled in her sheets. She would hug her dog for just a minute. She told herself she would scratch his belly, spending quality time with her favorite man before—

Teeth ripped into her flesh, and Bel jerked awake so hard, Cerberus grunted as her arm tightened around his ribs. Fear raced through her. Her scar burned, and it took a solid thirty seconds before she realized the pain in her neck was only a memory. Sweat clung to her skin, plastering her shirt to her chest as she pushed to a seat. Something about this nightmare alarmed her. It was the same panic that plagued her nights. The same attack, same teeth, same stench of blood, but this one possessed an anomaly. Something that had never entered her nightmares before. Black eyes. Watching her, taunting her, terrifying her. They stared through the darkness with their violent threats, and even though she had escaped the dream, Bel still felt them on her. They watched her, hunted her, and the longer she sat in the dark, the more the fear crept in. Instead of dissipating upon waking like it always had, it grew and multiplied, coating her skin, spilling into her lungs.

Bel scanned the cabin. Cerberus would have warned her of a break-in, but the tugging at her gut unnerved her. Someone was watching her. She could feel it in her bones, in the way the hair on the back of her neck rose with electric fear.

The room was empty, though. Her dog lounging unbothered on the pillows. The clock read 3:00 a.m., and Bel told herself she was paranoid. No one was here. No one was stalking her. This case was dredging up repressed memories. That was it.

She scratched the pitbull's ears as she shimmied off the bed to grab a drink when a shadow outside her kitchen window moved. Bel froze, for a pair of black eyes hovered on the opposite side of the glass panes, watching her every move.

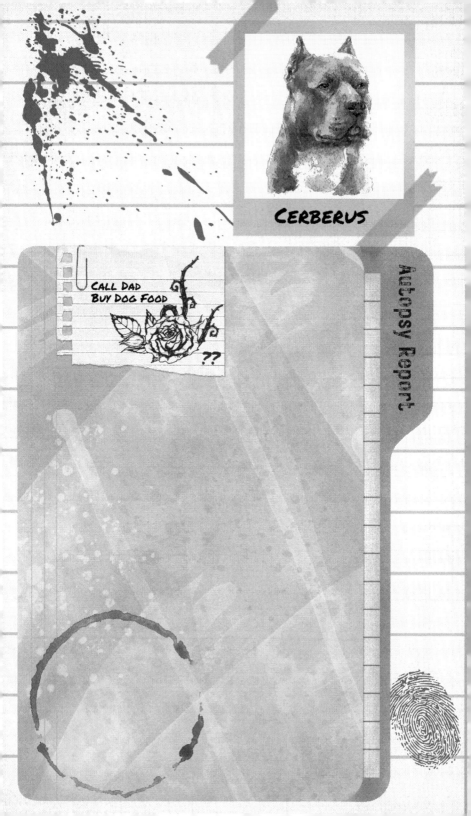

CERBERUS

CALL DAD
BUY DOG FOOD

??

Autopsy Report

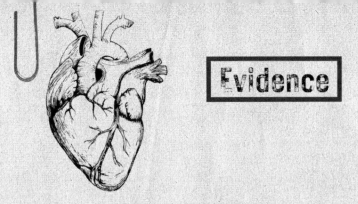

Evidence

Chapter Nine

BEL HAD HER SIDEARM IN HER GRIP BEFORE SHE COULD EXHALE her panicked breath, thumbing the safety off as she bolted for the door. She flung it open, the thud of wood colliding with the wall a resounding gong in the silence, and she lunged out into the moonlight, bare legs shining in the pale light.

Nothing.

She found nothing. No monster lurked outside her window. No black eyes. No angel of death. Only the crickets mocked her state of undress. Bel clicked the safety back into place and rubbed her eyes, but the view before her remained unchanged. She was alone in the darkness.

Her bare feet padded over the dew-drenched grass, and she locked herself inside her cabin. The eyes had appeared so real, the stare so oppressive, that she almost felt them drag across her skin, but Cerberus lay undisturbed on the mattress, watching her lazily. If someone had tried to break in, the dog would have reacted, but the only things bothering his sleep were her and her nightmares. Bel sighed, sliding the gun back into the bedside table's drawer before collapsing next to the pitbull. She didn't want to worry him, but maybe she should call her dad. She wasn't sure she was ready for a case like this. It was making her see things, convincing her that a reclusive millionaire found her sleep worth observing.

Bel shuddered at the memory of Eamon's hungry gaze tormenting her skin, at the way his mouth twitched as if he wanted to learn what her fear tasted like, what her moans against his lips sounded like. She grabbed Cerberus and pulled him closer. Evil had come to this town. Evil in its most beautiful form, and the dread in her gut promised that the violence plaguing her new home had only just begun. She never jumped to conclusions, but Eamon Stone was a predator on the hunt. He was involved in this darkness, and she needed to figure out how before his sin swallowed her whole…

The blare of the alarm jerked both Bel and Cerberus violently from their dreamless sleep, and she slapped the clock, desperate for silence. She didn't remember falling asleep, her adrenaline high after her nightmare, but the dog's warm body had obviously lulled her to safety. She kissed his head and fumbled with her shorts before clicking the leash onto his collar. Thank heavens for this animal. She desperately needed the rest, and if not for his snoring and heavy weight, she would have stared at her ceiling for most of the night. Bel smirked at Vera's cabin as she led him out into the early morning. She didn't need a husband or kids. She had Cerberus, and he was the only man she trusted besides her father… and Garrett. The thought surprised her as the pitbull dragged her around the yard. It had taken her partner months to ask her out, and she realized perhaps it wasn't because he was shy, but because he understood she needed time to adjust.

Business handled, Cerberus towed her toward the house, but then he veered sideways, pulling her along the plants lining the cabin. Bel's heart lodged in her throat when she saw where he stopped, where he insisted on sniffing. The leaves under her kitchen window were crushed, as if a person had stepped on them. Black eyes flooded her vision as the dog refused to leave, insisting on smelling every inch of the bent stems. She told herself a rabbit had visited in the dead of night, and that was what the pitbull scented, but her lies were flimsily thin. Someone had stood here. Someone had been watching her.

THE FOREBODING DREAD STILL CLOAKED her flesh as she ordered a vanilla latte and an Americano at The Espresso Shot. Bel barely registered Emily's teasing her about buying Garrett's favorite coffee drink. She didn't even notice Abel Reus until she almost knocked his oatmeal out of his hands.

"No harm done, Detective," Abel said softly as she apologized for nearly painting his shirt with his breakfast. In his late forties with thinning hair, Abel was a nice enough oddity in town. Like most of the locals, he got his coffee from The Espresso Shot, but he always insisted on ordering oatmeal to go, regardless of Emily's irresistible homemade pastries. Bel had tried it once, and Emily Kaffe could turn anything into gold, the oats rich and creamy with brown sugar and cinnamon, but Bel didn't understand how anyone could stare at her display of blueberry muffins, glazed apple donuts, or cranberry vanilla scones and choose hot cereal. This morning, Emily was selling kiwi fruit tarts, and Bel essentially had to physically peel herself away from the pastry case, reminding herself of the container of Vera's chocolate chip cookies sitting in her car.

"I heard about Lumen," Abel said as she snagged some of the complimentary napkins. "Such a shame. Do you have any leads?"

"I can't talk about ongoing cases, sorry," Bel said distractedly.

"Of course." He stepped closer. "I hope you are taking care of yourself with such a dangerous killer on the loose."

Bel paused and stared at the man. He often greeted her as she rushed through the coffee line on the way to work, but after last night, his comment set her on edge.

"I am, thank you." Her phone vibrated in her pocket, and she thanked whoever it was for giving her an excuse to leave this conversation. "I have to take this. Have a good day," she called over her shoulder as she fished out her cell, not noticing how Abel watched her every move until she disappeared down the street.

"Lina texted me," she said by way of greeting when she arrived at the station. "She wants us to meet with her to discuss the autopsy." She shoved the Americano at Garrett and leaned forward to set the Tupperware onto the desk. To his credit, her partner simply nodded, his face relatively neutral as he attempted to mask his eagerness for her answer to his date request.

"I have cookies from my neighbor," Bel called loud enough for the small station to hear. "Someone please eat these before I do."

Deputies descended on her like locusts, Sheriff Griffin not far behind.

"We are on our way to discuss the autopsy result," Bel said to her boss as he smiled at her for sharing.

"Excellent." He grabbed four cookies. "Keep me updated and let me know if you need anything."

"Will do."

"Thanks for these... like I need them." He laughed as he saluted her with his full fist, and Bel mockingly rolled her eyes. Sheriff Griffin looked like a man who could eat whatever he wanted and still have it transform into muscle. That was why she brought the baked goods for the deputies instead of leaving them all at home. Their instant sugar was too convenient for her to eat rather than forcing herself to cook a proper dinner, but she had saved a small batch for herself. Chocolate was healthy for the soul, after all.

"You ready?" She looked at Garrett. He nodded his agreement, his mouth full of chocolaty goodness, and Bel gripped the latte tightly for courage.

"Yes."

He choked behind her, almost spitting crumbs, before he gulped his coffee. "Yes... as in?" he croaked.

"One date." Bel opened the car door and slid into the driver's seat. "As a trial run."

Garrett practically tripped over himself as he sat next to her. "I'll take it."

"CAUSE OF DEATH was exsanguination from the chest wound," Lina Thum began when they arrived at the morgue. "Since I have not received it, I assume we still have not located the heart?" Both Garrett and Bel shook their heads.

"Right." Lina nodded. "This is where it gets weird." The detectives squinted at her, and she amended her statement. "Weirder. The wound was caused by curved blades digging into his skin in four equal gouges before both the flesh and the rib cage ripped free."

"Do you know what kind of blades were used?" Garrett asked.

"No." Lina shook her head. "Since part of the chest and the heart are missing, I only have the surrounding torn muscles and the outermost portion of the blade's wounds to measure. I didn't find fibers or any trace evidence in the chest cavity, either. This is going to sound bizarre—trust me, I don't even like saying it —but honestly, the injury reminds me of a clawed fist. As if someone reached into his ribcage and ripped it out with a hand."

The claw-foot base of the chandelier flashed through Bel's memory. "Like the carvings?" She asked.

"Yes, almost like a larger version," Lina confirmed. "I know a beast didn't kill Brett Lumen, but whoever murdered him wanted it to look like it."

"It fits the narrative," Bel said. "He turns the body into a work of furniture art, making it appear like a monster killed him and replacing his heart with roses. I can't help but feel the killer is trying to tell a story. I'm just not sure what that story is yet."

"That's not all," Lina continued. "The only antemortem wound on Brett Lumen's body was the chest wound. The killer drilled the screws in postmortem after he had been drained of blood, but besides those, he sustained no other injuries."

"No defenses wounds?" Bel asked.

"None. No blood or tissue under his nails. No bruising on his knuckles. No cuts or scrapes. Not even a paper cut. No blunt force trauma to knock him out or stun him."

Garrett shuttered. "So, he was drugged to keep him compliant?"

"That's what I assumed," Lina said. "I put in a rush for a Tox screening. It came back negative."

"Negative?" Bel wasn't sure she had heard the medical examiner correctly.

"Negative," Lina repeated. "Brett Lumen had no drugs or sedatives in his system when he died. No alcohol. Nothing that would impair his senses or reflexes."

Bel stepped backward reflexively, Garrett's muscular chest absorbing her shock as she bumped into him.

"He did not fight back. He was not sedated or unconscious." Lina sucked in a fortifying breath. "From what I can tell, Brett Lumen sat there and willingly let someone carve out his heart."

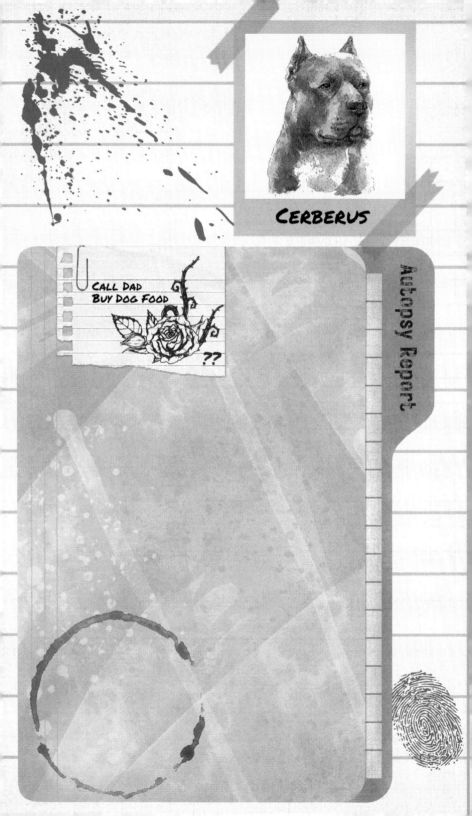

CERBERUS

CALL DAD
BUY DOG FOOD
??

Autopsy Report

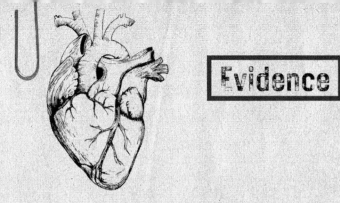

Chapter Ten

HOURS OF PAPERWORK DID LITTLE TO LESSEN THE KNOT IN BEL'S stomach. Who stood by and let someone rip open their chest? Why had Lumen not resisted? Her fingers drifted to the scar on her neck. She had been helpless against her attacker that night, his power far surpassing hers, yet she had fought tooth and nail to escape. It wasn't until she had nearly bled out that she finally stopped struggling, her strength pooling on the pavement with her blood. Defensive wounds had coated her arms, but whoever her assailant was, he had been careful of her nails. She had scraped no DNA from him despite her best efforts, but that was what made this case so confusing. She had put in great effort not to die. Even when hope abandoned her, she still fought to survive, to keep breathing. Bel fiercely wished to see another second, another day, another year, and she refused to go gently into that dark night. But Brett Lumen had just accepted an excruciating death without fighting, without inhibitors to subdue him.

"I'm starving." Garrett pushed away from the desk, the sun setting behind the station. The idea of lunch after their meeting with Lina appealed to neither of them, so they had worked through their breaks, but now Bel's stomach growled at his statement.

"Me too."

"Do you want to go get dinner?" Garrett stood and stepped before her chair, offering her his hand. She slipped her fingers into his and let him pull her to her feet.

"Sure." She noticed his expression and froze. "Did you mean?"

"Kind of." He didn't release her hand. "We both have to eat, and…" He trailed off. "Never mind. I'm screwing this up."

"No, you're not." Bel smiled. "It's just I still have a lot of paperwork. When you said dinner, I thought you meant quick takeout."

"Yeah, that's fine. Chinese?" His voice sounded enthusiastic, but Bel read the disappointment in his eyes. An impromptu date was the best way to get her to agree. She wouldn't have time to overthink her answer. She could tell his eagerness and lack of romance embarrassed him, but she needed not to think. Vera's encouragement flooded her mind. Garrett was handsome and kind. How long would he wait before someone like Violet scooped him up?

"What about takeout from La Signora?" she offered. "Like a work date?"

"I've been wanting to try that place," Garrett said. "I would prefer to take you there, though." His face lit up. "How about a compromise? Agree to accompany me there when we don't have as much work on our plates, and I'll cook for you tonight. You can finish up while I make dinner, and when the food is ready, we'll open a bottle of wine and ignore this case for an hour."

"I didn't know you could cook?"

"I'm an excellent chef." He puffed out his chest with exaggerated pride and stepped closer, grabbing her other hand. "Both of my parents worked, so I spent a lot of time with my grandmother, who believed life wasn't worth living without good food. She taught me so that one day I could trick some girl into putting up with me." He raised his eyebrows in a teasing expression.

"This I have to see," Bel laughed. "I'll come over after I take care of Cerberus, and I might have to call your grandmother if this dinner isn't the best I've ever eaten."

"Anything but that." He feigned pain in his chest as he released her hands. "And bring the dog. I'll stop and grab some wine while you get him."

Bel grinned. Smart man. The way to her heart was definitely through her pitbull.

Forty-five minutes later, Cerberus lay next to her on Garrett's couch while he worked in the kitchen. His apartment was bigger than her entire cabin, and while it was nothing fancy, it was clean and well decorated.

"Hey?" Garrett called over his shoulder, dragging her eyes from her laptop. He held a slice of raw chicken for her to see. "Before I put this all in the pan, does he want a plate?" He nodded at the pitbull whose thick head jerked off the couch so fast, Bel's neck hurt just watching him.

"I think you have to now," she laughed. "Careful, or my dog might end up liking you more than me."

"That's my master plan." Garrett winked as he turned back to the stove. "Bribe him into becoming my friend so that you have to come over."

"I'm pretty sure you could convince me to visit with the smell of that alone." Bel inhaled deeply, the aroma of herbs and pasta filling her lungs. Garrett chuckled at her statement, and she picked up her laptop and carried it to the kitchen island, where two bottles of red and white wine waited.

"Help yourself." Garrett nodded toward them as he dumped the plain cubed chicken into a small pan to cook for Cerberus. "I wasn't sure which you preferred, so I got both."

Bel grabbed the red and uncorked it, pouring Garrett a glass before filling one for herself. She hoisted herself onto one of the island's stools and took a sip as she stared at her laptop.

"They didn't find fingerprints on the furniture encasing Lumen's body," she said.

"You clean a scene that well, I doubt you would leave prints." Garrett scooped the dog's chicken into a small bowl before turning back to their meal.

"The sterile nature of this homicide makes me wonder if the killer has a forensics background."

"You think he's a cop?"

"Or he was. He prepared for everything we would look for. Besides, we have little else to go on. The only person we know who could make furniture of that caliber was the victim."

"Eamon Stone seems pretty handy."

"Handy, yes." Bel took another sip. "But construction differs from carving a floor-standing chandelier around a body," Garrett grunted his agreement. "And then there is the missing heart. We haven't found it, and many killers take souvenirs."

"You think he kept it?" Garrett met her gaze with a slightly nauseous expression.

"If he has a forensic or medical background, he might know how to preserve the organ, keeping it as a trophy, or…" Bel sighed, realizing this wasn't an appropriate dinner date conversation, but with her nerves firing all at once, work felt like the safest topic. "Or I'm grasping at straws. None of this makes sense." She rubbed her face, leaving her skin blotchy.

"How about you take a break?" Garrett gently pushed her laptop closed and slid it away from her. "You have bags under your eyes. You won't solve this on an empty stomach or without sleep. Breathe for a few hours, and tomorrow, we'll start fresh." His fingers slowly reached up and tucked her hair behind her ear. Bel leaned into his palm, surprised by how comforting it was. She hadn't let many besides her father and her dog touch her since New York, and she couldn't stop the grin that curved her lips. Maybe this was what she needed. A kind boyfriend in a small town. Eamon's intoxicating gaze flashed through her mind at the thought, but she shoved it aside, shocked by how often his dangerously handsome face seemed to find its way into her thoughts.

"Come on, buddy." Garrett released her and grabbed the cooled cubed chicken off the counter. Cerberus raced across the floor, his muscular body lumbering for the kitchen like a dog possessed. The meat disappeared in seconds, the pitbull grunting and snorting like a little pig as he ate while Garrett chuckled in amusement.

"Does he always sound like that when he eats?" he asked, still watching Cerberus' wagging tail.

"Especially when it's something he likes." Bel nodded.

Cerberus licked the bowl within an inch of its life and then looked expectantly at Garrett.

"Sorry, buddy, that's all there is." He scratched behind one of the dog's cropped ears. "Convince your mom to visit again, and I'll make you some more."

"He'll definitely want to return, now." Bel slid off the stool and settled beside Garrett, his hand instinctively wrapping around her waist before either of them realized what he was doing. Bel felt his body stiffen against hers as if bracing for rejection, but she slipped her arm around him in reassurance. "I want to come back too."

Garrett looked down at her with hope falling from his eyes, and the expression never vacated his gaze as they ate. Bel prayed that the peace dinner had brought her would fill her dreams with curly brown hair and laughter. Instead, those dangerous black eyes haunted her nightmares, waking her with their teeth, always the teeth, and while no dark irises hunted her through her windows, Bel could not shake the feeling that someone was watching her. That the shadow hovering among the trees was not foliage, but something human. Something predatory.

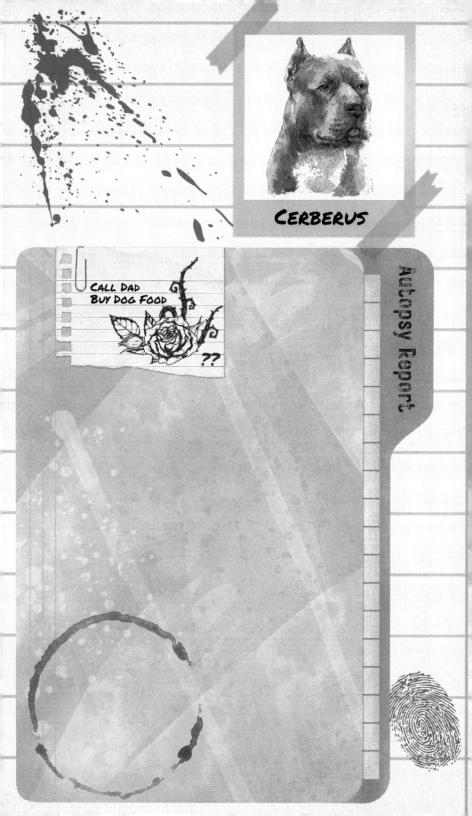

CERBERUS

CALL DAD
BUY DOG FOOD

??

Autopsy Report

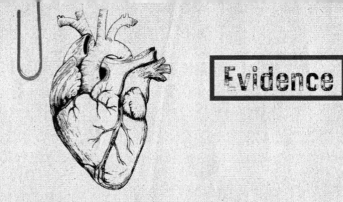

Chapter Eleven

DESPITE DROWNING HERSELF IN COFFEE AFTER SLEEP ABANDONED her, Bel found her autopilot steering her car toward The Espresso Shot. She should call her father. She should accept that she wasn't ready for a case this severe, for the lack of blood to remind her how much had spilled from her own veins, but she was afraid to admit her weakness. So instead, she would exist on caffeine and sheer determination of will. She would force her body and mind into submission because she understood the devastation of an unsolved crime. Her attacker had vanished without a trace. Brett Lumen's murderer would not be granted the same lenience.

Bel parked, only half aware of her surroundings as she exited the vehicle until she collided with an immobile Abel. The surprise firmly deposited her into the present, and only then did she realize a crowd hovered before the coffee shop's front door.

"Good morning, Detective," Abel said, trying to capture Bel's attention, but it was of little use. The unopened shop had already claimed it.

"What's going on?" Bel asked, checking her phone for the

time. It was early, but Emily was always open at this hour, catering to the half-awake on their commutes. "Why isn't she open?"

"Don't know," Abel said. "Perhaps she's running late?"

"Emily never runs late." Bel unlocked her phone and searched the internet for The Espresso Shot's number. Finding it quickly, she dialed, raising her cell to her ear as she chewed on her lip. The phone rang, but no one answered, so she hung up and opened her text thread with Garrett.

BEL

> Do you have Emily Kaffe's personal number?

GARRETT

> Yeah, why?

> Call her. Let me know if you're able to reach her.

> Okay... 2 seconds.

Bel shoved her cell in her back pocket and walked to the front door. In the short time she had lived here, The Espresso Shot had always opened before the sun's rays graced the earth, and Emily thrived on surprising her patrons with different, freshly baked pastries. From the stories Bel heard, the woman rarely took vacations. Not that she didn't trust the shop with her employees. She was simply obsessed with everything coffee and sugar. She was usually the first to arrive so she could bake, and then her daughters or another employee would show up for the morning rush. Emily claimed she was a reverse night owl. She would get up so early that it was still night. Apparently, as a teen, she had horrible insomnia, but baking helped calm her. The schedule stuck, and she figured if she was awake at that god-awful hour, there was no need to force a college student to come and unlock the doors for the few early birds.

Bel peered in through the glass door, but the shop's eclectic design hid the counter from the street's view. Mismatched furniture sprawled about the floor. Bookshelves lined the walls. The Espresso Shot's unofficial library was something Bel had taken advantage of herself. People left their old books on the shelves for patrons to read. Bel had borrowed a few, donated others, and kept three because they spoke to her soul. She loved Emily's shop. Everyone did. The coffee, the food, the atmosphere, but at the moment, Bel cursed the crowded decor obscuring her view. She tested the door as her phone vibrated, but it didn't budge.

> She didn't answer me. Want to tell me what's up?

Bel stared at Garrett's text, hoping she wasn't being paranoid.

> The Espresso Shot isn't open. No one knows why.

> That's not like Emily.

> I know.

> Should I call her husband?

> I don't want to alarm him... hold on. There is a window in the back. Let me check it first.

Bel returned the phone to her pocket and walked around the side of the building. She stared through the glass, but every angle obscured the counter. She tested the door, but it, too, stood locked. Bel sighed, hands on her hips as she scanned the alley. She didn't like this. She prayed there was a simple explanation. That Emily would race out any second in an embarrassed flash of flour to confess that she had fallen asleep while the muffins baked, but Bel knew that wouldn't happen. The air surrounding the Espresso Shot normally curled with fragrance, but all she smelled was the dumpster. Nothing was baking within these walls.

Bel's eyes landed on the SUV parked behind the shop, and her heart wrenched free of its arteries and plummeted through her chest cavity. Emily's car.

She raced for the vehicle, but it took her all of five seconds to discover it was empty. The hood of the car was cool, the engine having sat idle for hours. Had Emily run out of an ingredient, deciding to pop over to the store to purchase it? Many of the town square's shops were within walking distance of one another, but at this hour? Most weren't open yet.

A window at the rear of the building hovered above the door. It was too high for her to look through, but that angle might offer a view of the counter. If someone could hoist her up?

Bel rushed back to the main street and settled close to Abel so no one else could hear. He was tall. He would have to do. "Can you help me?"

"Of course, Detective." He followed her to the alley.

"Would you mind lifting me?" She pointed to the window, trying not to think about the man wrapping his arms around her thighs.

"Sure." He bent, jerking her upwards, and her muscles went rigid to avoid leaning against him more than necessary. When he hoisted her over his head, she gripped the small ledge and peered through. The shop was empty. Emily was not inside.

"Where is she?" Bel whispered to herself before speaking aloud. "You can put me down now—Wait!" She stiffened against Abel's pull, and he pushed her back up.

"What is it?" He grunted below her.

"I see something, hold on…" Bel trailed off, straining to make out the flash of pale coloring that caught her attention. "Can you shift to the right?"

Abel groaned under her weight but complied, and the

object came into view. Bel froze. Everything within her both stilled in terror and screamed in panic, and forgetting to use her words, she shoved herself down. The pale sight? It was a hand.

"Detective?" Able stumbled.

Bel cursed as her feet hit the pavement hard, but she ignored the tweak in her knees and scanned the alley. She should call for help. She should call Garrett, but what if…?

"Stand back," she ordered Abel as her gaze snagged on the fractured parking block, and she raced for it.

"Detective, what are you doing?"

"Get back," Bel repeated, and Abel barely had time to leap sideways before she launched the concrete through the air. This panicked act would probably come back to haunt her, but she couldn't think of that at the moment. All she knew was there was a hand inside this shop, and if she delayed, her hesitation could cause devastating consequences.

"*Please be alive. Please be alive. Please be alive,*" Bel's mind chanted as she tucked her blazer protectively around her arm and reached through the shattered glass to unlock the door. The second it was free, she was moving, and she was suddenly back in New York, blindly running for her life, fear eating away at her like a vulture upon the carrion.

The distance took seconds, but to Bel, it was a lifetime. And then she rounded the counter corner, her feet skidding to a stop. Her entire body went numb, and nausea roiled in her stomach like a Kraken-whipped storm. Her fingers shook. Her muscles froze. She was too late. Too late. Too late.

She wasn't sure how long she stood there, but the sound of crunching glass jarred her back to the present. Able hovered in the doorway, inching closer.

"Get back." Bel threw her hand up in an order. He opened his mouth to argue, but she pinned him with a glare of vengeance. "Get outside now, Abel. No one comes in."

Sensing the severity in her tone, the older man slipped outside, and she dug her phone out, dialing with shaking fingers.

"Hey," Garrett answered on the first ring. "Bel?" he asked when nothing but silence greeted him.

"I found Emily."

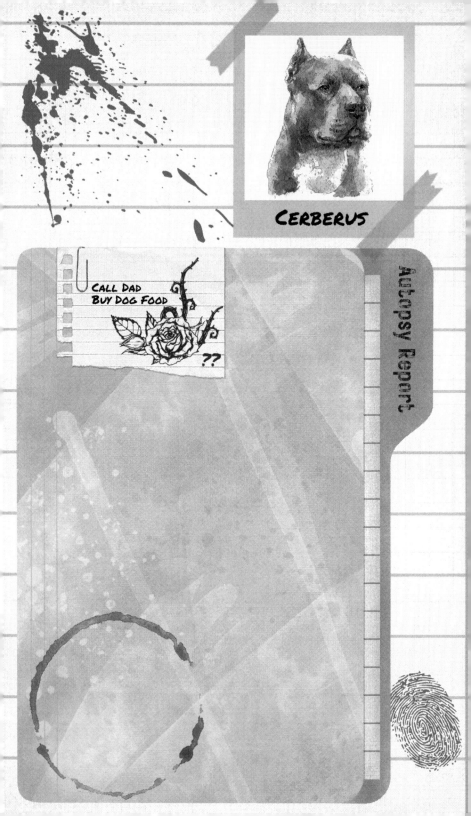

CERBERUS

Autopsy Report

CALL DAD
BUY DOG FOOD

??

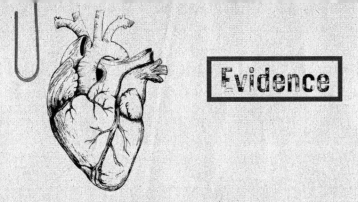

Chapter Twelve

THE STATION WAS MERE BLOCKS FROM THE ESPRESSO SHOT, BUT as Bel stood motionless before Emily's body, the few minutes it took to hear the sirens blaring seemed to stretch into hours. Emily Kaffe leaned against the counter in the only spot invisible from the street. Her upraised hands, the only part of her Bel had seen from the high window. She had wanted to believe the shop owner had fallen, her hands reaching for help, but instinct warned her what she would find. But even then, Bel was not prepared.

Emily sat, knees to her chest, in a small circular ceramic tub. Custom made, its claw foot base was forged from a bronze metal, the claws as severe as the chandelier's foundation below Brett Lumen. The ceramic tub was bone white, only just big enough to support Emily's naked form, and delicate green leaves and thorns illustrated its circumference. Bel didn't need to look further to understand. Just as someone had carved the chandelier, so had they painted this tub. A rose bush.

Emily's bare ankles were crossed, her knees propped up on the sides, and her torso leaned back against the counter. Her arms were raised above her head and bound with thin, ornately twisted bands of metal, entwining her fingers in a delicate pattern with her palms side by side and facing forward. Bel studied the design, but it was the fact that Emily's lower half was submerged beneath black coffee that triggered her recognition. A spoon.

Bel almost choked at the realization. Brett Lumen had been carved into a chandelier, turned into the furniture he cherished. Emily had been shaped into a spoon to stir the life-sized mug of coffee, becoming one with the liquid she claimed flowed through her veins instead of blood.

The desecration of her body was not the only thing to mimic Lumen's macabre display. Bel desperately wanted to avoid it, to drape her jacket over Emily's bare and pale chest, but she had already altered the scene enough with the broken glass. She could not contaminate it further, and so she forced herself to witness the ruptured flesh. Emily's heart was gone, the beating organ replaced by delicate roses.

"Emerson...? Detective Emerson!" Bel jerked at Sheriff Griffin's voice, startled by how close he stood to her. How long had he been there? How many times had he called her name?

"Are you okay?" he asked as their gazes met, and she nodded. "Did you touch anything?"

"I had probable cause," Bel whispered, not sure if she was trying to convince him or herself.

"I know." Kindness mixed with authority in the man's eyes. Unlike Garrett, he knew every excruciating detail behind her transfer to Bajka. "Did you touch anything?"

"I covered my hands with my sleeve when I unlocked the door." Bel shook her head in confirmation. "I saw her fingers peaking over the counter. I worried she had fallen or..." she trailed off.

"It's all right, Emerson." He extended a hand to her. "Deputies are setting up a perimeter. Come outside and tell me what happened."

Bel nodded numbly, following his commanding lead as they

exited the way they entered. The moment she stepped out into the morning light, Garrett was at her side.

"You okay?" he asked, and she nodded before launching into a recount of her steps, starting with parking her car and ending with the Sheriff's arrival.

Griffin opened his mouth to speak as she finished, but a cry of anguish ignited the air. Every head turned, watching in horror as a middle-aged man barreled for the police tape.

"Emily? Oh my God, Emily," David Kaffe screamed as he ran. Time stood still. No one moved. No one breathed. Nothing existed outside of that husband's fear. "My wife? Where is she? Oh god, is she okay? Please say she is okay."

He reached the police tape, ripping through it, and time sped up, careening almost too fast. Sheriff Griffin raced for him, catching his screaming mass. The distraught husband was no match for the Sheriff's honed power, but he did not give up flailing as Griffin and three deputies attempted to calm him.

"Did you call David?" Bel whispered, struggling to maintain her composure as the man collapsed in the officers' arms.

"No." Bewilderment colored Garrett's tone. "But…" He gestured to the gathered crowd, and Bel rubbed her eyes with the heels of her hands. A bystander had obviously alerted the husband, and all she could see as he screamed was her father's face. How must he have looked when they notified him she might never wake up?

"I…" Bel refused to stand idly by while Emily's husband lost his entire world. She couldn't bring her friend back from the dead, but she would nail the guilty to the stake for this crime. She stormed for the protective gear, donning it in angry jerks, and Garrett followed suit.

"I had assumed since Brett Lumen's scene was tailored to him that we were dealing with a single homicide," she said to those flocking to her command. "Emily appears to have been killed the same way he was. One perfect crime scene is an anomaly, but two? The killer will make a mistake, and so help me God, we will find it."

The Espresso Shot flared to life as the detectives led the charge inside. Every inch of the shop was photographed. Every angle was sketched. Every surface dusted for prints, but as the hours slipped by, yet another similarity to Lumen's Custom's crept in. The scene was immaculate. Not a cup stood out of place. No stray coffee beans littered the floor. Not a single fingerprint smudged the places dozens of people touched daily.

They didn't need Lina Thum to estimate the time of death. Emily had been alive and well yesterday. Bel had seen her, and even though the thought turned her stomach, they would ask her husband to confirm when she left the house that morning. Like Lumen, she was most likely killed where she was laid to rest, her rigor mortis confirming that she had not been moved from her death pose.

"No sign of forced entry... except for mine," Bel said. "The cameras were disabled the same as Lumen's."

"Her footage was kept on site," Garrett said, "but their aims focus only on the register and both entrances." Bel quirked an eyebrow at him, and he added, "She showed me when she first installed this. Asked if I thought it was adequate."

"Do you know how to use it?" Bel asked.

"Yes." Garrett rebooted the system, pulling up the recorded footage. They watched in silence as some of Emily's last moments played before them. It showed Emily from the night before as she locked up, chatting all the while with Vera as Bel's elderly neighbor clutched a bag of coffee beans. The women smiled and conversed animatedly, and then the front door shut, sealing the shop in its solitude. Night fell, and Garrett scrolled through the emptiness, but as soon as the clock struck 10:00 p.m., nothingness consumed the screens. No one entered. No one physically disabled the cameras. They just stopped working.

"Brett turned his off." Garrett replayed the blackout, but it cut out at the exact same timecode. The image was there, then it wasn't. "No one touched these cameras, though."

"Is this a less expensive security system than Lumen's Customs'?" Bel asked.

"Definitely." Garrett nodded. "But Brett's showroom was worth far more than this shop."

"Could someone disrupt it from outside the building?" Bel asked.

"Possibly."

"But if Lumen's was more extensive, perhaps disabling it was too difficult for the killer," Bel said.

"So, they requested Lumen turn it off under the guise of privacy." Garrett finished the thought for her. "It's possible. Someone as rich as Eamon Stone would have the resources to disrupt the security."

"But why? Why kill Emily?" Bel asked. "It's a stretch, but I can almost decipher a motive for Lumen. Perhaps they disagreed on pricing or design, but Emily? How could you not like her? She sold joy in a cup."

Garrett shrugged as he continued scrolling through the footage.

"There is another explanation," Bel said, studying the three limited views on the monitor. "There are blind spots. It's feasible someone hid in the bathroom until Emily locked up and then shut down the system. If the killer stalked Emily like he did Brett, he would have known where the cameras were aimed."

"And you believe whoever killed Lumen killed Emily?" Garrett asked.

"The details are exact. Details we haven't released to the public. It's the same person."

"Do you…?" He paused and then looked over his shoulder to meet her gaze. "Do you think we have a serial killer on our hands?"

"To be categorized as a serial, he would need a third kill."

Bel clenched her fists. "We can't let him do this again... Wait, stop. Go back." She stepped closer to Garret's seated form, and he rewound the footage at her outburst. "Okay, play it."

All three angles restarted simultaneously, but nothing out of the ordinary popped up on the screen.

"What are—?" he started

"There," Bel cut him off, pointing at the camera aimed at the rear of the shop.

"I don't see anything?"

"Play it again, and can you go slow?"

Garrett nodded as he rewound, replaying the footage of the back alley as an employee walked inside for their shift. Garrett paused the video and then stepped through the frames, one by one. Right before their view of the alley was cut off, a blonde entered the frame. Her hair obscured her face, but as she tried to walk past the still-closing door, a broad hand captured her elbow and jerked her to a halt. The woman whirled on whoever restrained her, and Garrett pressed pause, leaning closer to the monitor.

"I don't recognize her," he said, looking up at Bel. "But she never turns toward the camera, so I can't be sure."

"Keep going," she encouraged, and her partner sighed, stepping through the footage until the door shut. He opened his mouth to question Bel, confused about why this particular moment was relevant, but then he froze. He wasn't sure how she had noticed it playing at regular speed. He barely appeared on the screen, but for that fraction of a second before the door obscured the alley, the person restraining the woman shifted into view.

Eamon Stone.

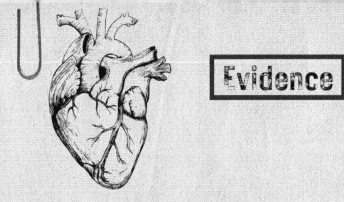

Chapter Thirteen

"WHAT TIME WAS THAT?" BEL ASKED, POINTING AT THE footage, Eamon's flawless jawline etched perfectly even in the grainy quality.

"Yesterday at... 3:24 p.m.," Garrett answered, and the partners shared a look that spoke volumes.

"And you don't recognize the woman?"

"No." He shrugged. "She never fully shows her face, but her visible features aren't familiar."

"Emerson? Cassidy?" Sheriff Griffin interrupted, and they both turned toward his voice. "David Kaffe would like to speak to you. He wants to help in any way he can."

The detectives nodded, wordlessly following their boss outside and shedding their protective wear. David stood small and defeated among the swarming throng, and Bel's heart ached. She often interacted with people on the worst days of their lives, and no matter how many moments like this she faced, they never got easier.

"Mr. Kaffe?" Bel said softly as she stepped closer with a comforting smile, extending her hand with a gentle invitation. The man took it, gripping her fingers weakly before shaking

Garrett's. "I'm Detective Isobel Emerson, and this is my partner, Garrett Cassidy. I am sorry for your loss. Emily was a treasure to this town."

"She was…" David wiped a tear from his eye before continuing, "I don't understand how anyone could have done this. Emily was kind. Well loved. She didn't have a cruel bone in her body. Why would someone do this to her?"

"We are going to do everything in our power to figure that out," Bel soothed, knowing the comment was a Band-Aid when stitches were needed. "I take it your wife didn't have any enemies that you were aware of?"

"No. Everyone liked her," David said. "It's hard to be mad at a woman who provides chocolate and caffeine."

"I certainly loved her for it." Bel smiled. "Aside from her customers, could she have been having problems with anyone else? Perhaps a supplier or someone she owed money?"

"Not that I know of. She would have told me if someone was giving her trouble. We talked about everything."

"Was she dealing with financial hardships? Debts?"

"No, the business does well." David gestured to the shop. "My father owned this building. He originally planned to sell it years ago, but one Christmas, I brought home this beautiful girl from college to meet my parents. I told my dad I was going to marry her, and when Emily made the dessert for Christmas dinner, my entire family fell in love with her baking. We married right after graduation, and when she moved to Bajka, my father gave us this shop as a wedding gift, so we own the Espresso Shot outright." David paused, the memory overwhelming his emotions. "My dad believed in his new daughter-in-law's talent, and he helped her renovate the storefront, transforming it into a bakery. Emily then added the coffee aspect. Said if she had to be up at dawn to bake, she needed liquid magic to fuel her."

"That's a beautiful story." Bel squeezed David's hand

comfortingly, knowing no amount of sympathy would ever heal his pain but needing to offer hers, anyway.

"Does the shop have anything designed by Lumen's Customs?" Garrett asked after a long silence passed between them.

"No. At the start, we had no savings, so we bought furniture from garage sales or second-hand shops. The eclectic decor became our trademark, so we continued the tradition."

"Did you or Emily interact with Brett Lumen? Were you friends, or did you travel in the same circles?" Bel asked, hoping for a connection between the two victims.

"Barely knew the guy," David said. "I've seen his work, but I've only crossed paths with him maybe a handful of times over the years…. Wait, his assistant? Viola?"

"Violet?" Bel corrected.

"Yes, her. I don't interact with the customers or deal with the baking. That was Emily and the girls' thing…" David's face crumpled. "How am I supposed to tell them about their mom?"

The man dissolved into tears, and Bel pressed a sympathetic palm to his shoulder. Flashbacks to when her own father sat her and her sisters down to inform them of their mother's passing assaulted her memory, and she had to push down the bitter bile climbing up her throat with a forceful swallow. It was a fate no family should have to endure.

"I'm sorry," David sniffled.

"Don't apologize." Bel rubbed his arm. "This is incredibly difficult. Take your time."

"I handled the books," David said after his breathing was under control. "I had a corporate job when we first got married, but when the Espresso Shot grew beyond what Emily could handle alone, I quit and took over the business aspects. Emily and my daughters—when they are home from college—deal with the customers, but I remember Violet. She stands out, and she always buys coffee in bulk. Other than her coming into the shop, we have no relationship with Lumen."

Bel and Garrett exchanged a look. It had been a long shot. Nothing about this case was obvious. Nothing made sense. Why would the choice of victims be different? And using Violet's purchases as a connection was grasping at straws. The entire town ordered their coffee from The Espresso Shot.

"So, this is a family business?" Garrett asked.

"Yes."

"Who will inherit the shop?" Bel asked, understanding where Garrett's line of questioning was headed.

"My daughters."

The detectives exchanged a wordless conversation. Unlike Lumen's Customs, where the assistant stood to inherit millions, The Espresso Shot was a family unit. It was unlikely that Emily's college-aged daughters had murdered their mother for ownership of a company they already had a hand in.

"David, we have to ask. Where were you last night?" Bel asked. In most homicides, the spouse was the killer, but the similarities to Lumen's scene made this question mostly a formality. She couldn't picture the slightly overweight, middle-aged husband of a baker having the power or cruelty to disfigure both bodies.

"I was in bed. Emily always leaves... left for work early. I got the girls ready for school when they were younger."

"Can anyone verify that?"

"My daughters are home for the summer. They were both there, but asleep."

"Would it be okay if we talked to them?" Bel asked, hating herself for having to mention it.

"Can I tell them first?" David asked. "They should find out from me."

"Of course." She doubted the girls knew anything, but there was a chance they were privy to their mother's secrets. In her line of work, it no longer surprised her just how often spouses were clueless. "I have a few more questions, and then we'll take a break. Did Emily come home last night?"

"Yes. She came right home after closing. We had dinner, watched tv, and then she went to bed early."

"What time did she leave for the shop?"

"We open at 6:00 a.m., so she usually got up at 3:30 so she could be there by 4:00. It gave her two hours to bake. It was her favorite part of the day."

"Did she leave on time this morning?" Garrett asked.

"Yes… no, actually," David said. "I'm not a morning person, but Emily always woke me up to say goodbye. It was two something, so, earlier than usual."

"Was she agitated? Upset? Did anything about her or her appearance seem off?" Bel asked, grasping for something, anything, to point her in the killer's direction.

"No, she was energetic. She had a recipe she was excited to try."

"What was it?" Bel's heart twinged, realizing that never again would Bajka wake up to a brand-new Emily concoction. She had touched the hearts of so many with her baking.

"Rose shortbread cookies," David answered, and Bel froze, roots of dread diving from her feet to embed into the asphalt, welding her where she stood. "With rose water buttercream."

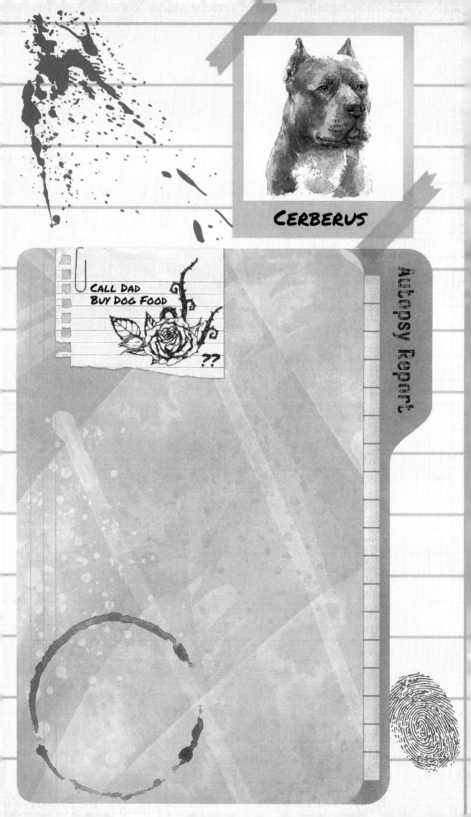

CERBERUS

CALL DAD
BUY DOG FOOD

??

Autopsy Report

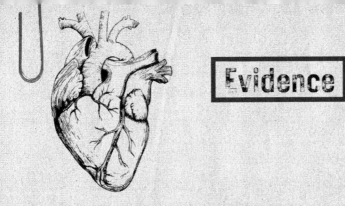

Chapter Fourteen

THE EMPLOYEE INTERVIEWS OFFERED WHAT BEL AND GARRETT already knew. Emily was well loved, and, like Lumen, she was unproblematic. The scene had been void of evidence save the ones the killer intended them to find, and as the detectives drove down the wooded road to the Reale Mansion, frustration coiled in Bel's gut like thorny branches scoring her organs.

"The killer's escalating," Bel said.

"How do you mean?" Garrett guided the vehicle with whitened knuckles.

"He's showing off. Not just in the display, but with his skill," she explained. "Lumen was killed on a Sunday, the timeline granting him almost a full day to perfect the scene. If Emily was still alive at 2:00 a.m., that gave our killer only a few hours to rip out her heart, pose her, and clean the shop before I arrived." Like Lumen's Customs, The Espresso Shot had been spotless. No signs of forced entry or a struggle. No fingerprints or blood or stray dustings of flour. Not even the scent of sugar. Only the fragrance of death and bleach and stale coffee bathing a corpse.

"Brett Lumen was drilled into an intricate floor-standing chandelier. Emily was merely seated in a tub, her arms wrapped in metal carvings. She would take significantly less time to pose." Garrett said.

"I know, but to clean the shop so thoroughly that forensics didn't even find stray coffee grinds? How is that possible in only a few hours?"

"Unless we revisit the multiple killers' theory."

"That scenario is looking more and more promising..." Bel paused. "And where are they getting these custom pieces? A ceramic tub shaped similar to a cup? Carved wood and metal. They look like Lumen's creations. He was the only one in town with the talent to build complex furniture."

"That I know of." Garrett slowed the car to a crunching halt on the gravel driveway and threw it into park. "Maybe Lumen did design these pieces."

"How do you mean?" Bel could practically see the wheels in her partner's head spinning with smoke-producing speed.

"Eamon Stone is a stranger. He moves to the outskirts of town, strives not to be caught on camera, and in a community unable to keep a secret, no one has heard of him. Shortly after he arrives, killings start, and he was Lumen's last client. What if the chandelier for his foyer was a mask for the true chandelier he commissioned?"

"You think he hired Lumen to design his own death shroud?" Bel shifted in her seat to stare at her partner.

"It's possible."

"What's the motive?"

"He's insane?" Garrett shrugged. "What if he commissioned the chandelier for his renovations to account for the crime scene parts he ordered? Perhaps Lumen was a loose end he needed to tie up. What if he isn't here for Lumen? Or Emily? What if someone in Bajka is the reason Eamon Stone moved here, and he's creating a spectacle to keep us running in circles so we don't see his true intentions?"

Fear crawled like spiders over Bel's skin as movement

caught the corner of her eye. The feeling of being watched hung heavy against her flesh, and she turned just in time to catch a dark shadow vacating one of the upper floor windows. She inhaled slowly, trying to force the fear from her body as she exhaled. What if Garrett was right? What if Eamon Stone was here for someone else, the killings a red herring for his true plans?

"It makes sense… if it were the plot of a thriller." Bel twitched as if to knock off the hundreds of invisible legs coating her arms, and Garrett looked crestfallen at her rejection.

"There's no evidence to support that theory." She placed a hand on his to soften the blow. "We won't throw it out, though. Maybe you're right, but ordering furniture and having an argument doesn't make you a killer. Suspicious? Yes. But we need more than just coincidences."

"I know." Garrett sighed, unbuckling his seatbelt and opening the car door. "But I can't shake the feeling that Eamon Stone is involved somehow."

"Me neither," Bel admitted as they walked toward the mansion. It was why they had driven to interview the stranger straight from The Espresso Shot. Lina Thum had seized control of Emily's body. The crime scene had been photographed and sketched, and final evidence collections and interviews were being overseen by the Sheriff. If Mr. Stone was involved, they didn't want to give him any more time than he already had to compose lies and alibis.

"Bajka Police!" Garrett knocked on the front door, and it swung wide, the latch not secure. "Mr. Stone, are you home?"

"Listen." Bel gestured toward the rear of the mansion. "Is that a saw?"

Garrett froze, his hand shifting to his sidearm. "Bajka Police!" The grating sound continued.

"Mr. Stone?" Bel yelled over the sinister song of metal teeth, and the saw silenced instantly at her voice.

"Back yard." Eamon's thundering rumble echoed through the decaying rooms. "Watch your step as you walk through. Wouldn't want you to fall and break your necks on my renovations."

The detectives exchanged a wary glance before plunging into the beast's lair. The saw continued its devastation, and they followed its siren's call until they found the owner of the house on the grass outside the back door.

"Good evening, Detectives." A low menace reverberated beneath Eamon's greeting, and Bel heaved a sigh of relief to find the towering man was fully dressed this time. Not that the black tee shirt stretched dangerously tight over his sculpted form offered him any modesty. He was sin wrapped in perfection, and the instant Bel stepped into his line of sight, his dark eyes snapped to hers. For a second, only the two of them existed as he lowered the power tool, his pull impossible to resist. And then Eamon took a deep breath, leaning almost imperceptibly toward her as if to capture her scent. Bel recoiled as the look in his haunted eyes changed from threatening to predatory, their intensity giving her the impression that the god-like man before her wanted to murder her where she stood. To carve her open and wear her blood. That or he wished to kiss her. A kiss that would leave her blind to his flaws, that would pin her shaking body up against the wall and not relent until she ceased to exist except in his arms.

"Detective Emerson." He said her name like the slice of a blade, like the taste of wine. "Detective, Cassidy. What can I do for you, fine officers?" Eamon released Bel from his hold, pinning Garrett with his death stare, and the air rushed back into her lungs.

"We would like to ask you a few questions about Emily Kaffe, the owner of the Espresso Shot," Garrett said, shifting slightly before Bel, as if to stake his claim on her.

"I can't imagine why." Eamon folded his muscled arms over

his chest, the movement revealing a peak of color over his shoulder in the distance. "I didn't know the woman. I only visited her shop once or twice to stock up on coffee... did something happen to her?"

"Yesterday at 3:24 p.m., you were seen on camera in the alley behind the Espresso Shot," Garrett continued, ignoring the man's question.

"My, my, something did happen to her." Eamon's eye flicked to Bel's, heat burning in their soulless black. "Did someone kill her? Was it like poor Mr. Lumen's death? What a shame. I thought small-town living was supposed to be safe and peaceful."

"You were arguing with a woman." Bel stepped forward, her ocean blue eyes meeting his gaze, challenge for challenge. "Why were you at The Espresso Shot?"

"To purchase coffee, of course."

"You never went inside, Mr. Stone." Bel crossed her arms to mimic his stance, and he leaned forward as if amused by her defiance. "Care to amend your story?"

"I planned to restock my coffee supply, but you are correct, I never made it inside," Eamon spoke to her as if only they stood in the garden, Garrett a distant memory. "I was distracted by my... friend."

"Does this friend have a name?"

"Alcina Magus."

"What was the nature of your conversation?"

"Nothing of importance, Detective Emerson. Simply two old acquittances having a discussion."

Bel ground her molars at his evasive answers, but she had said it herself. It wasn't illegal to disagree.

"Where were you last night between the hours of 1:00 a.m. and 6:00 a.m.?" she asked.

"Home in bed. Why, where were you, Detective?" He spoke

with an expression that hinted he knew exactly where she had been.

"Can anyone confirm your alibi?" Garrett seized control of the conversation.

"Just my renovations, Detective Cassidy. Now, if you'll excuse me, I'd like to finish this before I lose the light." Eamon turned back to his project, effectively murdering the interview. "My sympathy goes out to the Kaffe family. Such a tragedy, but I am new to Bajka, remember? Why would I be involved with this?"

Why would anyone do this was indeed the question, and Bel's hands flexed. Something was happening in her town. Something sinister, and she couldn't see the path through the thicket. These deaths didn't make sense. The victims didn't make sense. This man before her didn't make sense.

"We will be in touch, Mr. Stone," Garrett said, as if it had been his idea to end the conversation. "Don't leave town."

"I wouldn't dream of it." Eamon stared at Bel as the words fell from his lips, and his heated gaze slid over her scars to the book charm necklace resting delicately on her chest. "What a lovely necklace, Detective Emerson." He said her name like a threat. He said it like a moan of pleasure. "Whoever gave that to you must care about you a lot." The murderous hunger slipped back into his irises as he studied her throat, and Bel had to fight her every muscle to keep from clutching the pendant protectively in her fist.

The truth was, she didn't know who had gifted this to her. It had appeared beside her hospital bed when she woke from her attack without a note or a box. She wasn't sure what about the simple book on the thin chain sang to her, but she had clasped it around her neck and never took it off. But the stare on Eamon's face pitched her stomach. It was too familiar, too hungry, too abrasive.

"Have a good evening, Detectives," Eamon said, dismissing them as he returned to his saw.

"Good night." Garrett slid a palm against Bel's back and ushered her back the way they came. They walked silently unnerved through the chaotic house, but Bel froze halfway to the front door, her partner bumping into her suddenly immobile form.

"Wait," she whispered, something nagging at her memory. She spotted the staircase and raced up the steps two at a time before Garrett could stop her.

"Bel?" He dashed after her, but she didn't halt until she found a room with a window that opened out onto the gardens. "What are you doing?" he asked as he followed her to where she stood motionless.

"I almost didn't register them. They were a single sliver of color hiding just behind his head," Bel said, staring out as the sun set.

"Didn't register what?"

"The roses." Bel pointed, and Garrett sucked in a sharp breath. The bushes had been hidden from view where they stood below, but from this height, their vivid blooms were obvious. Behind Eamon Stone's crumbling mansion was a garden of damning crimson.

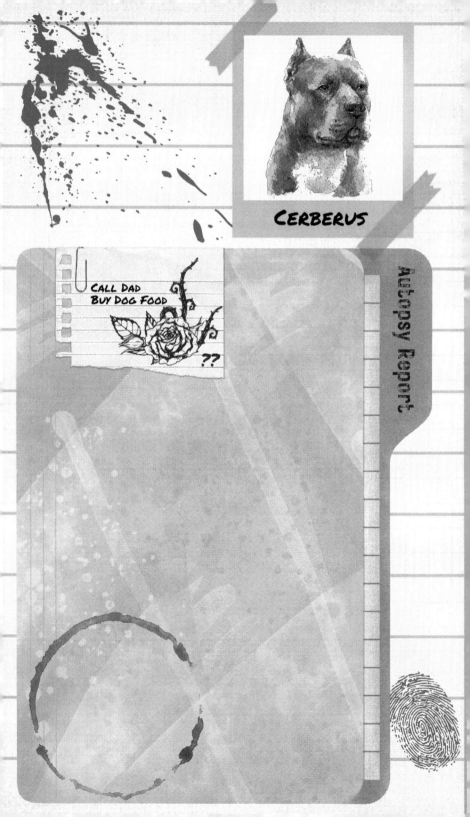

CERBERUS

Autopsy Report

CALL DAD
BUY DOG FOOD

??

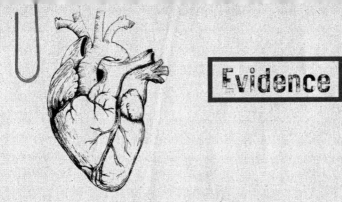

Evidence

Chapter Fifteen

"BUT A GARDEN DOESN'T MAKE SOMEONE GUILTY." BEL RUBBED her bloodshot eyes. They were getting nowhere. She and Garrett had arrived at the Medical Examiner's early that morning for Emily Kaffe's autopsy, but like Lumen's, it offered more questions than answers. Her body bore no defensive wounds, her blood had been drained, her heart was mysteriously absent, and the curved tears in her chest were indecipherable without the missing flesh.

Garrett and Bel had spent the rest of the day drowning in paperwork and examining evidence, but as evening turned to night, and the station quieted, Bel's frustration grew as they circled the same theories.

"If it did, we would have to arrest half of Bajka." Bel grabbed the Chinese takeout container and scooped rice into her mouth. "I'll admit Eamon Stone's arrival and his presence at each scene the day before are concerning, but there is no evidence that directly links him. And the killer's profile doesn't seem to align with what we know about him."

Garrett quirked an eyebrow in question as he held his fork

over the last spring roll. Bel glanced down at it and nodded, and he speared it, lifting it to his lips.

"Both homicides have been a show, a display of human art," Bel explained. "The killer wants us to see his work, to marvel at it, to obsess over it. It points to a personality that craves attention. The guilty party will often return as a spectator. They love the thrill of possibly being recognized, and while they don't want to get caught so they can continue to perform, they also long to take credit for their masterpiece. Eamon Stone is practically a hermit. You know the town gossips would drool over the presence of an eligible millionaire, but not one person breathed his name before this case. No one has seen him around town, and he never ventured to the crime scenes after the fact. I could be wrong, but I believe the killer enjoys the spotlight. He wants to draw our eyes to his superiority."

"There were plenty of spectators," Garrett agreed, shuffling through the folders on the desk. "We should have photos of the crowds. You think we caught the killer on camera?"

"With crimes this prolific, I'd bet money he was outside at some point. The killer had to stalk each victim to learn their schedules. These murders were premeditated, and those custom pieces required time to prepare. He would have stalked their lives for weeks, maybe even months. I believe he would want to witness the aftermath."

"He must be someone the town was used to seeing since he observed them for so long, unnoticed," Garrett said, and Abel Reus and his daily oatmeal order popped into Bel's head. "Someone who flew under the radar. If your profile is correct, Eamon Stone isn't invisible. He is too tall, too handsome, too rich to be ignored, and the killer would be someone we wouldn't blink an eye at." Garrett purposely avoided Bel's gaze, and she blushed, knowing full well how captivated she had been by Eamon's presence.

"There is something else," Bel said, expertly moving the

conversation away from the millionaire's sex appeal. "Emily always opened the shop herself, and then her employees would arrive for the morning rush hour. If I hadn't seen her hand and broken the door, one of her subordinates would have discovered her. Brett Lumen was found by his assistant. In both cases, an employee should have found the body."

"And both victims were bosses," Garrett continued. "Could the killer resent authority? Perhaps he's someone who was passed over for a promotion or who worked under a terrorizing manager. Perhaps by killing business owners, he is reclaiming his dominance over a boss who humiliated him?"

"To afford the Reale Mansion and surrounding estate, Eamon Stone is clearly not a disgruntled employee. Commissioning multiple designs from Lumen's Customs would cost a fortune, hinting that his status is most likely that of an executive and not a subordinate," Bel said.

"But…" Garrett swallowed the last bite of the spring roll and snagged his laptop, dragging it closer. "What was her name again? The woman Stone argued with?"

Bel opened her notes. "Alcina Magus."

"He was evasive when we spoke to him yesterday about her. He called her 'a friend', but based on the way his body tensed at the mention of her and the surveillance footage fight, I'm guessing they aren't actually friends." Garrett started typing.

"Are you thinking she is his employee?" Bel asked, scooting closer to her partner to watch him.

"Or maybe she is an old girlfriend who broke his heart. I don't know." Garrett shrugged, and Bel pulled her laptop beside his, entering Eamon's name into the search bar.

They worked in comfortable silence as the night bled past them. Back cramping and eyes exhausted, Bel finally pushed her chair away from the desk and stood, stretching with a groan. "I'm not finding much on Stone," she said as she drained her water bottle. Her gaze caught the clock's accusing time, and she groaned again. They had gotten takeout for dinner, but no one was home to feed Cerberus. She needed to find her little beast a sitter until she solved this case. "A few news articles mention him, but there are no photos except for this from a few years ago." She pointed at her screen, the photo capturing his profile behind a well-dressed couple at a black-tie event.

"That doesn't look like him," Garrett said, leaning closer to the image. "Except for the height."

"It's older, and the background is blurry." Bel attempted to explain the discrepancies, but she had to agree with her partner. Eamon's jaw line played on repeat in her mind, too defined to be muddled by a grainy photo. "There is a charity that lists him as their CEO. Looks like they provide shelters for displaced families and victims of disasters... which explains his renovation skills, but I can't find much else." She continued her search. "The man is an online ghost. No social media. No photos. No interviews."

"Well, you found more than me." Garrett pushed his chair back and looked at her. "I found absolutely nothing. Based on what I can tell, Alcina Magus doesn't exist."

———

THE NEXT FEW days were quiet, too quiet, setting Bel's teeth on edge. Lina Thum had placed a rush on the toxicology report, but it was no surprise when it revealed Emily Kaffe had not been under the influence at the time of her death. Just like Brett Lumen, she had allowed her heart to be stolen without drugs to subdue her or a single defensive wound on her body. She had not struggled, not fought to survive. Bel hated that fact most of all. Emily hadn't tried to live.

The detectives buried themselves in paperwork. They interviewed family and coworkers until they repeated the questions so often, their mouths moved on autopilot. They studied every crime scene photo and examined the ceramic Emily had been posed in, but nothing new presented itself. The mug and the chandelier were handmade, giving them no manufacturer to track purchases from. The victim's hearts were still missing, and before both security footages were disabled, the only people caught on tape were townsfolk going about their business. If being filmed on camera at The Espresso Shot was a sign of guilt, then Bel, Garrett, Sheriff Griffin, Violet, Abel, Vera, and occasionally Cerberus were all to blame. Lumen's footage was similar. Friends, tourists, neighbors. The only exception was Eamon Stone. Besides the few frames where his face was captured on the coffee shop surveillance, his likeness was nowhere to be seen. After their conversation about the killer's profile, Bel paid attention to the stranger's presence in town, but her vigilance didn't matter. Eamon was a ghost, a monster locked away in a castle in the woods. No one spoke of him, knew of him, thought of him. Only she did.

By the end of the third silent night, Bel was more police station coffee than human. Garrett had stood up as she scanned a takeout menu, and not so subtly insisted he was making her dinner. She protested, pointing to the mountain of work taunting them with a solution she couldn't find, but her partner made it very clear that she could not help the dead if she worked herself into the grave. Emily and Brett were gone, and chaining herself to her desk while surviving on vending machine chips would not bring them back. She needed sleep and real food, and the best way to avenge the fallen was to not fall herself.

Bel relented to his wisdom, despite her stubborn streak raising its hackles, but the moment she set foot in her partner's apartment, she knew it had been the right call. He made spicy chicken kabobs served over rice, and the meal settled her soul. By her second glass of wine, she couldn't keep the yawns from her lips. Garrett's presence was comforting, lulling her into peace.

Since he had only finished one beer, Garrett drove her home and walked her to the front door with an agitated hesitation in his steps. Bel opened her mouth to ask him what was wrong as she fished her keys out of her pocket, but Garrett's hands caught her face in a grip of adoration before she could utter a word.

"Bel," he whispered, lowering his forehead to hers. "I wanted to wait for our date, but I have the worst timing. I... Can I kiss you?"

Her feet grew roots, binding her in place as her heart fought to escape her chest. Her extremities and her organ warred with each other, threatening to tear her apart. No one had stood this close to her since the attack. The last time breath had brushed against her skin had been seconds before teeth had carved through her flesh.

"Are you all right?" Garrett pulled back to gaze into her eyes, and only then did Bel realize how rapidly her breathing assaulted her lungs. She forced herself to nod as she studied his brown irises. They were kind. Gentle. Not the stare of a monster. No, this was Garrett, her Garrett. The man who cooked her dinner when she was too stressed to eat and who didn't pressure her into confessing her secrets.

Hesitantly, Bel lifted herself onto her toes and placed nervous fingers on his chest. His heart leaped at her touch as if it wanted to escape his ribs and meet her palm. The tenderness in his eyes and the thunder of his heartbeat swelled the emotions in her own chest, and before fear convinced her to flee, she kissed him. Their lips met feather-light. Soft and sweet and gentle, and when they broke away, Garrett's smile was oceans wide.

"Good night, Bel." He tucked a loose chestnut curl behind her ear. "Sweet dreams." He leaned forward, kissing her cheek in farewell.

"Good night." She grabbed his hand; their fingers locked together until the distance separated them. She watched him walk to the car and waved as he drove away. The kiss hadn't been earth-shattering, but then again, she was impressed that her anxiety allowed anyone to get that close. She liked Garrett. He was a good man. Someone without drama or danger. Once the case was over and her stress reduced, they could work on the fireworks.

Bel turned to go inside when her sight snagged on Vera. Her elderly neighbor was watching Garrett leave with laser-sharp vision, her eyes cold and aggressive. The expression was foreign on her normally sweet face. As if sensing she was being watched, she jerked her gaze to Bel and smiled bright enough to charm the heavens. Bel smirked and waved back, fighting the urge to roll her eyes. Vera wanted her married and with a family so badly, she was practically salivating at Garrett's Prince Charming form.

Safely locked away in her cabin, Bel spent the rest of her evening with her main man, the one she trusted more than any human besides her father. As she cuddled the furry beast, she read, hoping to dream of curly brown hair.

The dreams started innocently, and even in sleep, she dared to hope. Garrett's kisses were warm. The sun shone. The birds sang. His lips were soft, soft, soft, but then his eyes changed. Black as midnight, as death, as destruction. The kiss turned rough, her body screaming for an escape. Begging for more, so much more. A hard chest pressed against hers, forcing a moan from her lips as a tongue slid inside her mouth. His dark eyes owned her. His tongue claimed her, and her skin burned. She was all fire and heat and desire. She craved more. She craved an end to the madness. And then the teeth came. It was always the teeth that woke her.

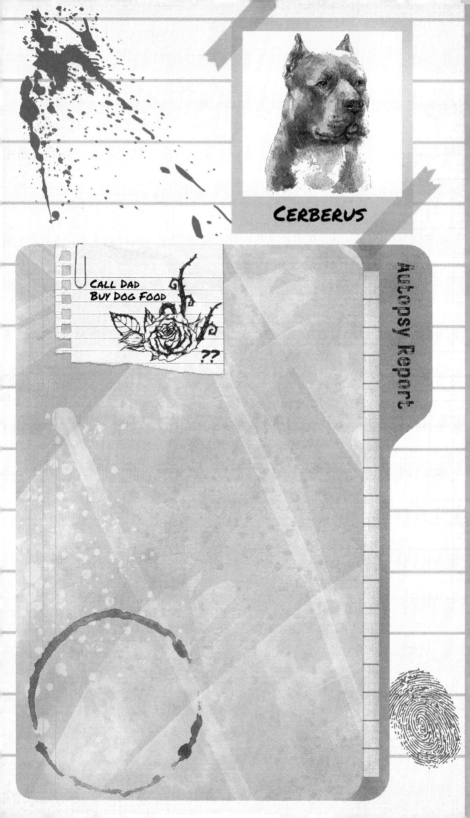

CERBERUS

CALL DAD
BUY DOG FOOD

??

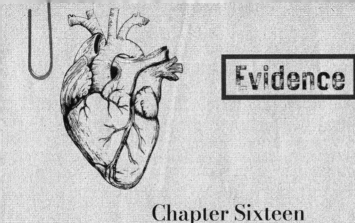

Chapter Sixteen

BEL STARED AT HER PHONE, THUMB HOVERING OVER HER father's number. She needed to call him. To tell him this case was drowning her in fear. He would understand. He wouldn't judge her. Her dad was the person she trusted most. They were cut from the same cloth, and he would never betray her trust. But it wasn't just her anxiety that kept her thumb from pressing his contact. The hesitation was darker, more complicated, and she was afraid of the truth. Unwilling to admit that the nightmares went beyond her fears.

Hiding in her terror was something else. Something new and equally unnerving. The black eyes. Their severity haunted her, and her instincts recognized Eamon Stone as evil. Every cell in her bones knew that a thirst for darkness simmered beneath his skin. With every molecule that vibrated within her heart, she knew he wanted her, but that was not the unsettling part. No, what shook Bel to her core was the fact that while Eamon Stone was the monster she was bred to hunt, she couldn't resist his call. He was her siren, her song in the deep.

"Cerberus?" Bel tossed her phone onto the bed and grabbed her leggings. "Want to go for a walk?"

The pitbull raced to the front door, tail whipping as if it was a propeller readying to launch him into flight. Bel laughed and shimmied into a sports bra before grabbing a tank top. It was hot outside, and revealing sportswear never used to embarrass her, but even running alone in the woods did not assuage her new insecurities over the scars that ran from her neck, down her chest to her stomach. They were thin pink stripes now, hardly noticeable, but she still let no one see them, so despite the heat, she donned long leggings and a shirt as armor.

Clicking on the dog's harness, Bel shoved her feet into sneakers, and then the two of them exploded into the early morning air. This was her favorite part of living in Bajka. A workout in the city meant traffic and sidewalks and crowds, but here, it was endless trails and peace behind her house. She loved these moments with her dog and couldn't imagine how frustrating it would be to lug a seventy-pound pitbull down four flights of stairs to the sidewalk just for a potty break.

The detective and her best friend plunged into the forest, and watching Cerberus chase squirrels, Bel almost forgot about her nightmares until the fur on the dog's neck bristled. His bulky muscles went rigid, and then she felt it prick her skin with icy awareness. Someone was following them.

Bel and Cerberus' eyes scanned the trees, but they were alone. There was no sound save her thundering heart. "Hello?" She clutched his leash tighter, but only the sounds of the forest answered her. They stood motionless for a moment, but when nothing happened, she gave the dog a gentle tug. "Come on, buddy, let's go home."

They turned back toward her cabin, but a twig snapped. Cerberus tensed, a low growl rumbling his throat, and the feeling of eyes on her skin increased. She couldn't breathe. She couldn't think. Fear took over, screaming for her to run as a second snapping branch reached their ears.

It happened so fast; she couldn't stop him. One instant,

Cerberus was at her side, and the next, he was running, powerful legs pounding through the trees. The force of his escape wrenched the leash from her fist, and within seconds, the black dog vanished into the underbrush.

"Cerberus?" she yelled at his disappearing shape. "Come back!" She stepped in the direction he had fled, but a paralyzing evil slipped over her skin. Whoever was watching her was closing in, their sight almost a palpable grip on her wrists. Bel's lungs constricted, her muscles tightened, and she bolted into a run. Gone was the sensible cop, replaced by raw instinct and terror. Fear pushed her forward, one foot pounding in front of the other. Escape. Escape. Escape. It was her mantra, her subconscious' desperation to keep her alive.

Branches whipped at her face. Roots tripped her. Her voice screamed for Cerberus, but she was alone. He had left her to be hunted. She choked on her panic. The scar on her throat itched, yet the eyes watching her never yielded. They stalked her. Haunted her. She ran until her muscles ached, until her lungs burned, until her mind blurred.

Whack! Bel slammed into a solid obstacle so hard she yelped in pain, stumbling as her momentum bounced her backward. She teetered, her body tilting dangerously when a powerful hand cemented itself to her spine and yanked her forward. She smacked into the obstacle again, her cheek slapping against cool, sweaty skin, and she froze. The palm at her back held her firmly against the formidable figure towering above her, killing any attempt at escape, and as she gasped for breath with stinging lungs, she recognized the coiled muscles caging her in.

Her terrified eyes shot up and found death-black irises staring cruelly down at her. Blond, sweaty hair hung over his brow, his sharply angled jaw tilted dangerously close to her face despite his towering height. His bare chest breathed steadily against her rapidly heaving breast, and with an unsettling smirk, Eamon Stone lowered his head slightly and inhaled her scent.

"Detective Emerson." He grinned with a wicked beauty, and Bel shoved his sweat-glistened abs away from her. The hand at her back resisted her escape long enough to make her panic before it released her.

"I was…" Her voice faltered. The sensation of someone following her had vanished, but she had run right into the arms of the devil himself. He was ungodly beautiful as he hovered before her, every inch of his bare skin sculpted for worship and sin, and she stepped backward again, putting a chasm of safety between them as if his beauty might carve her to pieces.

"Looking for him?" Eamon finished her sentence for her, his voice as deep as the ocean floor. Bel squinted at his words, and he jerked his chiseled jaw to his left. She followed his line of sight and simultaneously almost burst into relieved tears, an annoyed huff, and a good-natured laugh at what she found. Cerberus was sniffing a massive tree fifteen feet away before deciding to pee on it. He was completely unbothered by Eamon's presence, and Bel's gaze shifted warily between man and dog.

"Yes," she agreed.

"Beautiful dog," he said with a damning smile, and at this close angle, Bel noticed his canines for the first time. His teeth were perfectly white and straight, a smile that undoubtedly cost him to achieve, but his canines stood out from the rest. They weren't overly large. They didn't protrude, and they were the same pristine color as the others, but they were slightly sharp, as if he had purposely asked the dentist to straighten all his teeth but leave those natural. They were oddly seductive, like a threat hidden in kind words. Everything about this man screamed danger from his deep voice to his enticing body, and Bel ripped her gaze from his tempting lips. She strode toward Cerberus, who had found yet another tree to pee on, and she captured his leash without an issue. The pitbull finally took notice of her, and he wagged his tail as if nothing had happened.

"Come on, baby beast." She gently tugged his leash,

desperate to flee Eamon's unblinking stare. Cerberus obeyed immediately, but they only made it a few feet before Eamon's rumbling voice shredded the silence.

"Detective Emerson?"

She should ignore him. She shouldn't respond, but his orbit was impossible to escape, to resist, and Bel turned to face his hell black eyes.

"Be careful." He smirked, showing off those beautifully sharp teeth. "You never know what kind of predators are out here."

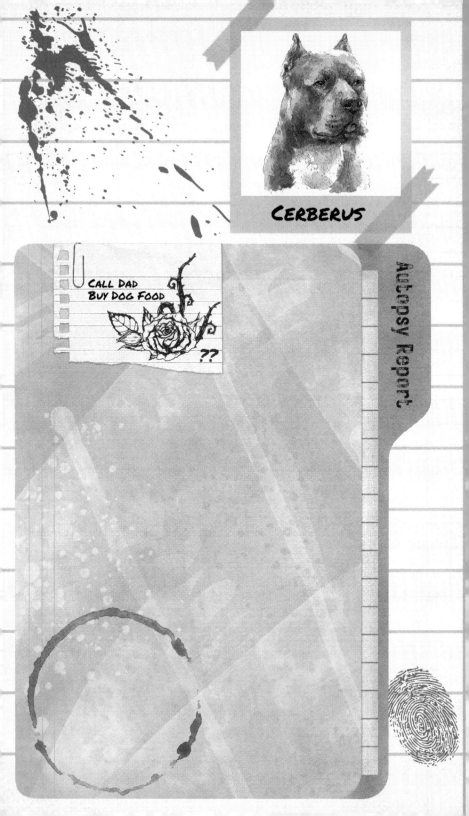

CERBERUS

CALL DAD
BUY DOG FOOD
??

Autopsy Report

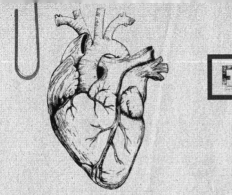

Chapter Seventeen

EAMON'S WORDS HAUNTED BEL FOR THE REST OF THE DAY, throwing her off kilter. Someone was watching her, hunting her. And while Eamon's presence so far from his home and so close to hers hinted that his black eyes were following her, she couldn't shake the feeling that despite the fear he inspired, there was an aura of safety surrounding him. She did not doubt that his skin contained a monster, but it was as if he was the king of the darkness, and no evil would dare challenge his dominance. Bel knew she was not safe from Eamon Stone, but when she stood within his grasp, he would protect her from the demons fighting for her soul.

Bel had the distinct sense that while his warning was meant for her, it was also a foreboding of deaths yet to come. An evil had claimed Bajka as its hunting ground, and she feared that its long night had only just fallen. More would die before the sun of justice rose, and the air felt too calm, too still. They were in the storm's eye. So, when the phone rang the next morning, waking her up, she knew.

"Emerson?" Sheriff Griffin's voice sounded raw through the

connection, and instantly, Bel understood the severity since he was calling and not Garrett.

"Sir," she answered, her voice rough with sleep. "Where?" She didn't need him to tell her it had happened again.

"The Ivory Keys."

"On my way." Bel fed and walked Cerberus at the speed of light before throwing on a clean pair of clothes. She would have to forgo coffee and breakfast, but she made it to the music shop in record time, the clock on her car dashboard reading 7:45 a.m. She knew for a fact The Ivory Keys kept 9-5 hours, so she was surprised someone had found a body this early until she saw him. Her heart leaped into her throat as he hovered in the shadows, dressed in black. His gaze found hers instantly, and he followed her every step as she moved toward the Sheriff. Unlike their other encounters, where his arrogance and dominance bled through his words and movements, Eamon seemed almost concerned as she arrived on the scene.

"Sheriff," Bel greeted Griffin, trying to avoid the caress of Eamon's gaze on her skin.

"Emerson." The Sheriff's voice was tight, his face drawn. Dread weighed heavily on both of them as Garrett parked and jumped from his vehicle.

"Victim is Victor Legat," Griffin said as her partner joined them. "Owner of The Ivory Keys."

"Did an employee find him?" Bel asked.

"No, Legat owns and runs this music shop by himself." Bel and Garrett exchanged a look as he answered. So much for her disgruntled employee theory.

"Who found him?" Garrett asked.

"Mr. Stone." Griffin jerked his head backward in Eamon's direction. "He had an appointment with Victor this morning before store hours. He called it in."

Bel's gaze slid to Eamon, his towering height stalking her from the shadows. Despite his pure beauty and intimidating size, none of the deputies paid him any attention, as if he existed for her and only her. Three deaths. Three crime scenes. Eamon Stone the only common denominator. Bel's stomach twisted. There was no evidence to support her conviction, but she knew. This beautifully dangerous man was a killer. He had done this, and she had been alone in the woods with him.

"Don't let him leave." Bell swallowed the fear choking her. "I want to talk to him after I see the body."

Sheriff Griffin nodded as the partners moved for the front door. "Legat has one adult son who lives a few towns over with his wife and her family. I'll notify him."

"Thank you," both detectives said in unison as they donned protective gear and slipped inside the music shop. Bel refused to meet Eamon's stare, but she felt his eyes follow her every step of the way. The thread of concern still weaved through his irises, and while she convinced herself that it was because they were closing in on him, a nagging in her gut whispered the concern was not for himself. It was for her.

The Ivory Keys had a cluttered eclectic feel, instruments decorating every inch of the space as they walked the straight path to the shop's main floor. A beautiful vintage piano stood proud and dazzling in the middle of the room, but its beauty was not the focal point. The piano bench was.

Victor Legat looked to be in his late sixties, his body posed on his hands and knees before the instrument, his spine creating the seat for the pianist to sit upon. Just as Lumen's nudity had been encased in carvings, so was Legat's. Starting at his wrists, claw foot wooden legs supported both of his wrinkled arms, the black sculpture drilled into his bloodless skin. A wooden table top stretched from his armpits to his pelvis to support his belly, delicately carved thorn bushes wrapping around his sides to hold him in place. Descending from his hips were another two legs encasing his own. Their delicate designs were screwed into his thighs to keep him steady. Two more gruesome claws protruded from where his knees pressed into the carpet. The killer had also broken Legat's bones so that he could push the man's calves against the back of his thighs, drilling his feet parallel to the ceiling to continue the flat stretch that reinforced the seat. The piano bench did not stop there. Beginning at his bare shoulders and extending all the way to the soles of his upturned feet was a cushion, thick threads stitching it bloodlessly to his flesh.

"My god," Garrett whispered at the mutilation. The black paint of the wood matched the piano's coloring exactly, the cushion as creamy as the ivory keys. "The wooded base covers his chest." Garrett pointed to where Legat's stomach lay pressed against the structure, hiding the man's ribs from view. "Do you think he is missing his heart?"

Bel stepped forward and studied the cushion sewed into Victor's back and realized that while the thick thread attached the fabric to flesh where a spectator could see it, the side of his body facing the piano was absent stitching. With gloved fingers, Bel gently tested it, and it lifted easily as if on hinges.

Garrett cursed under his breath as the lifted cushion revealed a gaping, bloodless hole in Legat's back, all flesh and muscle and bone missing to create a cavity where his heart should have been. An organ of roses rested in its place, the vibrant petals the only crimson on the scene.

"Do you think pulling the heart from his back is significant?" Garrett asked.

"No." Bel gestured to the immaculate piano. "This is important. A musician becoming part of his instruments."

"The floor is carpeted." Garrett rubbed the toe of his shoe over the fibers slightly to emphasize his point. "If the killer left blood behind, this is where we might find it. Bleaching tile is one thing, but carpet?"

"My god," Lina Thum's voice interrupted them, and the detectives watched as the medical examiner got to work. "Rigor Mortis is still in full swing," she said as cameras flashed from every angle. "Time of death was most likely sometime last night. My guess is before midnight, and like the others, it appears he was killed and posed here right away. The killer didn't break rigor to get him into this position." Lina cursed softly. "Who does this to an old man?"

"We'll let you work." Bel stepped out of Lina's way to allow her the space. She scanned the shop. The building was too clean, too spotless, and she prayed they would find something embedded in the carpet.

"Are there cameras?" she asked Garrett, not finding any hanging from the ceiling.

"Victor didn't have any," Sheriff Griffin's voice sounded behind them, his large frame hovering by the door. "He was old school that way. I told him he should invest, but he didn't like technology."

For a split second, frustration threatened to boil over in Bel's gut. This killer had claimed three lives, and he showed no signs of slowing. If he didn't make a mistake soon, if they didn't find evidence, he would undoubtedly kill again, and Bel couldn't help but feel that this town's blood was on her hands. Griffin had made her lead on this case because she was a New York City Detective. She had caught monsters before, but this one? This one was too smart. Too good. Too perfect. No crime was ever this pristine, this flawlessly executed. What kind of killer were they dealing with?

"I got in touch with Legat's son," the Sheriff continued, his voice somber. "He'll be at the station in a few hours."

"Thanks, Sheriff," Bel said, passing her boss as she walked outside. "Let me know when he gets here. I want to talk to him."

Griffin nodded, Lina mumbling in the background about how to safely dismantle Legat's piano bench, and Bel stormed for Eamon. She was done with his evasive answers and intimidating stares, and with determined resolve, she planted herself before his towering height.

"Good morning, Detective." Eamon's lips quirked in a smile that was decidedly threatening.

"Sheriff Griffin tells me you were the one who discovered the body and called it in?" Bel didn't bother returning his pleasantries.

"I did."

If he didn't start answering her, she was going to find pliers and pry them out of him. "What time was that, and why are you here before store hours?"

"I arrived for a 7:00 a.m. appointment, but by 7:15, he had yet to answer my knocks. I tested the door and found it unlocked, so I went inside. That was when I discovered him."

"Did you touch anything?" she asked.

"Only the front door to enter."

Bel glanced at Garrett, their partner bond speaking wordlessly, and he nodded, leaving to print the doors to confirm his statement. She watched him go, practically praying that they would find Eamon's prints elsewhere just to prove he was lying, that he was involved. She turned back to the towering blond and recoiled at his expression. His arrogant mask had dropped now that they were unobserved, as if he refused to allow anyone but her to see the predator beneath. Normally confident and sophisticated, his hungry eyes and hunched posture lost all pretenses of civility, flushing icy fear through her veins.

"I find it suspicious that, once again, you had dealings with a victim right before their death." She forced her voice to remain steady as she regained control of the conversation. "It's a stretch to believe you conveniently had a meeting with Victor Legat this morning."

"Think what you will, Detective," Eamon growled, "but I was not the one to request this appointment."

"What do you mean?"

"Mr. Legat called me last night, requesting I meet him today before the store opened. He knows I prefer privacy."

"Our victim called you? Forgive me if I don't believe that."

"It is not so hard to believe, Detective." Eamon said detective as if it was her name, as if he was tasting every syllable, savoring each letter. "I had business with his shop."

"What kind?"

"There was a piano left in the Reale Mansion when I arrived." He leaned forward further and inhaled as if he didn't even realize he was breathing in her scent. "It's an antique, damaged from years of abandonment, but its skeleton is good. I had hired Mr. Legat to restore it for me."

"You hired Lumen to design furniture and Legat to repair a piano?" Bel wanted to lean back, to escape his hold, but she couldn't. She was trapped in his orbit, letting his predacious gaze drink her down as he breathed her in, and she would never admit it, but the look of pure desire that flooded his eyes at her scent set her heart racing. "And you purchased your coffee from The Espresso Shot?"

"Of course I did, Detective." Honey… her title on his tongue was like honey. "Doesn't everyone in Bajka?"

"You had dealings with all three of our victims, saw them right before their deaths, and now discovered Victor Legat's body. If you did this, if you killed him… I won't stop until I find who's responsible, and if it was you, so help me God."

"I wouldn't expect anything less," he said reverently, surprising her. "But I can assure you, Detective, I may be evil, but I am not the evil you're hunting."

"I'll be the judge of that."

Eamon smiled, sharp canines capturing her sight. He was beautiful when he smiled. He was the devil.

"You said Legat called you?" Bel ripped her view from his teeth and planted them on his soulless eyes. "What time?"

"Around 9:00 p.m.," he answered, and she made a mental note to both check the phone records and tell Lina. It would help her narrow the time of death window.

"Did you speak to him, or did he leave a message?"

"Spoke to him."

"How did he sound? Was he agitated? Did he come off nervous? Coerced? Relaxed?"

"He sounded matter of fact…" Eamon paused, as if just realizing something. "Perhaps a little too much. I didn't find it out of the ordinary, but I suppose it was robotic."

Bel refused to say it out loud because she wanted to believe this man who terrified her was the killer, but her gut resisted her suspicions. She knew Garrett was convinced of Eamon's guilt, but what if someone forced Victor to make the call to place him in her line of fire? Eamon was involved. Of that, she had no doubt, but the small part of her that didn't fear him whispered that while he was a monster come to plague her town, he was not this monster.

"Did he give you a reason for wanting to meet?" Bel asked.

"It was about the piano. He wanted me to see it."

"Did he mention why he needed you to?"

"No, but when I found his body, I understood the meaning."

"How so?" Dread filled her belly. She didn't want him to say it.

"Because," he spoke slowly so she would understand his every word. "The piano he's kneeling before is mine."

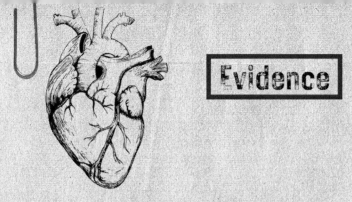

Chapter Eighteen

"I MAY BE EVIL, BUT I AM NOT THE EVIL YOU'RE HUNTING." THOSE words repeated in her mind as they processed the scene, hanging over her like a storm cloud as they interviewed potential witnesses. They taunted her as she handled the paperwork, walked Cerberus, and tried to sleep. This dread warned her that considering it was foolish, but what if he told the truth? What if something darker than Eamon had infiltrated her town, wanting her so focused on the handsome millionaire that she never saw the true villain before he came for her? Before he came for them all?

Bel mulled over the evidence while Sheriff Griffin spoke, hoping to see things from a new angle, to form a fresh theory. The killings were too elaborate, the scenes too clean. The carpet at The Ivory Keys had been absent blood, but as the autopsy she attended this morning proved before the Sheriff's press conference, Victor Legat had exsanguinated like Lumen and Kaffe. The human body held on average one and a half gallons of blood, and to drain every vein without so much as misplacing a single drop? It was impossible. She had not lost nearly that much, but after her attack, her blood had been everywhere. In her ears, under her nails, woven into her clothes. The stench had lingered in her nostrils for days, coating her skin with its phantom slickness. Maybe she had died that night and this unreasonable case was a Hell tailored specifically for her. It was as if a beast had clawed out its victims' hearts and drank them dry, but there was no such thing as monsters. Only men who were often more terrifying than the beasts of mythology. Human depravity ran deep and ugly.

The Sheriff's voice yanked her back to the present, and Bel surveyed the crowd. After they interviewed Legat's son yesterday—who stood to inherit his father's business—only to discover the music store owner was a well-loved member of society and his family without enemies, debts, or vices, word of a third gruesome murder spread like wildfire. Bajka had erupted in fear, and Griffin had called a press conference to answer questions and ask people to stay home at night, preferably not alone. He avoided the case's specifics, which Bel could tell annoyed those gathered. Not that she could blame them. The townsfolk had never witnessed terror like this, and to suddenly have unspeakable horrors committed against their friends? Their families? Their fear begged to be indulged.

Bel studied the crowd as the Sheriff slowly drew the press conference to an end. Based on her theory that the killer lived for the thrill of attention, she assumed he would be present, but the faces staring back at her were those of friends. Of good people. Of townsfolk who were welcomed here. David Kaffe and his heartbroken daughters stood arm in arm as they watched the police before them. Violet huddled among a group of girlfriends; her delicate black-tipped fingernails pressed against her mouth in horror. Abel Reus hovered on jittery legs at the edge of the throng. No one stood out. No anomalies caught her scrutiny—

A wisp of gold fluttered in the corner of her eye, and Bel's gaze snapped to the side street. Blonde hair. Long blonde hair just like Alcina Magus, Eamon's nonexistent friend from outside of The Espresso Shot. The woman was slowly walking away from the press conference, clearly restraining her escape as to not raise suspicion. Bel froze for a second, for a fraction of a breath, and then she was moving.

Careful not to draw attention to herself, she slipped from where the officers stood and into the outskirts of the crowd. Some spectators regarded her with curiosity, but most were too intent on the Sheriff's nerve-wracking words to notice the pretty brunette walking calmly. The second Bel rounded the corner, though, her pace quickened, and she ran past the small shops and offices until she came to a cross street. She scanned the side-walks, but they were painfully empty. Not a single life in sight. Bel paused, wondering if exhaustion and frustration were playing tricks on her vision, but then a flash of blonde stepped out from the shield of a car.

Bel burst into a run, her muscular legs chasing the stranger. She slid her sidearm out of its holster as the woman bolted into an alley.

"Freeze, police," Bel called, but the blonde picked up her pace, vanishing from sight. Bel hesitated slightly before plunging into the alley, but the narrow space was empty. She moved carefully over the asphalt, but when she emerged on the opposite end, that street too was void of pedestrians. A single car drove past as she spun in search of the stranger, but the driver was a curly-haired teenage boy. Not her fleeing mystery woman.

Bel cursed softly and scanned the streets again, but the blonde was gone as if she had vanished into thin air. Maybe she had. Maybe Bel needed sleep more than she realized, and with that thought polluting her brain, she slid her weapon back into its holster. She returned to the press conference in defeat and slipped silently into the crowd, hoping to go unnoticed and unquestioned.

"Bel?" The detective jerked but relaxed when she noticed

Nicole Scarano

Vera peering up at her, clutching a purse to her chest with crooked knuckles. "Are you okay? You look exhausted."

"I'm fine," she lied, and Vera tilted her head with that all-knowing stare grandmothers worldwide had perfected. "I'm tired. Bajka was supposed to be a quiet town." Bel subtly gestured to the press conference winding down.

"I know, dear." Vera slipped an arm comfortingly around Bel's waist. "This is so scary. I'm afraid to leave my house now. Thank goodness I have my very own police officer next door." She squeezed her for emphasis.

"Don't worry." Bel draped a toned arm over her neighbor's shoulders. "I won't let anything happen to you."

"I know. You're such a sweet girl."

A LOW GROWL rumbled from Eamon Stone's throat as Isobel Emerson rejoined the crowd and slipped arm-in-arm with her neighbor. For a second, he thought he had scented something, and he almost abandoned his hiding spot to chase after his pretty detective as she fled the press conference, but then the scent vanished as she reemerged. He settled back into the shadows, studying her, stalking her, and as if the elderly woman's protective nature sensed his obsession, she twisted her gaze to where he stood. She couldn't see him. No one could. He had made sure of it, but he could see her, and he stared the woman down with violence burning through his veins. That should be him out there with his detective. Those should be his arms surrounding her waist. His lips against her mouth. His fist around her throat. He bit his lip until he tasted blood as his muscles clenched painfully tight. Isobel Emerson was his. Not Vera's. Not Garrett's. Not this town's.

His.

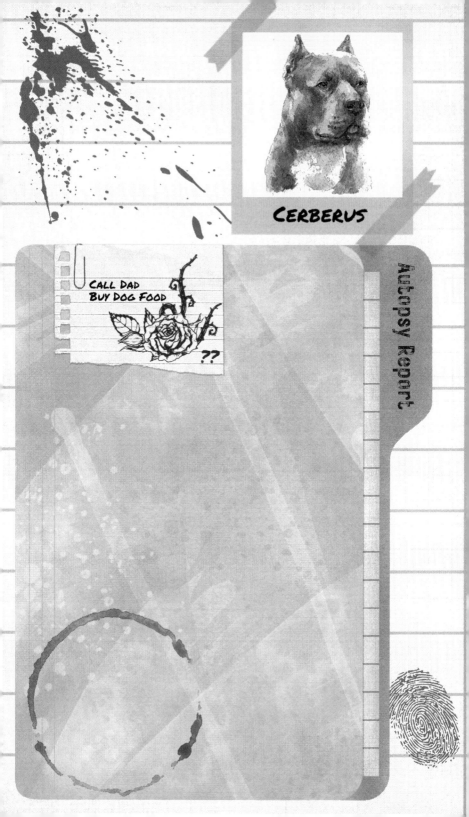

CERBERUS

CALL DAD
BUY DOG FOOD
??

Autopsy Report

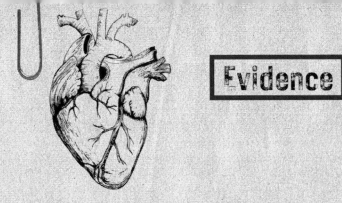

Chapter Nineteen

BEL STOOD, FIST RAISED BEFORE GARRETT'S APARTMENT DOOR, contemplating if she should knock. She hadn't texted him to say she was coming over. She didn't even know if he was home, but her world felt unsettled. She hadn't told anyone about Eamon's warning in the woods, nor had she mentioned why she raced off during the press conference. She hadn't planned on confessing either event, but earlier, when she walked Cerberus, he had pulled towards the forest. It was the first time since moving to Bajka that she feared those trees, feared what stalked it as its hunting ground.

She had contemplated visiting Vera, but when a sharp wind rattled her neighbor's bushes, forcing a low growl to escape her dog's throat, she reconsidered. Hence why she now stood unannounced at Garrett's door; the fact that he might kiss her, a bonus.

With a fortifying breath, Bel knocked, but silence answered. Her knuckles rapped against the wood a second time, but the door remained closed. With a disappointed sigh, she slid her phone from her pocket and pulled up their text thread.

"Hey… I stopped by, but you aren't home. Call me when you get this?"

She hit send, waiting to see if the notification pinged inside his apartment, but after a minute she felt like a stalker and turned to leave.

"Hello?" The door cracked open, and she twisted at the voice. "Bel?" Garrett leaned out into the hall slightly, revealing soap still in his hair and only a towel clothing his lean body. For a second, words escaped Bel. She knew her partner was in shape, but seeing him dripping wet and half naked was an entirely different experience. The idea of kissing him being a bonus for her visit doubled and then tripled as she watched a drop of water trail down his abs.

"What are you doing here?" His flustered question jerked her gaze away from dangerous territory and back to his brown eyes.

"I…" she choked, as if the words had wedged in her throat. "I texted you." She cleared her throat, but the act didn't clear her thoughts. "I wanted to see you." She tried and failed to keep her eyes from dipping. "To talk," she clarified.

Garrett glanced behind him awkwardly, and Bel got the horrifying sensation he was hiding something. *Oh god, please don't let it be another woman.*

"Um… yeah, come on in." He blushed, gripping the towel as he opened the door, and much to Bel's relief, no woman popped out at her. "Is everything okay?"

"Yes." Bel brushed past him, painfully aware of how wet and naked and close he was. "I don't know. Some thoughts are nagging me, and I need someone to talk to."

"Me?" Garrett smiled wide and stepped closer, momentarily forgetting the shampoo dripping from his brunette curls. "I'm glad you came." He leaned forward and then froze, blushing when he remembered that nothing but a damp towel separated them.

"Me too," Bel teased, quirking her eyebrows to place him at

ease, and he seized the opportunity. Closing the distance, his lips pressed against hers, and she closed her eyes, letting the kiss steal her from the present. Her fingers cupped his jaw, and when they broke apart, Garrett was all heartbeats and smiles. No fireworks for her, but this kiss was significantly better than their first, and Bel brushed her thumb gently over his bottom lip. Maybe they would come. Until then, she would enjoy trying.

"Um…" Garrett looked down at his body and then back at her. "Can you give me five minutes?"

"Yeah." Bel laughed as her partner rushed to the bathroom. She hoped getting involved with a coworker wasn't a bad idea. She hoped getting involved with anyone wasn't a bad idea. Her sisters found romance easy, but in her line of work, she had seen too many domestic fights turn ugly, too many marriages sour because of the job. Her parents had been the exception. Their passion never faltered. Even years after her mother made her father a widower, he still loved her with every cell in his heart. It was another reason love terrified her. Even if it worked, even if it was beautiful, it might still end in suffering.

The shower switched on, and Bel wandered around the living room. She sat on the couch for a full five seconds before anxiety pushed her back to her feet. She paced the carpet, pausing long enough to scan his abysmally small bookshelf before moving to the narrow hallway that led to the rear of the apartment. Family photos lined the walls, and she studied each version of Garrett as she walked, smiling at the images of him as a child, his curly brown hair as captivating then as it was now. She was almost sad when her toes hit the hall's end, alerting her to the conclusion of the photo history. The shower still ran, and Bel peaked into his bedroom. She shouldn't go inside. She shouldn't snoop, but the investigator in her won out. She wouldn't peek in any drawers or invade his privacy. She would just look, doubting he would be mad. He had left the door wide open.

Justifying her curiosity, Bel scanned Garrett's room. It was clean and organized, like the rest of his apartment, with dark grey bedding and matching dressers. Atop one of them stood an opened jewelry box of sorts, and Bel drifted toward it. A cluttering of cuff links, watches, and jewelry lay inside. Some rings were decidedly masculine, but a few were elegantly studded with jewels. She plucked a delicate gold band with an emerald stone from its hiding spot and experimentally slipped it on her finger. It was beautiful, and she guessed the more feminine pieces were family heirlooms.

Bel wiggled the ring off her finger and placed it back where she found it, deciding she should stop snooping before Garrett caught her. She twisted to leave when something buried among the watches and necklaces captured her attention. Bel froze, every muscle in her body going deathly still. It couldn't be. It had to be her mind playing tricks. With a suddenly dry mouth, she scanned the jewelry with a more attentive eye, picking through the gold and silver—

Her eyes snagged on a second object, and she felt sick. Her stomach threatened to heave itself onto the floor, and her head spun. *No. No. No. No. No. No. No.*

Her brain wouldn't stop repeating her denial. *It wasn't. He couldn't.* Most killers took souvenirs. Most liked a reminder of their conquests, and it seemed Garrett was no different.

So caught up with the discovery terrorizing her eyes, Bel didn't hear the shower turn off or the bathroom door open. She didn't notice the heavy footfalls thudding toward her. She was blind to all but that jewelry box. Deaf to all but her racing heart, she never heard his weight settle behind her.

"Bel?" Garrett's tone was ice. "What are you doing in here?"

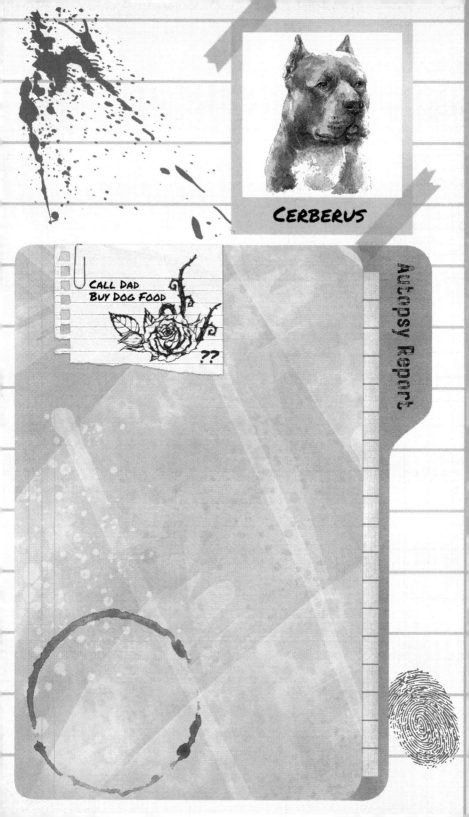

CERBERUS

Autopsy Report

CALL DAD
BUY DOG FOOD
??

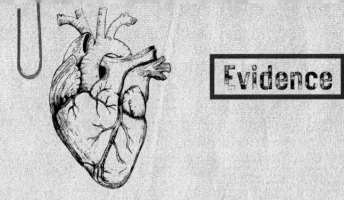

Chapter Twenty

BEL FROZE, FINGERS FLINCHING FOR HER HIP, BUT HER GUN wasn't there. She was alone, cornered against the wall without a weapon. Panic ripped its way up her throat with razor-sharp claws, choking her on its bile. Stupid. She had been so, so stupid.

"It was you," she croaked, her back still turned to Garrett as she stared at the damning evidence before her. His bloody souvenirs. A delicately carved wooden leaf spotting a few drops of dried blood rested under a watch band... the same kind that had been sculpted into Brett Lumen's death chandelier. Scattered throughout the jewelry box were whole coffee beans coated in dried blood, and to complete the ensemble, a single ivory piano key lay nestled beneath a twisted metal chain, it too splattered in old blood... blood Bel would stake her life on that belonged to Lumen, Kaffe, and Legat.

"It was you." Her voice shook.

"What are you talking about?" Garrett stepped forward, and Bel whirled on the balls of her feet, jerking away from him until her hips hit the dresser.

"You killed them. It's been you this whole time." Tears welled in her eyes. This man was her partner, her friend. She had kissed him. "It makes sense." The words poured from her mouth as the puzzle pieces clicked together in her brain. She should run. She should escape and call Griffin, but all she could do was grip the dresser, rage and fear and betrayal spilling from her lips.

"There was no evidence." Her chest heaved. If she didn't get herself under control soon, she would start hyperventilating. "We found nothing because the murderer is a cop who anticipated what we would look for."

"What are you talking about?" Garrett's normally kind eyes hardened.

"You, Garrett!" Bel practically screamed. "It was you this whole time! You killed them, and I've been working alongside you with no idea." She swore, a tear escaping to trail a line down her cheek. "We had wondered if the killer had a law enforcement or medical background, and as a detective, you certainly know how to cover your tracks."

"Bel—"

"Is that why you had me take lead on this case?" she interrupted. "You didn't want to investigate yourself? Leave it to poor, damaged Isobel Emerson, whose anxiety won't let her see what is right in front of her face."

"Bel—"

"Were you aware Brett had turned off his cameras? Is that why you started with him? And Emily asked you for help with her security system. How easy it would have been for you to tamper with her feed. Plus, you've been a cop in this town long enough to learn Legat didn't have a security system."

"Bel, what are you talking about?" Garret lunged forward, grabbing her biceps, and she flinched, slamming the heels of her palms against his chest.

"The souvenirs, Garrett!" She pointed to the jewelry box as he stumbled backward. "Most killers keep a memento, and you just couldn't help yourself. What did you do with the blood, Garrett? What did you do with the hearts?"

"What souvenirs?" He looked genuinely confused as he pushed forward to peer into the jewelry box, but the moment his eyes landed on the bloody objects, his face paled.

"You thought they would be safe here? That no one would come snooping through your things?" Bel slowly started inching toward the hallway while her partner stared transfixed. "Not a drop of blood at the scenes, yet you saved a few drops for yourself. What did you do with it, Garrett?"

"I…" He turned around, noticing how close to the door she stood, and his jaw set in a harsh line. "Bel?"

"You have everyone fooled." She was practically shouting as she inched backward. "This entire town thinks you are this Prince Charming. I thought you were Prince Charming." Tears flooded her vision, and as her heels crossed the bedroom threshold, Garrett stepped for her like a wolf stalking its prey. "I trusted you!" She should shut up. She should run. "I let you in. You were my friend."

"Bel, stop moving."

"I trusted you, and you're a monster! Why, Garrett? Why kill them?"

"I didn't kill anyone." He stalked closer. Too close.

"Don't lie to me. I know what I saw."

"Bel, come here, and we'll talk about it."

"Is this the reason you wanted to date me? So I would be oblivious to the evil coursing through your veins."

"Bel, stop!" He lunged for her, large hands grasping for her arms, but Bel whirled on her heels and raced for the door. She was blind with terror. She had to get out. To find help.

Garrett's heavy weight pounded behind her, and a second before she reached the exit, his hand captured the back of her shirt. With a cry of alarm, she lost her balance and plummeted to the carpet, her chest smacking hard as she fell. Garrett toppled onto her, but she kicked viciously, connecting with his shins. Her partner grunted, and she used the opportunity to scramble forward.

"Bel!" He roared, grabbing her ankle and dragging her backward. Bel was strong, her body pure power, but Garrett was larger than her, and he rolled her over, pinning her beneath him.

"Let me go!" She thrashed, but he grabbed her arms and restrained them above her head, his thighs caging her below him.

"Stop moving!" He shouted, and something in his voice froze Bel. Her muscles went rigid, and their gazes met. They stared at one another, saying nothing, only their heaving breaths polluting the air, and then Garrett seemed to register the fear in her eyes and his fingers binding her wrist.

With a curse, he scrambled off her as if she were burning coals, and Bel scurried backward like an injured crab across the floor until her spine hit the wall.

"I'm sorry." Garret shuddered. "I am so sorry. It's just you're freaking me out."

"How—"

"I didn't do this," Garrett forcefully interrupted her outburst. "I understand how this looks, but you know me. I could never do something like this."

"How would I know that?" she spat. "I barely know you."

"You know me well enough to recognize I didn't kill those people." He raised his hands placatingly, as if trying to calm a cornered animal. "I have no clue how those things got into my room. I swear to you, I didn't put those there."

"And you expect me to just believe you?"

"Yes!" He shouted, and Bel flinched. His face fell at her fear, and he ran his fingers through his still damp hair. "You were with me on the nights they happened. How could I have killed them?"

"I always left well before the time of death windows."

"Isobel," he said her full name softly as he crept closer. He captured her hands. She recoiled at his touch, but he held firm. "How do I convince you I'm innocent?" Bel tried to pull free from his grip, and after a few seconds, he released her. Arms still extended, he stared at his wrists before pinching them together. "Arrest me."

"What?" Bel's eyes flew to his.

"I swear to you. I'm not the killer. I am the guy you believed me to be. The Prince Charming who is good for you, who likes you." He stretched his wrists out further. "Get my cuffs from my room and do this by the book. You're a brilliant detective. You can do this. You'll find the evidence that proves I'm innocent." His gaze met hers, eyes brimming with sincerity. "I trust you. Arrest me."

Bel nodded and wiped the tears from her cheeks. Garrett remained kneeling while she pulled herself to her feet. She found his handcuffs and padded back to where he knelt, clicking them on his wrist.

"You have the right to remain silent," she began.

"I have gloves and evidence bags in my kit, too." Garrett gestured to the closet as soon as she finished reciting his rights. "Prove I didn't do this. I know you will."

Bel nodded, the life draining out of her as she collected what she needed. She took her time photographing the room and the jewelry box with her phone before dusting for prints and collecting the souvenirs. Garrett made no movements to struggle or escape. He simply knelt on the floor, patiently waiting for her. When she finished, she called Sheriff Griffin, who told her he would meet her at the station, but since it was so late, they would leave his questioning until the morning. He claimed it was because a night in jail might rattle Garrett. That the hours alone to sweat it out might loosen his tongue, but she recognized the truth behind the delay. Griffin was rattled, as was she, and if they interviewed him now, they would make mistakes. There could be no mistakes. Not with this. Garrett's arrest and interrogation had to be by the book.

Disconnecting the call, Bel collected the evidence and fished out her keys before grabbing her partner's arm. She took a forti-fying breath, afraid to leave his apartment. The second they stepped foot outside, this would be real. There was no going back.

"It's okay," Garrett urged.

"I don't want it to be you," Bel sobbed, wiping her tears on her sleeve.

"Good." He smiled weakly at her. "Because it isn't me, and you are going to prove that. I have faith in you."

"I'll find who did this," Bel promised. "I'll find this killer and nail them to the wall for this. I need it not to be you. I'm praying the evidence confirms your innocence, but understand this, Garrett. If you are guilty, not even God can save you from me."

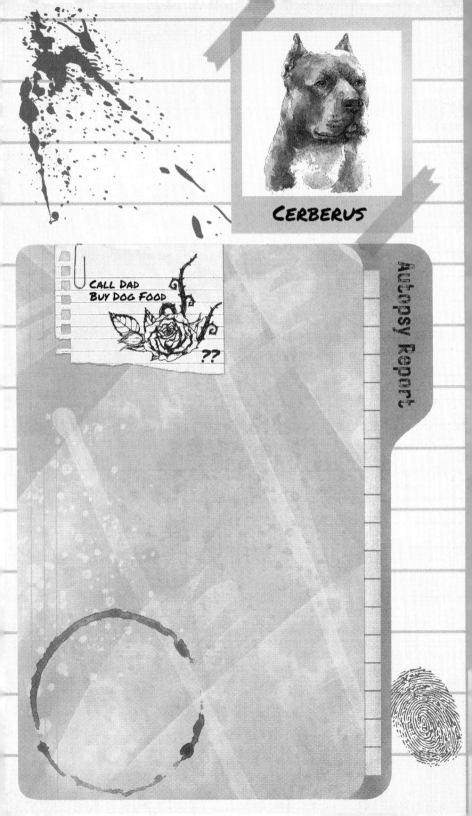

CERBERUS

CALL DAD
BUY DOG FOOD
??

Autopsy Report

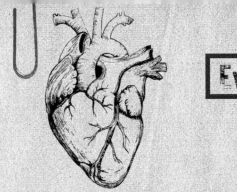

Chapter Twenty One

SLEEP DID NOT COME FOR HER. IT LEFT HER ABANDONED AND wandering the night, a ghost in the darkness.

Sheriff Griffin had met her at the station after she called him, and the sight of his blue jeans and plain tee shirt unnerved her. She had never seen him like that, a testament to how devastating her call had been. Two deputies worked the overnight shift while they booked Garrett, and Griffin threatened both of their jobs if they so much as breathed a word of this before he had the chance to address the situation. He promised to meet Bel first thing in the morning before the shift change to interview Garrett. He had then sent her home to rest before the impossible task ahead, but there was no peace. Only tears and fear. Tears that she had made a mistake accusing her partner. Fear that the first person she had opened up to after her attack was a killer.

The sun had yet to bless the land, but Bel gave up on any chance of sleep. Instead, she slipped into her workout gear and strapped Cerberus into his harness. It was foolish going into the woods at this hour, but she couldn't breathe in her house, in her bed. All she saw were Garrett's pleading eyes. All she remembered was him tackling her, her attacker tackling her. Death and murder and betrayal painted the backs of her eyelids, and she needed air.

"Keep an eye out for your mamma, okay, baby beast?" She scratched the dog's meaty head. "If you hear something, you let me know." Cerberus looked up at her as if he understood, and she booped his nose. "You are mamma's good boy." At that phrase, he wagged his tail aggressively, whacking everything in his wake, and then they plunged into the darkness, the steady glow of the moon and her flashlight the only beacons in the night.

The walk was uneventful, Cerberus taking full advantage of his mother's insomnia, and as the sun peeked between the trees, Bel pulled her cell from its slot in her leggings. She unlocked it, the time still too early to meet the Sheriff, and so she thumbed through her contacts, finding the name she needed most.

"What's wrong?" Her father's voice surged through the phone as she sank to a tree stump.

"Hello to you too," Bel said, hoping her greeting came off teasing when, in reality, his voice made her want to cry. She might be thirty-four, but there was nothing quite like a parent when the storms raged.

"Sorry, hi, sweetheart," he groaned, and Bel realized she must have woken him. "It's early, and…" he trailed off, but he didn't need to say it. She already knew. Every time his phone rang at an odd hour, he was transported to the past, listening to strangers tell him his youngest daughter was in the hospital and they weren't sure if she would make it.

"Sorry, Dad." Cerberus started pulling to get to something, and she dropped his leash.

"Is everything okay?"

"Yeah…" Her father's silence was so accusing, she finally continued, "No."

"Are you safe? Are you hurt?"

"I'm fine, but I can't talk about it. It's a case… a bad one."

"In Bajka?" Her father sounded surprised.

"My thoughts exactly." Cerberus trotted back to her, holding a thick stick in his teeth. Bel smiled at her dog and accepted his invitation to play, launching the makeshift toy down the trail. "I know there is crime everywhere," she continued, "but this? I don't think I'm ready."

"Do you need me to come? Say the word, and I can be in the car in a half hour."

Bel laughed. "No, you don't have to come. Well, I would love you to visit, but not like this." Cerberus returned the stick to her, and she tossed it again. "It's just... something happened, and it... it feels personal."

"I'm serious, sweetheart, I'm awake now. I'll start packing immediately."

"No. I just wanted to hear your voice. I've been meaning to call, but I was nervous to."

"Why on earth would you be nervous to call your old man?" She didn't answer him. "Bel... are the nightmares back?"

"Yes... but they never really left. They only got better when I adopted Cerberus."

"He isn't helping anymore?"

"He is the only thing that helps." Bel kissed her dog's head before tossing the stick again. "It's this case. I wasn't ready for one this aggressive, and... there have been more than one. Then something happened with someone I care about."

Her father let out a low whistle. "Sweetheart, multiple homicides are tough on anyone, especially if it involves someone you know. I realize I can be the overprotective dad, but can you cut me some slack? I worry for two parents now." Bel laughed softly at his words. "Call me, okay? Always call me. I don't care what time it is or how silly the reason is. If you won't let me come see you, then at least pick up the phone. Every day if you have to."

"Okay, Dad." Bel smiled. "But I'll try not to call at weird hours since you answer so sweetly when I do." It was her father's turn to laugh. "All right, I should probably go. I need to feed Cerberus before I meet Sheriff Griffin."

"Call me, Isobel. I'm serious."

"You must be if you're using my full name."

"You and your sisters…" she could practically see her father shaking his head. "Too much of your mother in you all. Gonna make me crazy."

"You love it."

"I do, sweetheart, I do. I love you so much. Let me know when I can visit you. I miss the dog."

"I'm sure he misses you too. Love you, dad."

Bel hung up the phone and searched for Cerberus. He had abandoned the stick and was sniffing a tree. She waited for him to finish his business, but it wasn't until she pushed off the stump that she saw him.

Eamon Stone hovered in the distance, his sweat-soaked skin blending in with the trees as he watched her. If Cerberus hadn't wandered off the trail, Bel would've never noticed him. She froze as their eyes met. How long had he been watching her, and why had she not sensed him? She had felt alone in these woods, almost safe with her father's voice and her dog's presence, yet there Eamon stood, hungry gaze never blinking as he stalked her.

"Cerberus, come." Her pitbull obeyed, and she seized his leash, pulling him toward her house. Against her better judgment, she glanced over her shoulder as they fled, but Eamon hadn't moved. He simply observed her, and Bel couldn't tell if it was because he was hunting her or guarding her.

Thankfully, he didn't follow, and she arrived at her cabin without an incident. Cerberus acted like nothing was wrong as she dragged him home. Both times they found Stone in the woods, her dog had behaved as if he was an old acquaintance, his presence barely worth a second glance. The same could not be said for her neighbor, and as they passed Vera's cabin, Bel spotted her cleaning her kitchen, curly grey hair bobbing in the window. The thought made her feel guilty, but she prayed the woman didn't notice her. She liked Vera, but she couldn't face her. Not today. Not when Vera loved that she was finally dating Garrett.

"Let's run," she whispered to her dog, and the two of them charged for their front door. Out of the corner of her eye, she thought she saw her neighbor spot them, but she ignored her, not stopping until they were safely locked inside.

The morning sped by after that, as if the countdown to the gallows had begun. Bel showered and fed Cerberus, making a pot of coffee as she dressed. She contemplated forcing herself to eat, but the reality of what awaited her turned her stomach. If she ate now, she might vomit the minute she saw Garrett's trusting face.

"Please," she whispered as she hugged her dog and left her house. "Please let it not be him."

Her prayer repeated over and over as she drove, the normally quick trip suddenly the longest drive she had ever endured. When she finally reached the station, she felt as if she had aged one hundred years.

Judging by the absence of his vehicle, she had beaten the Sheriff to work, and she contemplated waiting in the car for him to arrive. She wasn't sure she should face Garrett alone. All of her rage from yesterday had evaporated, anguish replacing it. She liked Garrett. Really liked him, and she couldn't bear the thought of him holding the guilt. He made a good suspect, the first real one they encountered, but could Prince Charming Garrett Cassidy truly be a monster? She tried picturing her partner ripping people's hearts out and stringing them up, but her imagination found it impossible. It didn't mean he was innocent, though. Plenty of serial killers had been charmingly handsome men who tricked women into trusting them.

Bel waited another ten minutes, but since there was still no sign of the Sheriff, she decided to venture inside. The overnight deputies were still on duty. She wouldn't be alone.

Mind made up, she scrambled from her car, locking the door behind her as she walked toward the station. Like every morning since her arrival in Bajka, Bel pulled open the doors, expecting to smell stale coffee and remnants of whatever had been reheated in the microwave, but as she stepped inside this morning, a wrongness washed over her. Gooseflesh pricked her skin, her hair standing up on end. Fear. Unadulterated fear. Something was wrong.

Bel walked further into the station, her hand drifting to the gun at her hip when something tripped her. She stumbled, using a desk to catch her fall as she glanced down. The sight ripped a scream from her throat. She didn't mean to scream. She couldn't help it, for there on the floor was one of the overnight deputies, his neck broken.

Bel's eyes snapped up as she drew her sidearm. She moved quietly, gaze scanning every inch of the room, but her gut already knew what her mind was still trying to process. The station was too still. Too quiet. These rooms were void of life.

Bel cleared each corner, each blind spot, and after forty-five seconds which felt like an hour, she found the second night deputy. His body sprawled across a chair, neck broken and hanging at an uncomfortable angle. Bel's mouth went dry as the evil in the air coated her skin. Something had come into the police station and overpowered two muscular, professionally trained men. It had snapped their necks like they were rabbits, and as she stared at the corpse, a fresh horror dawned on her.

Blind with terror, Bel bolted across the floor, feet slipping as she tried to gain traction, and her shoulder smashed into a corner as she took it too hard. She was no longer human. She was fear and instinct. She ran, her mind screaming in silence. Begging and pleading and praying, but they did no good. Her prayers would not be answered. It was already done. Already over, and as she burst into the jail cell, the first thing she registered was red.

Drying crimson blood pooled on the floor, and she barely skid to a stop in time to keep her toes from sliding in the slickness.

She did not scream this time when her gaze lifted from the stained tiles, for the sight stole her breath. It stole her everything, leaving her an empty, pain-riddled shell as she stared up at Garrett hanging from the jail cell bars... his heart missing.

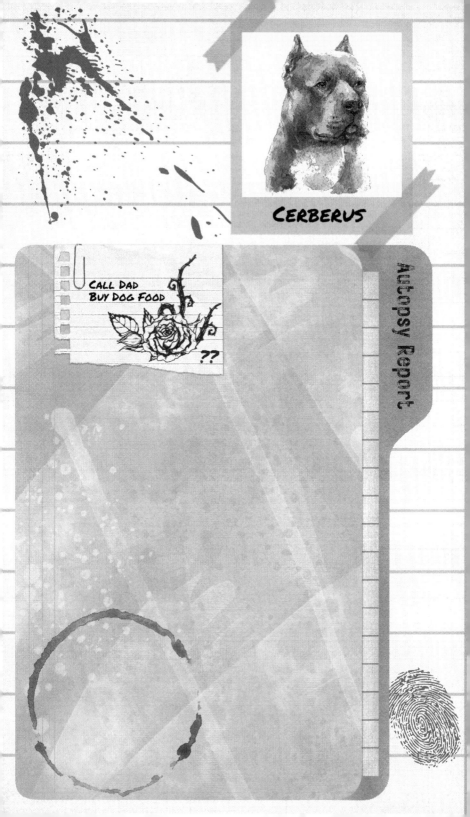

CERBERUS

CALL DAD
BUY DOG FOOD

??

Autopsy Report

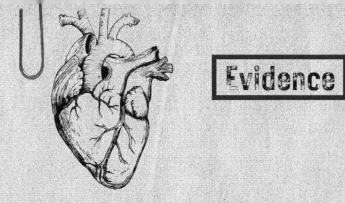

Chapter Twenty Two

THE EARTH STOPPED SPINNING ON ITS AXIS, TILTING dangerously beneath her feet... or maybe she was the one tilting. Tilting. Tilting. The crimson pool rushed for her face, and then Bel was moving, lunging forward with reckless abandon.

She barely moved three inches before a powerful arm caught her waist, hauling her backward against a solid chest, and that was when the dam blocking her voice burst. Bel screamed as she thrashed against her captor. She raged and kicked and cursed, her own ears unable to decipher the words of pain pouring from her mouth. She needed to help him, to cut him down and save him.

"Emerson!" A deep voice ripped through her haze of blinding insanity. "Calm down."

She could not calm down. She would never calm down.

"You're going to hurt yourself!" Sheriff Griffin jerked her around to face the wall, Garrett's and the deputies' bodies hidden from her view, and she choked as he lowered her feet to the ground. "Breathe," he ordered, his arms still cementing her spine to his chest so that she could feel his lungs inhale and exhale. "Breathe, Emerson."

She couldn't. She couldn't. She couldn't.

Bel gagged, bile racing up her throat, and with an uncoordinated jerk, she ripped herself from Griffin's hold. She barely made it to the bathroom before she heaved into the toilet, the retching painful.

"Deep breaths, Isobel." The Sheriff's palms found her back, gathering her hair as she sobbed and choked. "Let it out. Get it all out." She had fled into the women's restroom, but it seemed Griffin knew not to leave her alone. He was the only person in Bajka who knew the truth about her transfer from New York.

She coughed, dry heaving, and then the floodgates opened, tears rolling down her cheeks as she collapsed against the stall wall. Sheriff Griffin stood and flushed the toilet before returning to her side, rubbing her shoulders. Nausea receding, Bel noticed for the first time just how horrified her boss looked.

"This is my fault," she whispered, Garrett's handsome and lifeless face accusing her from her memory.

"Don't." Griffin's voice was tight. "Don't go there. The evidence you found was serious. Any of us, Garrett included, would have done what you did. This isn't on you. This station is supposed to be secure. For God's sake, two officers were on duty here last night, and..." he cursed viciously before continuing. "And someone came into my house and killed three of my men. My house!" He pounded his fist against the stall door, causing Bel to flinch.

"This is not on you." Griffin stood and ran his hands through his hair. "I'm going to get everyone in here, and I mean everyone. I will find who did this and crucify them."

"He can't be dead," Bel whispered from the floor. "He was my..." *Partner? Friend? Boyfriend?* They never got the chance to have their first date, and a fresh wave of guilt washed over her.

Griffin stepped out of the stall and pulled out his phone. He made a few calls Bel barely heard, and when he was done, he bent and scooped her off the floor. He guided her to the sink, turning on the faucet so she could wash out her mouth and drink some water before he led her out of the bathroom into his office. He placed her on the soft leather couch beside his desk as a flurry of movement sounded from outside as the first of the officers arrived.

"Stay here." The Sheriff gently brushed her hair away from her face, the gesture reminding her of her father. "Someone will be in shortly to get your statement."

When she failed to acknowledge his words, he left the office, clicking the door shut behind him. Bel sat in the silence. For how long? She wasn't sure. Pain constricted her heart like a ravenous snake. Garrett. Sweet, handsome Garrett. Her partner. Her friend. He didn't deserve this. No one did, and seeing him strung up confirmed his confession last night. He was innocent. She had arrested an innocent man, a man she cared for, and now he was dead.

The numbness in her soul was so severe, she could no longer sit still, and Bel stood and quietly escaped her boss' office. The station was a storm of movement and rage. Lina Thum was just walking through the doors as Bel emerged, and on silent feet, the detective slipped through the swarm. She didn't trust anyone to do as thorough a job as she would. This was her case. Her partner. She needed to see it through.

An officer mentioned the security system was experiencing technical difficulties as she moved for Garrett's body, but she ignored that information. She already knew what they would find. They weren't dealing with someone holding a grudge or someone killing for the first time. The skill of the crimes. The devastation of their station. Whoever did this was skilled and potentially wealthy enough to invade the police without detection, and Bel knew of only one person who came even close to filling those shoes.

There were similarities about Garrett's death that matched the previous victims, and she could see from where she stood that roses had replaced his missing heart, but they weren't what caught her scrutiny. The killer had changed his M.O. He had altered his routine, and that was what screamed for her attention. Killers followed their rituals with almost religious devotion, so to break the cycle? It had to be important. It had to mean something.

Bel looked at the blood pooling below Garrett's feet. His cell door had been unlocked and his body moved to the outside of the bars. His wrists were strung up by handcuffs on either side of him like a crucifix, blood leaking from his gaping chest wound to stain the floor. The killer hadn't transformed him into an object of significance. He had not been meticulously cleaned or posed, which made Bel wonder if Garrett wasn't originally a target. He wasn't supposed to die. There was no plan, no elaborate scene for him. Just a graphic display of brutality enacted on him and the two deputies. This killing occurred to make a point. Bel thought she found her suspect, but one look at Garrett told her she had made a grave mistake, and the killer demanded she acknowledge it. He wanted her to understand she caused these deaths. Perhaps he hadn't intended for her to find those souvenirs in the jewelry box yet. She and Garrett had only just begun dating, and perhaps the killer was banking on the fact that she would not jump into bed with him immediately, allowing more time to pass before she discovered the bloody objects. Her partner was most likely the scapegoat meant to take the fall when the killer was finished, but by the spectacle playing out before her, he was nowhere near his finale.

Garrett still wore clothes, unlike the other victims, but it was the blood that she kept circling back to. The other three had been drained, yet Garrett's body dripped blood everywhere. Based on the pooling pattern below him, passive drips had formed the puddle, gravity pulling the blood down. She assumed there would be high-velocity spatter somewhere from when his chest had been ripped open, but there were no walls or objects close enough to Garrett to catch the spray. Any spatter peppering the tiles would have been erased by the pool, offering, yet again, no clue what weapon caused those wounds. But as she studied the red, hoping something would speak to her, Bel remembered her accusations. She asked her partner what he had done with the blood. Was someone listening to their conversation? Watching their movement? For here it was, his every drop for her to find.

Bel drifted toward her desk after a rushing deputy plowed into her, unable to shake the feeling that this scene was for her benefit. This death was aimed at her specifically. But why? She had barely been in town long enough to warrant enemies, but why else break M.O. and go after her partner? The killer wanted her to see this. To appreciate what he was capable of and that he wasn't done. That realization terrified her, and she sank to a seat, suddenly drained of energy. She longed to move closer, to be in the thick of it, but the second Griffin noticed her, he would banish her back to his office. Her reaction this morning had been raw. Primal. Visceral. That he held her hair while she vomited was proof enough that the Sheriff suspected just how close to the victim she was.

So, Bel sat at her desk and watched the chaos unfold, taking everything in, making notes of every conversation, every discovery. She would observe from afar, ensuring the investigation happened by the book and no stone was left unturned. Garrett deserved Bajka's all, and this town couldn't give that to him if she sat out and—

Bel froze, noticing a fingerprint on her desk for the first time. Dozens of prints smeared this piece of furniture, mostly hers and Garrett's, and most were either unnoticeable or messy smudges, but this? It was crystal clear, as if coated in dirt. As if the owner had been in the woods… or filthy from renovations.

Thundering heart forcing too much blood through her veins, Bel slipped silently to her forensics case and snapped on gloves before capturing her fingerprinting kit. She made quick work of lifting the print from her desk, and after scanning it into the database, she settled in to wait. It might take hours to identify a match. It might find nothing, but she was going to sit there until—

"Emerson, I told you to stay in my office." Bel stiffened. Griffin had finally noticed her escape.

"I can't just sit here and do nothing."

"I understand. Trust me, I do." He moved closer, sympathy and terror warring in his eyes. "But Emerson, I know… about you two."

"Sir?"

"It was as plain as day that Cassidy liked you." The Sheriff's voice softened. "I wasn't born yesterday. I know there was something between you two, and I figured when you guys worked it out, you would tell me. So, trust me, I understand why this is important, but you can't be here. If anyone discovers that Cassidy's girlfriend was the lead investigator, they could call all the evidence into question. You are no longer objective."

"Please, don't do this," Bel begged. "Don't take me off the case. I need to help him." Her tears fought for dominance over her control.

"I don't want to do this, Emerson." The Sheriff sighed as if the fight had left him. "You are the best I've got, but we must be careful… for Cassidy. We can't solve these homicides only for them to get thrown out in court because someone calls your motives into question."

"I would never jeopardize this case, and you know—"

"I do, but I'm sorry. You were too close to him." Griffin patted her arm sympathetically, and Bel saw the conflict in his eyes. He wanted her to stay, just as much as she did, but he was right. Minutes before she arrested Garrett, she had kissed him. She was no longer objective. She would never jeopardize a case, but she was aware of how it looked from the outside. How many times had she made this same call in New York?

"I'll get a deputy to take your statement, okay? And then… why are you running Eamon Stone's prints?"

"I'm not," Bel squinted at the Sheriff, and then the realization hit like a bulldozer. She wasn't running Eamon's prints. She was running the odd one from her desk. The one that shouldn't have been there, and it seemed the system had found a match.

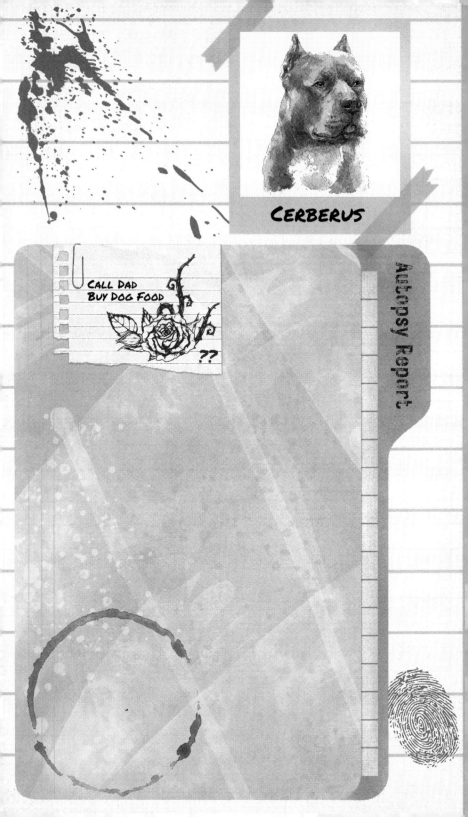

CERBERUS

CALL DAD
BUY DOG FOOD

??

Autopsy Report

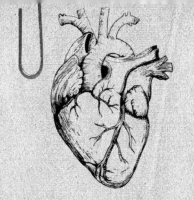

Chapter Twenty Three

BEL SAT IN HER CAR, UNABLE TO STAY BUT UNWILLING TO LEAVE. The station was a swarming hive, curious bystanders surrounding the chaos on their way to work, and she wanted to scream at every one of them to leave her partner in peace. She didn't want news of his death to leak. She didn't want this town to hear her guilt. No matter how Sheriff Griffin tried to convince her this wasn't her fault, she had been the one to tighten the handcuffs on Garrett's wrists. She left him here overnight to meet his horrifying end alone, and the tears refused to stop. What she wouldn't give to rewind time and ignore that jewelry box, to not abandon her innocent partner for the wolves.

Griffin was right. She was too close to this. He had promised to keep her informed of the case's developments and to look into Eamon Stone, but then he forced her to leave the station after she gave her statement. It was the right call. Her heart was a wreck, her guilt eating her alive like a parasite, but she couldn't move. She couldn't abandon Garrett.

"You'll find the evidence that proves I'm innocent. I trust you." He shouldn't have trusted her. Look where it got him.

"I'm sorry, Garrett," she whispered as she twisted the key in the ignition. If she sat in the parking lot any longer, she would find a way back inside, and her presence would only jeopardize the case. Emily noticed Garrett had feelings for her. Vera had practically pushed the two together. Griffin—as it turned out—suspected it too, and if they had spotted their relationship, then the entire town probably knew. She needed to leave, to give Garrett the best chance of finding justice.

The minute Bel got home and saw Cerberus, she burst into tears again. She was never this emotional during a case, but memories of her own bloody attack and kissing Garrett flooded the reasonable side of her brain. Perhaps Griffin taking her off the case was a good thing. She couldn't handle these killings at the moment.

The afternoon passed in a blur. She was a shell, a ghost haunting her own home. Even Cerberus was wary of her, both following her every movement and keeping his distance. Not knowing what was happening at the station was almost too much to bear, yet every time she tried to eat, the sight of Garrett's blood burned her memory, turning her stomach. The hours dragged in an agonizing haze of nothingness. The day lasted a century. It lasted seconds.

Then, a little after 9:00 p.m., her cell rang, and Bel practically dove across her furniture to answer it.

"Emerson?" The Sheriff's exhausted voice sounded through the phone. "I asked Thum to rush the autopsy instead of waiting until tomorrow. He was killed the same way as Lumen, Kaffe, and Legat, but you already knew that."

"What happened to the security system?" Bel asked, that fact bothering her more than most. Disrupting a local coffee shop's surveillance and the police station's were two vastly different things.

"You aren't going to like this. Deputy Saltz disabled it."

Bel froze. She had tripped over Saltz's body on her way into the building. "Why?"

"No idea." Griffin sighed. "From what footage we have, he stepped outside to smoke shortly after you and I left. He spoke to no one while he smoked. He received no calls, didn't appear to be under duress, and then when he came inside, he walked over to the cameras and started cutting wires."

"Cutting them?"

"Destroyed every camera, one after another."

"And Marcus didn't stop him?" Bel asked. The third victim, Deputy Marcus, had been very much alive when they left in the middle of the night.

"Didn't even blink at what Saltz was doing," Griffin confirmed.

"The killer's profile suggests a police background and possibly multiple perpetrators due to the complexity of the scenes. Could Saltz and Marcus have been involved? Perhaps the killer wanted to tie up loose ends and killed them after they turned off the cameras."

"God, I hate that idea, but I can't understand why else they would have disabled the security unless they were bribed. Maybe they demanded more money, and the killer decided it was cleaner to remove all witnesses."

Bel's mind instantly pictured Eamon following her in the woods. He certainly possessed the funds to bribe police officers. He had been watching her yesterday morning while she talked to her father. Had he just come from murdering her partner? Was he there to gloat over her?

"Eamon Stone?" Bel asked, and Cerberus went to the front door and touched his leash with his nose. It had been a few hours since she'd taken him out. He was probably crossing his legs in desperation.

"We called him down to the station, but he arrived with his lawyer," Griffin answered. "He explained he came looking for you last night. Said he had a concern he wished to discuss with you."

"What concern?" Bel asked as she hooked Cerberus into his harness and opened the door.

"Wouldn't say. He claimed he searched for paper to write you a note, which is how his print ended up on your desk. Explained his fingerprints are in the system because of his job for security purposes."

"Did you find a note?"

"No."

"Convenient."

"I know, but unfortunately, without the surveillance footage, we can't be certain."

"Sheriff, he was at the scene."

"Yes, but there was one print on your desk, which is in a different room than the cells. There was no evidence of him on either deputy or Cassidy. He explained his hands were dirty from the renovations, so it stands to reason there would be fingerprints elsewhere if he was involved."

"He could have left the darker one on purpose." If Eamon was smart enough to clean a crime scene, he would know how to plant misleading prints.

"I realize that, but with his lawyer present and no concrete proof of his involvement, there's nothing I can do. My hands are tied, Emerson." Griffin sighed. "I want to find who did this, but Stone came to the station willingly. We don't have enough evidence to arrest him, so he left."

Bel groaned, but her voice caught in her throat as the shadows moved in the woods bordering Vera's garden.

"We'll find something," Griffin said. "Just promise me you won't do anything stupid."

"Sheriff—"

"I may not know you well, Emerson, but I understand that not working this is killing you. It would kill me too. So, I need you to trust that I'll do everything I can."

"I know you will." Bel moved closer to the movement. *Was*

that… blonde hair?

"I'll call you when I have another update."

"Thanks, Sheriff." She pulled Cerberus across the yard.

"Good night, Emerson."

"Goodnight." She hung up the phone, slipping it into her pocket as a feminine silhouette darted through the woods.

"Who's there?" Bel yelled, pulling her dog into a run after the mystery woman. "Stop! Police."

The woman's shadow vanished, and Bel stopped short, her heart in her throat, a confused pitbull dragging behind her. For a moment, both woman and pet stared into the darkness, and then Cerberus loosed a low growl.

———

"Bel, dear?" Vera appeared from behind the bushes, and Cerberus' growls increased. "What's going on?"

"I don't know." Bel pulled the dog closer to her legs. "I thought… never mind."

"Thought what?" her neighbor pressed, stepping back so that the shrubbery separated her from the pitbull.

"Did you see a woman? A blonde?"

"No." An odd look passed over Vera's face. "Where, here?"

"Yeah…" Bel realized how crazy she sounded. She needed sleep. Real sleep. "I thought I saw someone… probably just the wind and shadows."

"Must be, you poor thing. There's no one over here. Just me." Vera smiled. Bel returned the expression, Cerberus still growling at the woods, and she pulled him away from her neighbor and back home, terrified that she was seeing things. This was the second time she had chased a blonde ghost. Women —tangible women who appeared as flesh and blood on security footage—didn't vanish into thin air… twice.

Bel locked herself and Cerberus inside their cabin and

dragged a recliner in front of the window. She resolved to stand guard, to stalk whatever was stalking her in the hopes of proving her mind wasn't conjuring blondes in the night. It wasn't healthy; she realized that. She desperately needed a good night's sleep, but the alternative was to lie silently in her bed, allowing thoughts of Garrett and death and vicious black eyes to consume her. No, she would keep watch and prove her sanity was not so far gone as to play tricks—

The phone rang, vibrating in her lap, and Bel jerked awake, her neck twinging at the sudden movement. She groaned as sunlight poured into her eyes, blinding her as she fumbled to answer the call.

"Emerson." Her voice escaped her lips like an irate frog, and she hunched forward to ease the sharp pain in her back. She was too old to sleep sitting up.

"Did I wake you?" the Sheriff grunted over the line.

"It's fine." Bel squinted at the digital clock above the microwave. The red numbers read 9:30 a.m., and a jolt of surprise ran through her. She couldn't believe she had slept so late, and in a chair no less. No wonder her body felt like it was cracking glass.

"Sorry, but I figured you would want an update," Griffin said. "The lab results came back on the souvenirs from Cassidy's apartment. As we suspected, the blood on the wooden leaf was Lumen's, the blood on the coffee beans was Kaffe's, and the blood on the piano key was Legat's. There was no other evidence on the leaf or the beans, but they found a print on the piano key." Griffin paused, but Bel already guessed his next words. "It belongs to Eamon Stone."

She sucked in a breath.

"But before you get excited, the lab also confirmed the key belonged to the piano at Legat's scene. That instrument is owned by Stone, so his print on the key is not exactly the smoking gun we were hoping for."

"Are you going to at least question him?" Bel asked, all hope fizzling like embers in a rainstorm.

"We're doing one better." She heard the smile in the Sheriff's voice. "Because of Stone's interactions with all three victims, the piano, the prints, and the officers' deaths, the judge issued a warrant for his house. We're on our way to serve it now."

"Oh, thank God."

"If something's there, we'll find it," Griffin promised. "I'll update you when we have news. Get some rest in the meantime."

"Will do," she lied. "Thanks, Sheriff."

"Of course, Emerson." He hung up, and Bel plugged her phone in to charge. She couldn't sit here and wait for another call. Not when she was the one who should be serving that warrant, the one searching every inch of Eamon's haunted ruins. She knew she was being reckless. Her New York self would freak out if she could see her now, but Bel needed this. She needed answers. To avenge Garrett. To prove she wasn't going insane.

But that wasn't the only driving force behind her decision to disobey orders. She wanted to believe in the darkness of Eamon's predatory gaze. Her soul knew that the man was capable of murder, that he could spill blood without remorse, but his lack of motive nagged at her as she fed Cerberus. Why would a successful millionaire move to a small town and turn murdered strangers into objects? Why stalk her through the woods? Why watch her sleep? Bel wasn't connected to the victims, so why hunt her through the trees and transform flesh into furniture? Except… that she was the lead investigator on the case. Why not drive the detective to insanity so she failed to do her job and recognize Stone's evil?

Bel growled at herself. Was she really so fooled by a handsome face? Eamon Stone was the most intoxicating man she'd ever laid eyes on. His skin begged to be pressed against hers; his lips dared hers to accept their invitation. Every curve of muscle, every strand of dark blond hair, every carefully executed movement was desire wrapped in flesh. Her body craved his in ways that terrified her. She wasn't a woman deceived by perfection. Not a woman blinded by men.

Bel snagged her keys and cell off the table too aggressively and stormed to the car as if to prove to herself that he didn't affect her. She wouldn't let Griffin catch her. She would park down the road from the Reale Mansion and walk the rest of the way. Her presence would simply observe to ensure that nothing was overlooked or ignored. If she spotted something worth inspecting, she would text the Sheriff a lie, informing him she remembered it from a previous interview.

Justification fully in place, Bel drove the short distance to the edge of town and pulled her car off the road. The gorgeous morning air made the walk through the woods almost enjoyable, and when the ever-watchful gargoyles emerged from the treetops to condemn her presence, she tucked herself behind the branches and watched the chaos. The Reale Estate swarmed with uniforms, and she prayed they would find something.

An hour later, her prayers went unanswered. The officers seemingly searched every room of that crumbling mansion, but Bel could tell by the defeated hunch of their shoulders that all they found inside Stone's home was dust and nails and drying paint. Bel's legs ached from standing, and when she noticed Sheriff Griffin's exasperated expression as he emerged briefly from the house, she felt suddenly foolish for stalking them through the trees. She could do nothing hiding among the leaves, and she turned to retreat when she caught sight of Eamon for the first time that morning.

Cloaked in darkness, he stepped out of a side door, his hulking frame hidden from the officers' view. He moved like a panther, all grace and savagery, and Bel watched mesmerized as he pulled his powerful body up to his full height before breathing deep. He lifted his nose into the air as if searching for a scent, and then with excruciatingly deliberate movements, his neck twisted until his eyes peered in her direction.

Bel's skin went icy. There was no way he could see her from that distance, but it was as if he knew she was there. As if he smelled her fear. Heard her terror. Her heart pounded against her ribs, angry and alarmed like a red warning of danger, but her feet had grown roots, welding her to the dirt. She couldn't move. She couldn't think. It was an endless eternity, but then Eamon's head snapped in the opposite direction as if he heard something. Air flooded her suffocating lungs as he launched into a run, disappearing into the trees.

Bel's curiosity waged a bloody war with her self-preservation, but in the end, the detective emerged as the victor. She flew deeper into the forest, feet racing after Eamon, but within ten minutes she knew it had been a stupid decision. He had vanished, not a single trace of him remaining to guide her path.

"What are you doing?" Bel whispered to herself as she searched for any hint as to where the man had gone, but every tree, leaf, and branch stood unhelpfully by, mocking her. Their only suspect had fled the Sheriff and a horde of deputies unnoticed by all to race through the woods, and she had followed him. No one knew she was here, and she bit her bottom lip to keep from cursing.

Her phone vibrated in her pocket before she could berate herself further, and she pulled it out to check the notification. It was a text from an unknown number, and she almost ignored it before an urging in the recesses of her mind forced her fingers to unlock the message. It was one word. Only one. But never had three letters inflicted such fear in her chest.

UNKNOWN

Run.

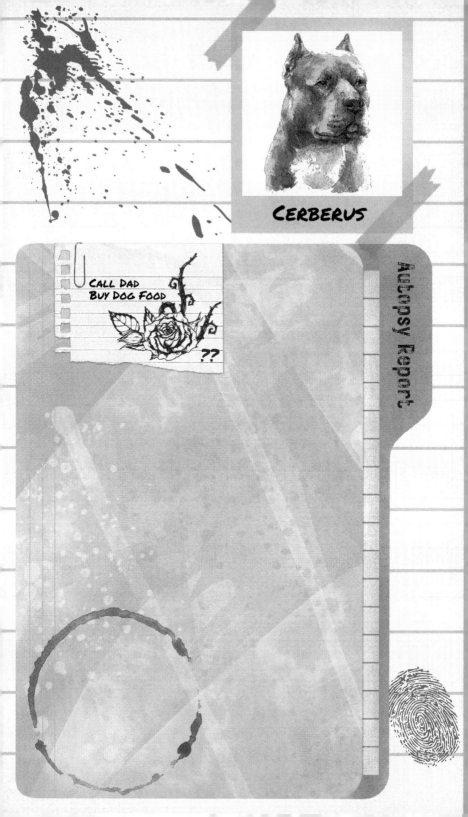

CERBERUS

CALL DAD
BUY DOG FOOD
??

Autopsy Report

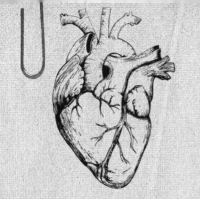

Chapter Twenty-Four

BEL EXPLODED IN MOVEMENT, RACING THROUGH THE TREES AS she obeyed the anonymous warning. She wasn't sure if the text inspired the sensation or if it merely alerted her to its presence, but someone was watching her. Their stalking eyes pricked the back of her neck. She ran faster, her heart crawling up her throat in an attempt to escape. A tree branch snapped behind her, and suddenly Bel was no longer in the woods beneath a warm, sunny sky but in a dark warehouse district, fleeing for her life. The slap of feet on concrete, the absence of life, the teeth. Always the teeth.

Her sight registered a twisted root at the last second, and she leaped over it, lungs burning. She was strong, a woman used to hiking and chasing a dog through the woods, but fear made breathing impossible. A branch whipped her face, the sting launching her back into the present as another footstep cracked to her left. She was not in the city, and her car was mere feet away. If she could just reach it.

Bel's speed was so intense, she couldn't stop in time to save her hip from slapping the side mirror. She hit the unlock button and jumped inside, bruised hip and welted cheek throbbing, but they were nothing compared to the pounding in her heart as she slammed her door shut and locked it. For long seconds, she sucked down painful breaths, her lungs protesting every inhale as she scanned the trees. No cars passed her on the road. No shadows moved among the leaves. All was silent. Peaceful. Picturesque.

Bel jammed her keys into the ignition and pulled out her phone, foot on the gas in case she needed to flee. She opened the text, her eyes tracing the curves of the unknown number. Had this one-word warning been meant to save her or increase her paranoia?

Bel lowered her forehead to the steering wheel. As the adrenaline bled from her muscles, exhaustion took its place. She was too tired to endure much more. She knew what it was like to be hunted, and she wasn't sure she would survive it a second time. Someone was stalking her. She might not be able to prove it, but she felt their eyes, and somehow it related to this case. It was as if she had only half the puzzle pieces but was being forced to assemble them anyway, the unmatched edges jamming together without reason.

She shifted the car into drive, but her ringing phone interrupted her. For a second, she feared it was the unknown number, but one glance at the I.D. settled her anxiety slightly.

"Emerson?" The Sheriff's voice greeted her. "We are finishing up at the Reale Estate." Bel opened her mouth to say she knew, but then bit her tongue, realizing she should move her car before Griffin drove past.

"We found nothing," he continued.

"Nothing?" Bel leaned back in her seat.

"He has plenty of tools scattered around his house, but none of them matched our victims' chest wounds. We found no blood, no remnants from the crime scenes, or signs of surveillance.

Besides a bag of coffee from the Espresso Shot in his kitchen, his missing piano, and the chandelier strung up in the foyer, nothing ties him to any of the victims."

"His roses?"

"I saw them. He has a receipt. Bought them from the same nursery my wife got hers. Half the town has flowers from there."

Bel hit the steering wheel with her palm. "There has to be something. You don't just kill six people and not leave a single shred of evidence."

"You do if you're innocent."

"He isn't."

"Emerson." The Sheriff's voice cut her off. "I'm as frustrated as you are. We have no suspects. No evidence. No motive. This killer shows no sign of stopping, and my best detective can't be on the case. Trust me, I'm at my wit's end, but we can't accuse a man because you don't like him. For all we know, Stone is simply seeking a quiet life away from the pressures of his job."

He didn't say it, but the *'just like you'* was implied. "Unless you know something I don't, my hands are tied. We'll examine the evidence again with a fine-tooth comb, but with custom pieces used at the scenes, we don't even have a company to inquire after."

"So, we look into who has carpentry skills," Bel said.

"The one person I knew capable of creating these is dead."

"Garrett and I had considered that. His theory was Stone commissioned those from Lumen before he murdered him."

"And it's a decent theory, but again, we have no proof. According to both his assistant and his records, Lumen's only job for Stone was the chandelier. They were supposed to have an ongoing relationship, but there was only one receipt."

"So, he paid cash. Insisted on no paperwork to accompany his demands of no surveillance." Bel was spiraling. She heard the desperation spilling from her mouth, but she couldn't stop it.

Nicole Scarano

"Emerson." Griffin stopped it for her. "You can theorize all you want, but without proof, we are at a stalemate. We found nothing else designed by Lumen at the Reale Estate. Not even a footstool, so unless Eamon's hiding the pieces somewhere on his acres of property, we can't do anything. The warrant only covered his house because of the piano key, and even that barely convinced the judge. If we hadn't lost three officers, I doubt he would have granted us one."

"Okay, so who else in town has carpentry abilities?" Bel refused to let it go.

"Emerson…"

"Please," she begged. "Is there someone else?"

"Abel Reus' father made furniture as a hobby years ago, but before you get too excited, he passed away. Abel didn't follow in his father's footsteps. He works at a bank. Doesn't have a single handy bone in his body."

Bel shifted through her memories, trying to picture the crowds at each scene. She had theorized that the killer was closely following the investigation. Had Abel been present at all three crime scenes? He had helped her at The Espresso Shot, but she couldn't remember the exact faces of those at Lumen's Customs. By the time they found Legat, it seemed the entire town had congregated to watch. He might have been there… as well as Emily's husband, Violet, Vera, Eamon, Garrett, the two deputies who were murdered, Saltz and Marcus, along with every other vaguely familiar face.

"Could he have furniture left over from when his father was alive?" she asked.

"I'll look into it," Griffin promised. "I'm going to take another pass at Cassidy's apartment, too. I won't stop until I find something."

"I hate this." Bel eased her car onto the road. "I hate sitting on the sidelines. I should be helping you."

"I know." Her boss sounded almost defeated. "But I can't

allow you back on the case. Not when you and Garrett were dating."

"It was only—" Bel started.

"Doesn't matter, and you know it. You were too close to him. Any prosecutor worth his salt will paint you as an unreliable investigator."

"It's because I was his friend that I should be the one finding his killer." She was careful to avoid the term the Sheriff had labeled their relationship with.

"That's why I'm keeping you in the loop, Emerson." Griffin's voice softened. "Don't make me regret that decision."

"I won't." Bel turned off the winding road toward her house, hoping that his last comment didn't mean he had spotted her car. "I'll let you go."

"Sounds good, and Isobel?" The way he said her first name made her insides go cold. "I never said it at the station, but I am sorry for your loss. I realize finding him like that was the worst thing a girlfriend could see. I'm so very sorry."

Bel fought back the tears, but their will was stronger than hers. "Thank you." She hung up, unable to talk about it. Concentrating on the case, on the guilt gave her purpose, but when she remembered the bloodless body of the first man she had kissed in years, the memory eviscerated her.

———

BEL SPENT the rest of the day toggling between avoiding her emotions and visualizing every face from her crime scene memories until all their features blurred together. Without the case photos, she couldn't confirm Abel's presence at any of the scenes save Kaffe's, and even if she had access to those, they wouldn't accurately represent the entire day. Spectators came and went. Parents, loved ones, elderly neighbors. They had drifted in and out on the tide of curiosity, but as Bel finally fell asleep, a thought of absolute certainty flickered in her brain. Almost every resident of Bajka had appeared at each crime scene to watch with horrified nosiness, except for Eamon Stone. He had been noticeably absent at all save for Legat's, and as sleep claimed her, Bel felt that his absence was more damning than his presence.

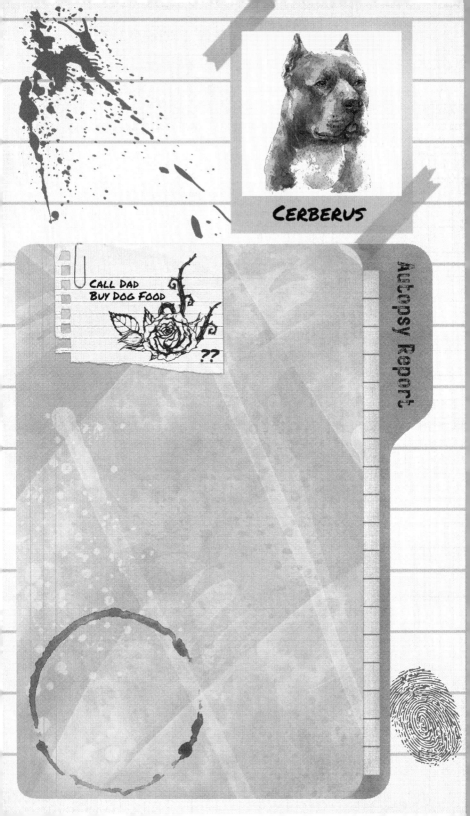

CERBERUS

CALL DAD
BUY DOG FOOD
??

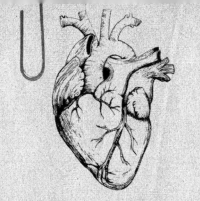

Chapter Twenty Five

TEETH TORE INTO HER SKIN, RIPPING HER WIDE AS THE SCENT OF blood and sweat filled her nostrils. The pain was excruciating as they flayed her open, starting at her throat and trailing down her breasts to her stomach. The pain was fire and ice, like burning coals and frozen metal. She screamed until her voice was hoarse, until her body no longer possessed the strength to scream, and then she surrendered to the darkness. It wouldn't be long now. She would wake up. She always woke up when the teeth carved into her.

Yet she didn't wake. She lay there in a pool of her own blood and fear, her vision blurring, her hearing dulling. Hands pinned her to the ground, breaking bones, bruising flesh, bursting veins, and then the teeth dragged back up her body to dig into her throat. Agony exploded in her neck, but she was too weak to fight. She would die this time. She knew it in those final moments as her attacker sliced her open wider. If she died in the dream, would she die in reality? Had she died that night, and Bajka was simply her own personal purgatory? The pain was so intense it ceased to exist. She was dying. This was her end.

And then the teeth halted their carnage. Her skin stopped

ripping in painfully wet tears, and her attacker surged away from her body, leaving her suddenly cold in his absence. She couldn't see him, her sight almost dark, but the massive form hovered over her as if at war with itself. It twitched and growled, fighting an unseen battle. And then he lowered his face to hers, breathing in her scent with a bloodied nose and lips. That's when she saw them. Eyes she knew all too well. Eyes that haunted her nights and stalked her days.

Bel jerked awake so violently, Cerberus grunted in surprise before crawling closer to her. She instinctively reached for him, wrapping her arms around his comforting mass. She buried her nose in his fur and inhaled, her nightmare shaking her to her core. It was unlike the previous ones. The second those razor-sharp canines shredded her skin, she always woke, but this time, the nightmare had continued. Only Bel knew it wasn't just a dream. It was a memory; one she had repressed until this moment. Her attacker had left her for dead, but his sudden disappearance had confused the detectives working her case. The signs on her body pointed to him wanting to watch her die, to ensure he killed her, but then, without warning, he vanished, allowing her the chance to survive. Bel always assumed something interrupted him, but she realized that wasn't the truth. Her attacker intended to bleed her dry, but as if a conviction clicked in his brain, he forced himself to leave her. She had been barely conscious, but she saw his struggle, witnessed the battle of wills playing out in the black eyes hovering over her.

The New York City detectives never found her assailant. He had vanished without a trace, and since the trauma caused her memory loss, they had nothing to go on. But there was no mistaking those Hell black eyes now. She craved them, feared them, hated them, wanted them. She knew who her attacker was, and he had followed her to Bajka.

Bel bolted from the bed, pulling on clothes before snapping a leash on Cerberus' collar. It was the middle of the night, but she couldn't wait. She couldn't sit idly by as her attempted murderer plagued the innocent lives of this town. She didn't care how long it took, but she was done playing defense, done being the prey. It was her turn to become the predator, and if she had to sit outside his haunted mansion every night to catch a break in this case, she would. Let Eamon Stone see how much he enjoyed being hunted like a beast.

Bel pulled a confused but willing Cerberus into her car before driving into the darkness. Without Garrett, the dog was the closest thing she had to a partner, and she had the sudden urge to train him as a police canine. He was the only man she genuinely trusted besides her father. Deputizing him would ensure that someone who loved her always guarded her back.

The empty roads delivered her to the desolate edge of town, and she turned the headlights off as she approached The Reale Estate so as to not alert Eamon of her presence. If she was lucky, she might catch him leaving on his way to destroy another life. She parked among the trees, ensuring she had a direct line of sight to his dark mansion, and she settled down to wait. For five minutes, Cerberus stared out the window, hoping they were at the park, but when he realized Bel had no intention of opening the car door, he curled his muscled body into a ball on the back seat.

Bel reached behind her, rubbing her fingertips over his short fur as she watched the lifeless house. The gargoyles perched high above glowered at her with callous intensity in the darkness. They appeared alarmingly alive in the dim moonlight, demons guarding their dark lord, and gooseflesh raced over her flesh. How could anyone willingly live in this monstrosity? Evil practically oozed from its pores.

The clock read 2:45 a.m. before her heart rate slowed enough for her anxiety to ease, but the overbearing sense of dread never truly left her as she—

Bel jerked with a start, blinking rapidly until the red lights on the dashboard stopped looking like electric cotton balls. *3:18 a.m.* She had foolishly fallen asleep, and she leaned forward in her seat, rubbing her eyes. She should have packed a thermos of coffee and snacks to help her stay awake. An unconscious half-hour gave Eamon plenty of time to slip out unnoticed.

Bel glanced back at Cerberus, who was out cold, and smiled. At least one of them got a decent sleep every night. She twisted further in her seat to pet him, but the moment her palm touched his warm body, his muscles flinched, and he jerked awake.

"Sorry, baby beast," she soothed, but her dog wasn't looking at her. His alarmed eyes were staring out the windshield, studying something closely as his gaze tracked its movements. Bel twisted slowly, half expecting a bloody knife to be poised outside her window, but there was no such dramatic villain. Instead, it was a pretty young woman slipping into Eamon's house. The same blonde from The Espresso Shot's surveillance. The one who legally didn't exist.

ALCINA MAGUS. Or whoever she was. Were they in on this together? It made no sense why a millionaire would try to carve a detective up with his teeth, but Bel knew Eamon Stone had been her attacker. Had he followed her here to finish the job? Was this mysterious blonde his girlfriend? His partner? Had they decided to add more blood to their resume before finishing what they started in New York?

Bel watched as the woman slipped into the mansion. The house remained dark for long moments, and then a dim light flipped on upstairs. Shadows passed behind the curtains, and Bel longed to know what their owners were saying. Were they plotting their next work of macabre art? Had she assumed wrong, and they were merely secret lovers meeting for a torrid affair between the sheets?

The shadows jerked, the image almost violent, and Bel's hand instinctively reached for the door handle. Had her nightmares been just that? Horrible dreams without truth, and Eamon was innocent? Was this woman here to kill him?

The dark images moved again, and a faint crash sounded as the lights flickered out. She launched herself from the car, locking Cerberus safely inside as she watched the dingy windows, hoping that she had not witnessed another homicide. For long moments, nothing happened, and then a light blinked to life in a dilapidated part of the mansion. By the looks of it, that section of the house was not safe to wander, and the shadows passing the grimy windowpanes were decidedly female. Where was Eamon? Bel stepped forward on undecided legs, pleading with whoever might be listening that he was still alive, that her assumptions about the man had not led to his murder before her eyes.

Bel crept closer to the mansion, undoing the buckle securing her sidearm. She told herself she would just check the perimeter to ensure Eamon wasn't inside, bleeding out from a missing heart. On silent feet, she sneaked around the house, but none of the windows offered her any view of him. After circling back to the front door, Bel considered returning to her car and leaving this insane plan in the dust when a light upstairs flickered and voices drifted to her ears. They were angry, hostile, and decidedly male. Eamon was still alive. She should leave before they found her, but then his deep, sultry voice exploded in what sounded like pain.

Instinct kicked in, and Bel tested the front door. Finding it unlocked, she pulled her weapon from its holster and slipped inside, thankful that the floorboards didn't creak under her weight. She paused in the foyer, noting Lumen's chandelier hanging above her head, and for a moment she forgot to breathe. She understood why people paid what they did for his work. It was single-handedly the most elaborate piece of furniture she had ever experienced… besides the chandelier Lumen himself had been encased in.

She shoved the murder scenes from her mind when the angry voices drifted down the grand staircase. She couldn't understand their words, but the tone was clear. The argument raging upstairs was on the verge of escalating into deadly territory, and Bel found her feet carrying her toward the ruined section before her brain could rationalize with her. The further up the stairs and down the hallways she ventured, the worse the structure became until she was creeping through a wooden skeleton of decay. What on earth were they doing in this part of the house? It wasn't safe, and Bel wondered if Sheriff Griffin had this area of the mansion searched when he served the warrant. She would have wanted to search these crumbling rooms, but if this wing was condemned, perhaps they left it untouched. Was that why Eamon allowed these halls to remain peeling and cracked? To hide his supplies, his trophies? Was that why the police hadn't uncovered evidence?

Bel's toes tested a floorboard, and it creaked below her hesitant weight. She froze, half expecting them to barrel out and find her guilty and alone, but their conversation continued. Eamon's raw sexuality argued with an unfamiliar feminine tone.

She still couldn't decipher their words. Their voices were nothing but melodies and harshness, and against her better judgment, Bel continued. This went against all of her training. Creeping around in the middle of the night without a warrant or backup was single-handedly the most reckless thing she had ever done, but she couldn't stop herself. The dream, the teeth, the demon-black eyes. They drove her to this, and she was powerless to resist.

"I will find a way." Eamon's voice sent a jolt of fear and excitement through her body as his clear words traced her skin like foreplay.

"We both know you won't," the woman answered him, her tone both nondescript and ice-cold.

"Do not—" Eamon grunted in pain.

"I'm tired of this same argument," the woman drawled. "It's exhausting, and it changes nothing. I can only lead you to water, my stubborn horse. Drink before there are consequences."

"You forget who you're dealing with."

"No, I know exactly who you are. It is why it must be done, why it must be you."

"Go to—" he grunted again, his words cutting off, and Bel surged closer. Their argument made no sense, but the way Eamon kept grunting concerned her. She should turn around and call for reinforcements. She should have never set foot inside this crumbling monstrosity.

"I'm over this. Do it. You have no choice," the woman said, and Bel heard footsteps moving toward her. She froze. She needed to get out of there. To hide, but it was so dark, and the floors were littered with dozens of ways to break her neck.

She slipped backward, thankful the floorboards didn't give her away. The arguing receded, and when she finally reached a less dilapidated hall, she sighed in relief. She could move easier without the rot hindering her, and when she escaped the mansion, she would lock herself in the car, wait for her heart to stop racing, and then decide what—

"You shouldn't be here, Detective." Bel froze as Eamon's powerful voice echoed through the house, booming off the walls and slicing into her nerves. "You can't hide from me, Detective. I can smell you."

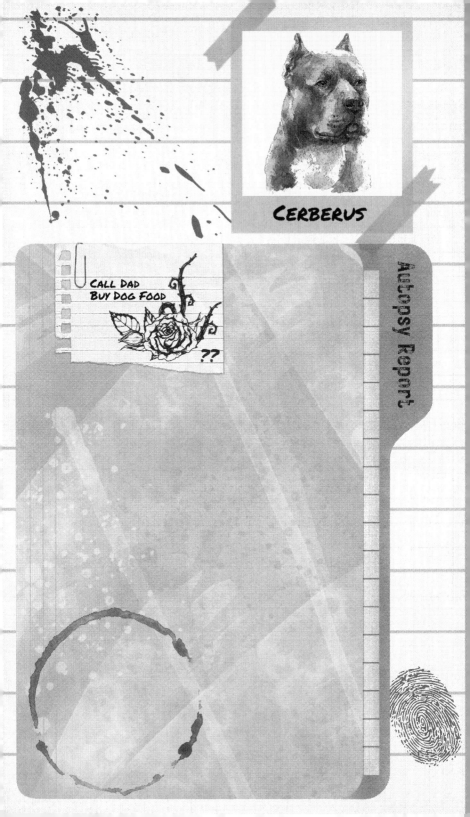

CERBERUS

CALL DAD
BUY DOG FOOD

??

Autopsy Report

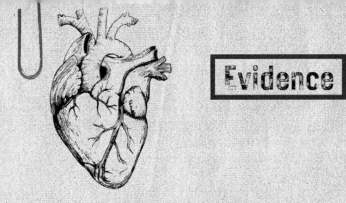

Chapter Twenty Six

BEL LAUNCHED INTO A RUN, NO LONGER CARING THAT HER BOOTS slapped heavily against the rotting floorboards.

"You can't run from me, Detective." Eamon's voice came from everywhere and nowhere all at once, surrounding her on every side.

Bel looked around the once grand hallways, suddenly disoriented. Panic danced heavily in her chest, and her breathing went erratic.

"Don't try to hide from me." The seductively low menace echoed through the rooms, and her eyes wildly searched for an escape. She couldn't tell where his voice was coming from, and with a rising tide of terror, she realized he was right. It was impossible to hide from a man who was everywhere.

"Detective?" His deep tone was a siren's song, pulling her down into the depths, but she refused to answer. Bel burst into a run, not caring which direction she fled as long as it was away from him. When did this mansion grow so many walls? So many crumbling hallways?

"I told you, you couldn't run from me." Eamon's voice was in her ear, his soft breath scraping her skin as a powerful hand snaked out of the darkness and caught her stomach. His other palm cut off Bel's cry of alarm, his callouses grating over her lips as he slammed her spine into his chest. Before she comprehended what he was doing, he pried her gun viciously from her grip and tucked it into the back of his pants. Bel realized just how tall, just how immensely strong he was as he welded her to his body, his massive hand slowly pushing over her belly in an erotic restraint before yanking her further against him. She felt every hard line of his abs, his chest, his thighs, and his fingers gripped her shirt as if it were his bedsheets.

"There's nowhere you can hide that I won't find you, my little Detective," he spoke against her ear, his lips brushing her skin as if he was declaring his undying love and not death threats. "I will always find you." His breathing grew erratic, his voice pitching lower than his already impossibly low gravel. "I can taste your scent on the air. Do you know how sweet you smell, my little Detective? Do you know how much it drives me crazy? How much it makes me want you?" With each word, his mouth dragged lower, lower, lower, until it pressed a soft kiss against her scar.

Bel screamed into his palm, bucking against his hold, but he was too strong, his embrace tightening seductively around her. His hand at her stomach moved lower, his knuckles brushing the tops of her jeans, and then his teeth were on her throat. Not hard enough to cause pain, and if this were any other scenario, the act might make her moan with pleasure, but the way his slightly sharp canines fit exactly over her scars had her mind screaming red and hot and vicious.

"You drive me to madness, to oblivion," Eamon growled against her neck, his lips brushing her skin reverently as he spoke. "I will always know where you are, my sweet, little Detective."

He kissed her throat as his teeth increased their pressure, and every tether tying Bel to this earth snapped. She roared into his palm, curling her arm and slamming her elbow into his gut. Eamon grunted, and she pitched sideways, knocking his nose with her skull. He stumbled at the force, releasing her as he tipped off balance, but that was all the opening she needed.

She vaulted into a run, legs pounding as she raced down the hallway. She tripped on a few strewn boxes but managed to right herself as she careened off the wall.

The staircase!

It was so close, she almost tasted the freedom, and Bel practically threw herself down the steps. She was instantly grateful for Cerberus' love of hiking. All those uneven trails and hidden rocks had prepared her for this.

She didn't dare look back as she raced down the stairs so fast, she would have met the floor with her teeth if she hadn't used the railing to propel her through the foyer. Eamon's steps thundered behind her. He was taller, stronger, faster, and he was gaining on her by the second. One misstep, and he would capture her, so Bel ran for her life, picturing Cerberus in the car. She just had to get to him. He would protect her.

Bel exploded from the front door and raced for the hidden vehicle when something stepped out of the trees, blocking her path. The blonde woman lunged from the darkness, and stifling a scream, Bel skidded to a stop so hard her knees jarred. She ignored the pain and whirled on her heels, aiming for the woods.

At that exact moment, Eamon burst from the house, his gaze finding hers in an instant. Bel pushed harder, racing for the tree line's protection. She was outnumbered, and he had her gun. Her only hope was to lose them in the forest. It was a decent hike back to her cabin, but close enough since she knew Eamon ran it often. If she could just get home, she could call the Sheriff.

"Detective, stop!" Eamon's voice had changed. Gone was the menace, the seduction, the dominance, replaced by genuine alarm. Bel snapped her head around, noticing that the blonde had disappeared, but Eamon was hard on her heels, his demeanor

Nicole Scarano

entirely altered as he ran faster than she had ever seen any grown man move.

"Isobel." Her name on his tongue was a beautiful warning. "Isobel, stop! Don't go into the woods!"

Bel did not stop despite her confusion at his sudden shift in temper. She would not fall prey to his tricks, and so she plunged into the darkness, the moon her only guide home. She prayed they wouldn't break into her car and harm Cerberus before she called the station. She hoped her dog would use all seventy pounds of his power if they so much as cracked her windows.

Bel's heartbeat was as erratic as her footfalls as she pounded through the darkness. She had lost all track of time, and she prayed she had not lost all sense of direction. She hoped she was still heading toward her cabin and not deeper into the woods. With the leaves in full bloom on the trees, the moon's light barely reached the underbrush.

Her lungs screamed as she pushed them to their limit. Her toes ached from constantly smashing them into concealed roots. Her thighs burned white hot, but she did not yield. She embraced the discomfort. It meant she yet lived.

The forest had gone quiet behind her, but she didn't dare slow. She couldn't afford to stop, to give her enemy a single moment to gain on her. She ran until every muscle in her body bled pain, and then she ran harder.

A familiar tree caught her attention, and she almost cried as she realized how close she was to home. Her legs surged with new energy, and as she began the slight descent toward her cabin, she saw a figure standing among the trees.

"Vera?" Bel's voice was hoarse, and her elderly neighbor looked up at her in surprise. "Oh, thank God!" she raced for the woman. "Please help me."

204

"Bel, sweetheart?" Vera squinted in confusion as the younger detective flung herself into her arms. "What on earth is going on?"

"We have to go." Bel thought she might throw up from that ungodly pace as she hugged Vera, pulling her toward the cabin. "I need to call the Sheriff."

"There, there, I got you," Vera soothed. "What happened, dear?"

"Eamon," Bel blurted out of breath. "Eamon Stone is chasing me. Please, we have to get inside and call the station."

"Eamon Stone is chasing you?" Vera asked. "Right now?"

"Yes, right now," Bel repeated urgently.

"Good." Vera's body stiffened against Bel's, and the detective froze, leaning her head away from the elderly woman to stare at her face. "That's wonderful news. A good hunt usually buries his conscious."

"What?" Bel tried to escape, but her neighbor's arms tightened around her waist, holding her captive with the strength of someone much younger. "I'm sorry, dear, but we won't be calling the Sheriff."

And then, right before Bel's eyes, Vera's body began to mutate. Her skin disfigured as it shifted, stretching and pulling unnaturally. Her grey, curly hair uncoiled and lightened, and her hunched height straightened until Vera completely vanished, leaving the blonde Alcina Magus in her place.

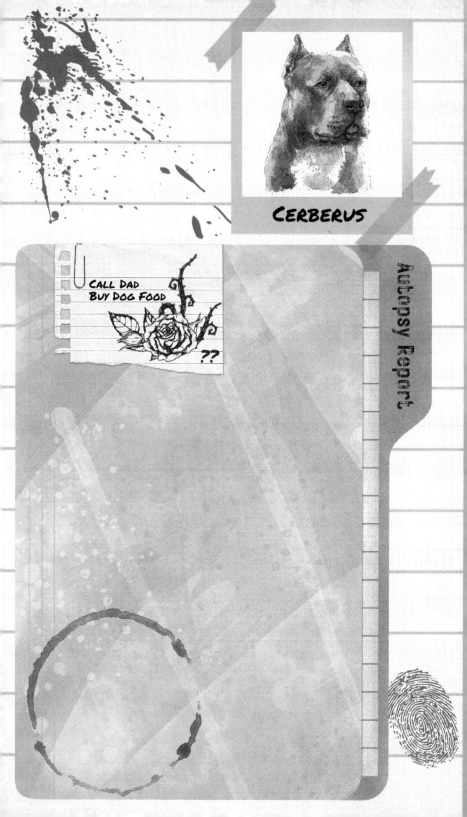

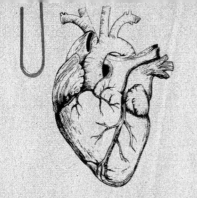

Evidence

Chapter Twenty Seven

BEL STUMBLED BACKWARD IN TERRIFIED DISBELIEF.

"Vera...?" Her eyes shot to her cabin, calculating how quickly she could get home.

"Don't worry. It will all be over soon." Alcina said with a twisted grin as the detective bolted for the clearing. She felt sick, her mind spinning. Vera? Alcina? They were the same person? Dizziness overtook her, and her shoulder slammed painfully into a tree trunk. How was this possible? What was happening? Had Eamon drugged her? There was no reality where a woman could transform her appearance. That was magic, but magic existed only in fairytales.

"I'm sorry, my dear," Alcina soothed, and suddenly Bel's entire body went rigid. She screamed as her legs stopped working; her arms stopped flailing. "But I cannot allow you to leave," the blonde continued as Bel's feet left the dirt. She twisted and bucked as she floated backward, coming to a stop only once her airborne form hovered before Alcina.

"Don't fight it, my dear," Alcina said, reaching an arm out, her hand clenched as if it was holding Bel in the air and not this strange unseen force.

"Put me down!" Bel spat.

"Or maybe you should fight," the woman laughed. "He will enjoy the kill more."

"What are you?" Bel thrashed against her invisible bonds, and Alcina squeezed her fist. Bel's body constricted painfully, forcing her muscles to still.

"This?" Bel spat, afraid if the invisible hold tightened any more, her ribs would snap and puncture her lungs. The pressure was already almost unbearable. "This is how you killed them?" she wheezed. "No drugs, no defensive wounds." Bel began to hyperventilate, the pain in her chest worsening. "This is why they didn't fight back. Magic."

"It's such a shame you have to die. You are an incredible specimen." Alcina shook her head. "Gorgeous, smart, resilient, but it must be done."

"Why?" Bel coughed. "Why kill all those people? Why kill Garrett?"

"Because, my dear, he wasn't doing what I wanted of him. I had to force his hand. Push you into his path. All that spilled blood. Seeing you in his new home. I knew it wouldn't be long before he couldn't control himself." A twig snapped behind the women. Instinct twitched Bel's neck to turn so she might see, but Alcina's magic held her in place, causing her muscles to burn as they resisted her hold.

"It's time," Alcina said, a sickly smile plastered on her lips. "It will hurt, but it'll be over soon."

"Help me!" Bel screamed, despite knowing no one would hear her. Only she and Vera—or whoever this terrifying woman was—lived this far off the road. "Someone, help!"

Bel's screams for aid turned into screams of agony as a piercing sharpness sliced through the flesh above her heart. She looked down in horror to watch as four wounds opened up on her chest, blood dripping down to her belly and soaking her shirt. With a strangled cry, Bel watched Alcina's free hand raise into the air. Her fingers curled as if they were claws, and the pain ripped through Bel again as her skin tore further. Blood pulsed down her breasts, and her ribs groaned against the unseen pressure. She screamed at both the torture and the realization. They hadn't been able to identify the weapon used to carve out the victims' hearts because there had been none. It had been magic, an invisible force carving them open.

Bel screamed as the pain intensified. Her heart raced; the speed was too fast, too erratic for her to survive much longer. Sweat poured from her brow. Her fingers itched to clamp down over her ribs as if to keep the organ firmly in her chest, but she couldn't move as she hovered over the earth, her blood slowly dripping down her belly to her pants.

Her vision blurred, and her hearing dulled. The tearing continued cell by cell, and when she was sure she could not endure the agony for another second, a hulking mass launched from the shadows with inhuman speed. The body of solid muscles slammed into her, and the two of them crashed to the dirt, bodies rolling over limbs. They jerked to a harsh jolt against a tree trunk, but Bel hardly felt the pain from the impact over the torture in her chest.

"That's it," Alcina soothed. "I prepared her for you. Made it easy. It's time to finish what we started."

Eamon hovered over Bel, his black eyes somehow even darker as they stared at her. All traces of humanity were gone from his gorgeous face, replaced by pure, unadulterated hunger. He was an animal, a ravenous predator, and she was his wounded prey. Bel had never seen a human face so void of life, and it was his soulless stare that scared her more than Alcina's brutal magic.

"Do it." Alcina's voice turned cruel. "Now."

As if drugged by the sight of her blood, Eamon dragged a finger through one of Bel's wounds and brought it to his lips. He sucked the crimson liquid off his skin, his eyes rolling back in ecstasy as he tasted her, and when his gaze found her again, a burning hunger raged in his irises. He gripped her biceps tight and thrust her harder into the ground, his body hovering over her with menace, and then he lowered his head to her bloodied chest, his sharp canines readying to rip her to shreds.

"Eamon," Bel coughed through the pain as she weakly grabbed his face. "You don't have to do this. You resisted once before. You can again." She remembered every detail, as if the magic had unlocked the chains imprisoning her memories. Eamon Stone had been the man who almost killed her in New York, but he had also stopped himself. She didn't understand the true gravity of her situation, but if he had fought whatever bloodlust this was before, perhaps he could now.

"Please," she sobbed, her tears mixing with her blood. "Don't do this."

Eamon paused, his empty eyes studying her before he tightened his grip.

"Please, stop." Bel pushed against his face, but he was too strong.

"He won't stop, my dear," Alcina laughed. "Not this time. You can fight all you want. It won't change anything, although he might enjoy the struggle. Predators love the hunt."

"Eamon, please." She tried to knee him in the groin. She couldn't die like this. It would destroy her father. "I don't want to die," she cried, and at her heartbreaking plea, Eamon looked up. A fraction of his humanity returned, as if he suddenly realized what he was doing. His grip on her loosened slightly, but before he could release her, Alcina lunged forward, seizing the back of his neck.

"That's enough!" Alcina roared as she drove Eamon's face into Bel's bloody chest, holding him there with inescapable force. For an unending second, Eamon hesitated, refusing to cave to the woman's cruelty, but then he lost all control. His teeth sank into Bel's flesh, and she screamed at the excruciating agony.

"Drink." Alcina shoved her power around them in palpable waves, and Eamon's bite increased. With each thrust of magic, his hold tightened. Bel's voice poured out of her in terror, in pain, in sorrow, and with every scream, her decibels quieted as she died. She vaguely registered Eamon's hands on her arms, pushing against her as he tried and failed to resist Alcina's dominance, and as much as Bel wanted to hate him for taking her life, she realized that at this moment, he was as helpless as she was. He was killing her, and she knew by the way his fingers clung to her biceps, he didn't want to. She didn't want him to either. She wanted to see her dad one more time. And Cerberus. She wanted her dog. She loved that animal, and—

Cerberus? Surely Bel's eyes were tricking her, because flying out of the darkness like a demon was her pitbull. The dog growled with a ferocity she had never heard from him, and he plowed into Alcina so hard, the force shook the ground. Cerberus didn't stop as he dug his teeth into the blonde's shoulder, and both witch and dog rolled violently to the forest floor.

The second Alcina's hand released its unforgiving hold on his head, the magic evaporated, and Eamon ripped himself away from Bel's flesh. He looked around wildly, drunk with blood, but the hollowness in his eyes had vanished, rage taking its place. He launched to his feet faster than humanly possible, and with powerful arms, he hauled Bel off the ground.

"Run," he growled.

"I can't." Bel fell to her side.

"Run!" he shouted so loud in her ear, it was like an adrenaline shot to her heart, and she crawled on unsteady limbs to her hands and knees.

"Go," Eamon ordered. "Get out of here." He didn't wait to see if she obeyed as he dove for Alcina, who was still wrestling the enraged pitbull. He dragged the seventy-pound animal off the woman as if he weighed no more than a pillow and launched him at his mother. Cerberus landed hard beside Bel, and Eamon gripped Alcina by the throat, slamming her back against the tree. "Go, dog! Get her out of here."

As if he understood, Cerberus lunged for Bel, shoving his snout under her arm. She wrapped an elbow around his neck, and together they began to crawl for her cabin, leaving a stream of blood behind them on the underbrush.

"Kill her!" Alcina screamed as Eamon smashed her skull into the tree again.

"No," he growled, and that solitary word was the single most terrifying sound Bel had ever heard. It was unrestrained anger and hatred. Despair and regret, but it was the underlying care braided with his rage that struck her through the heart like an arrow on the battlefield. The two unnatural beings raged in and out of her peripheral vision, and out of the corner of her eye, she noticed the witch lift her hand to throw magic.

"Eamon!" Bel's warning was weak, but he heard, and he caught the witch's wrist. He slammed it against a tree so hard, Bel flinched as the bones audibly snapped in half.

"You are supposed to kill her!" Alcina screeched.

The further Bel crawled, the darker the world became. Sounds muted. Her skin had stopped hurting. She barely felt Cerberus pushing her along.

"I will never." Eamon threw the blonde to the dirt, but Alcina launched a punch of magic at his face, and he flew across the clearing to slam into a tree.

"You shouldn't be able to resist her blood!" Alcina stood, cradling her broken wrist, but Eamon was faster, his fist around her neck as he lifted her off the ground. "You shouldn't be able to defy me."

"I told you I would find a way," he said, and then as Bel's vision blurred to blindness, he fought with a speed not even a witch could survive. Cerberus nudged Bel, trying to get her to move, but she couldn't. She had lost too much blood. This was it. This was her end. At least her dog was by her side. At least Eamon had found some redemption in resisting this monster, and the last thing she saw before losing consciousness was Eamon Stone fighting a brutal assault of magic that ripped into his body to give her the chance to escape.

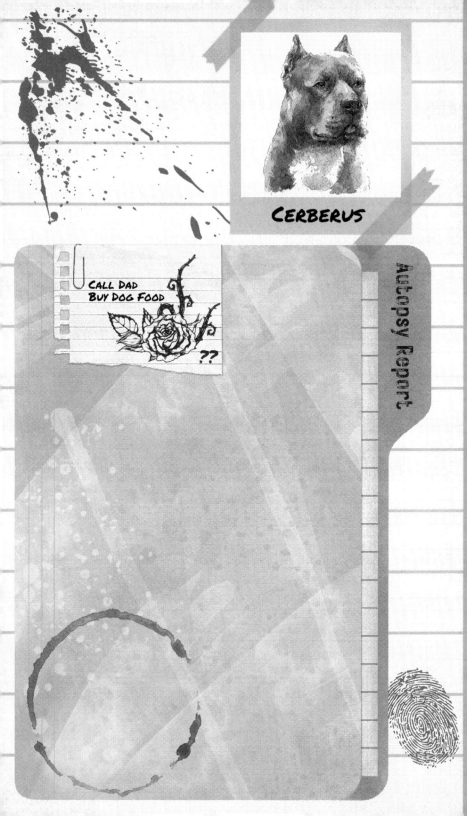

CERBERUS

CALL DAD
BUY DOG FOOD

??

Autopsy Report

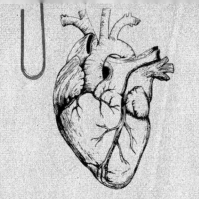

Chapter Twenty Eight

BEL KNEW THREE THINGS. SHE WAS NOT DEAD, CERBERUS' heavy head was lying on her stomach, and a solid wall of muscles supported her back. She blinked slowly in the darkness, registering that the excruciating pain in her chest had faded significantly, and her eyes trailed down to her heart. Her bloody shirt had been ripped open to reveal what should have been deep puncture wounds and a ruthless bite, but the teeth marks had vanished and her torn flesh looked less like claws had dug into her and more like aggressive scrapes surrounded by sickly purple bruises.

Bel lifted a tentative finger to her skin, the excessive blood coating almost every inch of her body not matching the barely-there wounds, and the movement jostled Cerberus' head. He jerked to attention and pushed his beefy snout against her cheeks, gifting her with slobbery kisses. Bel smiled as she pulled him closer, burying her face in his neck, and that was when she noticed the powerful hand resting on the dog's black coat. She stiffened, suddenly aware of who sat at her back. She was still mostly laying on the forest floor, but someone had settled behind her, cradling her shoulders and head on their chest as one muscled arm held her possessively while the other pet her pitbull.

"Any witch worth her salt keeps healing potions on hand." Eamon's voice rumbled through his ribcage, vibrating her back with its roughness.

"He's letting you pet him." Bel ignored Eamon's statement, transfixed by the closeness of her dog and her attacker. The pitbull was clearly a better judge of character than she, and he lay beside this dangerous man as if he was a long-lost friend.

"He's a good dog," Eamon said into her hair.

"He hated Vera... Alcina," she corrected, studying Cerberus' face for signs of discomfort, but the animal seemed to enjoy the man's attention. "He knew something was wrong."

"Like I said. He is a good dog."

"And he likes you." Bel tried to twist in Eamon's arms, but the pain in her chest froze her in place with a gasp. "Wait? Healing potion?"

"I found some in her cabin. I put it on your wounds to save you. You wouldn't have survived the trip to a hospital."

Bel looked down again at her bare chest, fingering the flesh where his teeth had ripped her open. The skin was whole and smooth, if not a little greasy. "Is there any more?"

"Yes."

"Could we use it?" She gently traced the purple bruise spreading viciously over her ribs.

"No." His tone was final, not allowing for arguments, and Bel twisted, trying to see his face. "We'll need to prove this was self-defense. I healed you as much as I could without erasing all the evidence."

"Self-defense?" Bel recalled where they were and scanned the forest floor, spotting a feminine hand poking out from behind a bush. "Is she...?"

"Yes." He didn't need to answer her, though. Alcina's hand was lifeless.

"I can't believe she was right under my nose, and I didn't see it." Bel scratched Cerberus' ears. "He did. He saw, and I should have listened to him. She killed all those people, and then I sat in her kitchen telling her about Garrett as if she was my friend." Emotions boiled over in her chest, and Bel swiped the tears that escaped with a bloody finger. Eamon's grip tightened possessively around her, and the fact that the thundering heart and warm embrace that kept her from spiraling into hysterics belonged to the man who had tried to carve her to pieces on two occasions baffled her. Yet here she lay, his possessive strength inexplicably comforting.

"No one suspected her," Eamon rumbled against her ear, and she was glad it was too dark to see him clearly. She could tell by the way his skin stuck to hers that he was still coated in her blood. "I didn't even know Vera and Alcina were the same person until just now."

"Is Vera…" Bel trailed off.

"Yes. In order to take her shape, Vera would have had to die. Your neighbor was most likely Alcina's first victim, since no one would suspect an old woman."

"I didn't." Bel's mind drifted back to the last time Emily Kaffe was seen alive in her security footage. Vera had been with her. Vera had been with all the victims, hunting them, stalking them… hunting Bel, and no one so much as blinked.

"I understand how," Bel huffed, wincing at the sharp pain the forceful breath shot through her ribs. *Understand?* That was an understatement. Until a few hours ago, she had refused to believe that magic existed outside of fiction. And Eamon…? She severed that train of thought at the root. Her mind could only process so much at once. "The impossibly clean crime scenes, the strength and skill required to kill those people. She used magic… like she did with me. Held me in the air and tried to rip out my heart." Bel flinched at the memory, fighting nausea at the knowledge that Garrett and the others had endured such an end.

"She was no ordinary witch," Eamon agreed. "Her power… it was darker. Stronger. Killing humans was easy for her."

"We thought it was multiple suspects, but if you possess magic, assembling furniture around a body would be simple. Disrupting security systems and convincing deputies to cut wires would have been easy, and the lack of sedatives." Bel wiped another tear from her eyes, knowing first-hand how Alcina's victims felt as magic held them still while she tore them open. "Her true nature explains the how, but why? Why kill innocent people and desecrate their bodies by turning them into monstrosities? Why kill Garrett?

"Isobel." He said her name as if she was his deity, his sovereign, his lover. "To explain her motive, I first must confess something unforgivable."

"You tried to kill me in New York," Bel said for him, and he stiffened against her back, his hand jerking softly against her belly as if unconsciously drawing her closer.

"You remember?"

"Only just last night… or tonight, actually." The conflict in his eyes played out again in her memory. "I dreamed about the attack, about you sinking your teeth into me and trying to flay me open, but this time, I didn't wake up like I usually did. The nightmare continued, and I remembered you stopping. I saw your face, the war you fought within yourself. It wore the same expression you did earlier when she forced you to drink."

"Isobel." This time her name was sorrow. "What I am… it is evil. Hunger. Death. It craves the darkness. It thirsts for blood. We are few, and I? I am unmatched. Alcina spent decades searching for one of my caliber, and when she found me in New York, she cursed me. She enacted an ancient ritual, one if completed, would bind me eternally to her. She would be my master, and I would have no choice but to obey. I refuse to even picture what this world would look like if a witch with Alcina's bloodlust gained control of my strength." Eamon shuddered against her, and the primal terror in his movement pricked Bel's skin with gooseflesh.

"The ritual requires a sacrifice to seal the curse," he continued. "One I had to slaughter." This time, it was Bel's turn to shudder. "Alcina set a trap, and a handful of officers arrived at the scene. The sacrifice could have been any of them, but fate chose you, and her magic trapped you. She began the ritual, and I lost all control of my body. My mind screamed for freedom, but then there you were, beautiful and alive, your skin impossibly sweet. The urge to kill you was so strong, your blood was on my tongue before I even knew I had moved."

"You were supposed to kill me?" Bel's voice was so soft, it almost disappeared on the wind. "But I saw you leave. You stopped yourself."

"Because." Eamon turned his face until his nose pressed against her jaw, and he breathed in deep. "You are the only person I cannot kill. I refuse to. The more I drank, the sweeter you tasted. I've never in all my years experienced anything like you." His lips brushed her jaw as he spoke, as if even his words wanted to kiss her. "I can't describe it. You wouldn't understand, but I recognized something in your blood. Fighting her curse was the most excruciating thing I've ever done, but I had to resist her for you. The pain was unbearable, but I finally ripped myself free and fled. I hated myself for leaving you to die, but if I stayed, I would have killed you. So, I ran, and you lived."

Eamon pulled back from her skin as if suddenly realizing what his lips were doing, and he cleared his throat. "It doesn't excuse my actions. I almost destroyed the most perfect thing I've ever experienced, but it wasn't my choice. I fought it, and even though I hate myself for harming you, I revel in the knowledge you lived." He released her dog and reached for her necklace, his fingers brushing the book charm gently, reverently. "I learned you liked to read, and I paid a witch to bless this. It offers protection, and then I left it in your hospital room. I vowed to stay away from you after that. The ritual was incomplete, the curse still half embedded in my DNA, and all it would take was one mistake on my part for Alcina to win."

"You gave this to me?" Bel reached up, their fingers brushing as they both gripped the pendant. Eamon didn't remove his hand, and while she should be terrified of him, should scream for help, she held her skin against his comforting warmth. "I always wondered who left it for me. I never take it off."

"I know," Eamon rumbled. "And promise me you never will. The witch who blessed it isn't the most powerful, but there's protection in her magic."

Bel nodded, lowering her hand as Eamon's words suddenly caught her attention. "The curse? If you killed me today, the ritual would be complete?" Eamon nodded against her hair. "That's why she forced you to bite me. She needed the sacrifice. Is that what you were arguing about when you said you would find a way?"

"Yes… and I'm sorry about how I behaved at the house. I was only trying to scare you. I wanted you gone, away from me and Alcina. I assumed you would get in your car since your dog was there, but then you ran into the woods."

Bel remembered the change in his voice as she fled, the reason for the shift suddenly making sense. "I only trespassed because I heard a struggle. I was worried she had come to murder you." Eamon smiled with a hint of triumph at her confession, and she squinted uncomfortably before adding, "Alcina was blocking my car door, so I decided to run to my cabin and call for help."

"She wasn't there when I came outside. I thought I scared you into that decision, but I should have known that even under pressure, you're never foolish." Understanding flooded his rough tone. "I left your dog in the car while I looked for her, figuring since you were heading home, you would be safe. It wasn't until Vera shifted back into Alcina that I caught her scent again. It mingled with yours, and I realized my mistake. I let your pitbull out then, but I'm faster. Thank goodness for him, though. I might have killed you this time if it weren't for that dog."

"When this is over, I'm making you a steak." Bel leaned forward and kissed Cerberus between the eyes, Eamon scratching his haunches. Cerberus practically smiled at her as the first greying signs of dawn encroached on the darkness. "So, she became Vera to hide her scent from you and get close to me, hoping you would complete the ritual. But why the other deaths? Why did they have to die?"

"Black magic always requires a sacrifice. She took their hearts to fuel her transformation. And the rest? Alcina was cruel, thriving on the suffering of others. It happens often to those cursed with immortality. What are humans with their decades-long lifespan to those who live forever? She was narcissistic and brutal, reveling in your fear. There is a reason they used to burn witches. Beings like Alcina, if left unchecked, will annihilate the earth.

"I also vowed to stay away from you. I never intended to move to Bajka, but I received word of an odd power here. I came to ensure you were safe, never intending to get close enough to scent you, but when I caught sight of Alcina in town, I decided to stick around and watch over you. She must have grown tired of waiting for my willpower to cave, and what better way to entice a detective into her trap than to give her unsolvable crimes? You are the only one with the experience needed for cases this bizarre. It was obvious you would be assigned to the investigation. She killed people I dealt with to force you to interact with me. She drained their blood to draw attention to what I am. If we met face to face, Alcina knew my control would eventually snap. She pushed you into my path, knowing you would be a dog with a bone if you found evidence of my guilt. And her predictions were correct, because there you were, invading my house in the middle of the night. Ever since that first day you interviewed me, my home has smelled of you, and it has driven me to madness."

"Was Garrett the scapegoat?" Bel couldn't focus on the constant reminders of his obsession with her scent, of the fact that he was not entirely human, and so she changed the subject, despite the pain Garrett's death brought her.

"I assume so. My guess is that she would have continued to kill, aiming the evidence against me until I could no longer stop myself from harming you, completing the bonding. We would have left Bajka, chained together for eternity, leaving Garrett to take the fall. She most likely didn't expect you to find the evidence in his bedroom so soon."

"I wasn't… we didn't…" Bel trailed off, unsure why she felt the need to justify her actions. "Why were you at the station that night?"

"The more dark magic she used, the more it drained her, and maintaining Vera's form would have been exhausting," he answered. "She rarely revealed her true self, but over the past few weeks, I scented Alcina more and more. Only in her own body could I locate her, and her hold on Vera's image must have been slipping. I followed her trail to the station, and I was terrified she had come for you."

"You've been protecting me this whole time?" Bel twisted to see him in the dimness, thankful that he had attempted to wipe most of her blood from his blond beard. "That text? The one warning me to run? That was you."

"Yes."

"How did you get my number?"

"I have my ways, Detective." He tucked her hair behind her ear, but she flinched, her mind spinning at his confession. She needed to escape his hold, to stop her heart from ruling her head. This man had tried to murder her twice, yet he was holding her like she was his entire world, his beloved beauty.

"I…" Bel pushed herself to her feet and stumbled, light-headed.

"Isobel?" Eamon stood, but she held a palm out to halt him.

"I'm a detective," she said. "I've lived for thirty-four years relying on facts and logic, so this—" she gestured between him and Alcina's corpse "—is a lot for me to take in. I believe you. I have to." She clutched her bruised chest as if to remind herself of the horrors. "You say you've been protecting me, but I'll never forget the way your teeth carved into my skin. The pain and sleepless nights you inflicted on me."

Eamon's face fell as if she had knifed him in the gut. His genuine care for her was an excruciatingly different picture than the monster from her memory, and she felt dizzy trying to reconcile the beauty before her to the beast from her past.

"I realize you're as much her victim as I am, but I need time."

"I'll give you all the time you need."

"You tried to kill me. I've been afraid for months because of you." Tears flooded her eyes with a vengeance. "You took something from me I can never get back. I fled my life and family because of you, and moving here brought Alcina hard on my heels. She destroyed so many lives, and now I'm the reason they're dead. The reason Garrett is dead." Bel ran her filthy fingers through her hair, and Eamon opened his mouth. She recognized by his expression that he was going to say this wasn't her fault, so she cut him off before his beautiful voice fell from his lips. "Bajka will expect answers. Demand justice. What am I supposed to tell them? That a witch cursed you and then used magic to slaughter people just to trap me? They'll lock me up and throw away the key for such a ridiculous tale. For God's sake, I saw her use magic, I felt it, and I'm not even sure I believe it." She was spiraling. Hyperventilating. The blood loss was making it difficult for her to stand.

"Isobel." Eamon stepped forward and placed a broad palm on

her chest, not over her heart, but on the right side where the scar ran down her breast. "Breathe," he ordered, and instinctively, she obeyed. "Good girl." He guided her breaths until she calmed.

"What am I supposed to do?" Bel sobbed. "What will I say to explain this?"

"I was just in her cabin." Eamon peeled his hand from her skin as if letting her go caused him pain. "The kitchen is clean, but the rest of the house is littered with magical objects and evidence of her crimes."

She met his gaze at his confession. *The kitchen is clean.* Her memory flashed to the nights when the nightmares stole her sleep. Vera had been cleaning her kitchen. Bel had assumed she was an insomniac with a passion for baking, but the only times she noticed her neighbor awake had been the nights of the murders. She hadn't been prepping cookies. She had been washing away the evidence.

"It's obvious she was stalking you," Eamon continued. "Combined with this scene of self-defense, you'll have no problem explaining her obsession with you. *Woman kills to entrap the object of her fixation.*" His voice mimicked a news headline.

"That will work, but... the magic? She became someone else. People saw a woman they believe was Vera. How do we explain Alcina? Or Vera's decayed body when we find it?"

"There's a reason I don't allow my photo to be taken." Eamon stepped closer, and Bel hated how the air burned electric between them. "It's why I requested that Brett Lumen turn off his cameras. It's difficult to explain why I don't age, especially when there's recorded proof. On the rare occasions where photography is necessary, I take... precautions. Ten minutes, and I can hide those precautions in Vera's house. Even your Sheriff would believe the narrative."

"You want to plant evidence?" Bel looked up at him in surprise, having to crane her neck at his towering height. The single photo of him she had found flashed in her memory, the reason for the differences between the image and the man suddenly making sense.

"Or we can tell him the truth." Eamon leaned down, closing the distance between them, causing Bel's breath to catch in her throat.

"Fine," she growled, annoyed at how angry she was at him and how badly she wanted him to fold her into his powerful embrace. "If we're going to do this, I need more than your *precautions*."

"Ask the world, and it's yours." Eamon's lips twitched in a smirk.

She rolled her eyes. "You're wealthy and extremely fast, correct?"

"I am."

"Good, because we've already wasted too much time." Bel shuddered at what she was about to ask Eamon to do. It went against every conviction her detective's heart clung to, but she saw no other way forward. "This is what I need from you."

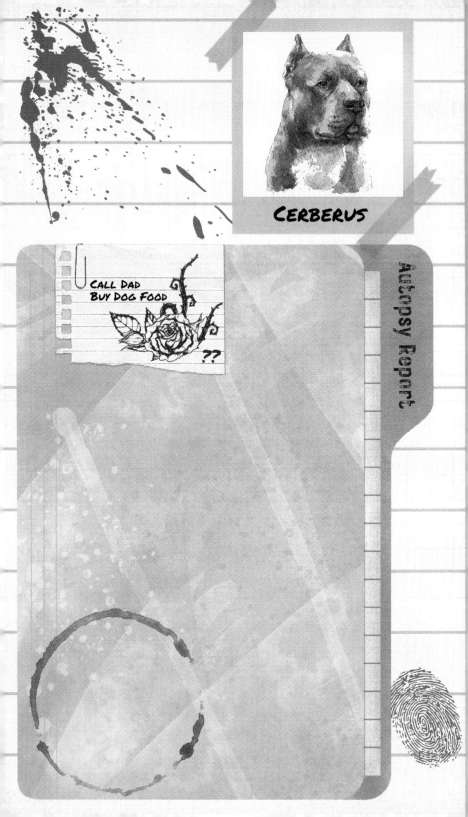

CERBERUS

CALL DAD
BUY DOG FOOD
??

Autopsy Report

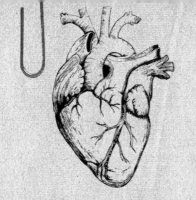

Chapter Twenty Nine

CERBERUS DID NOT LEAVE BEL'S SIDE AS DAWN APPROACHED. Light crept quickly through the trees, but Eamon was faster. A fact Bel was thankful for. Time would only tempt her to reconsider, and this was the only path she saw out of this chaos without sounding insane. But maybe she had lost her mind. Magic, witches, curses… beasts. She wanted to believe she hallucinated the whole thing, but her soul recognized the truth. An ancient darkness had followed her to this town, turning Bajka into its hunting grounds. There were unexplained evils in this world. Evils she had faced and survived. An evil that currently stalked through the trees toward her, a clean shirt in his fist.

Eamon paused before Bel, and she realized it was one of her tee shirts from her bedside dresser, ripped in ways it had not been the last time she saw it, and she chose to ignore the fact that she hadn't given him her house keys. Eamon crouched before her, rubbing the fabric along the ground to coat it in dirt and grass stains. He then dragged a broad palm caringly over her ruined shirt before wiping her blood onto the new one.

"Lean forward," he ordered, and when she obeyed, he ripped the shredded remains of her bloody top from her back before gently sliding the new one over her head. His movements were soft, worshipful, and if she hadn't been in such intense pain, she would have blushed that he saw her in only a bra. When he smoothed the tee shirt over her stomach, she realized the rips he created lined up with her injuries, the small hints of crimson making more sense with her healed cuts than the soaked shirt. She was glad he thought of it for her. Griffin would have taken one look at the blood oozing from her clothing and known something about their story didn't add up. The sheer volume of blood that had spilled from her chest should have killed her, but her current bruising and gouges weren't life-threatening.

"I'll be here the whole time," Eamon said, his hand still pressed possessively against her stomach, and Bel wasn't sure if it was the blood loss or the relief of survival, but his promise comforted her. He should scare her. She should hate him, and in a way she did, but she also felt dangerous threads stitching their souls together.

Bel nodded, unable to voice her emotions with words, and Eamon handed her the phone. She unlocked it and found the Sheriff's name, sucking in a lungful of air as she hit the call button.

"Emerson?" It was early, but Griffin answered on the second ring.

"Sheriff." She let the breath escape. "I've been attacked."

THE FOREST WAS a flurry of activity as Griffin led an army of officers and techs to her rescue. Lina arrived at the same time as the deputies, seizing control of Alcina Magus' body, and as the EMTs examined Bel, the Sheriff took her statement with panic stiffening his every muscle.

Bel and Eamon gave the same story. Alcina, posing as Vera, had attacked Bel in the woods while she was walking Cerberus.

The dog protected her until the commotion alerted Eamon, who was going for his customary early morning run. He came to their aid, but the altercation resulted in Alcina's death. Between the injuries coloring Bel's chest a disgusting purple, the blood staining her dog's fur, and the disturbance in the forest floor, it was obvious the killing had been in self-defense. Having already lost three officers, Griffin was more than happy to thank Eamon for saving Bel's life even if her insistence that Eamon was innocent confused him. She had been convinced he was the murderer, but when she explained how Alcina was masquerading as Vera, he understood as she did that Mr. Stone was merely a man in the wrong places at the wrong times. Bel told him of the woman's confession, and though most of it still baffled the Sheriff, understanding dawned in his eyes. No one, not even his own deputies, suspected the elderly Vera. A wolf in sheep's clothing until it was too late.

Griffin had tried to force Bel to go to the hospital, but she refused, and so there she stood in Vera's normal and cozy kitchen, mentally preparing herself to plunge into the woman's house. Eamon had done as she requested, but they would find more than just his *convenient* explanations.

"You don't have to do this," Sheriff Griffin said as he settled beside her in his matching protective gear. Eamon waited with Cerberus outside, but she needed to know. She needed to witness what she had lived next to for months, and as soon as the paramedics finished their exam, she pulled on the protective wear despite the onlookers' shock.

"Yes, I do," she answered, her eyes catching on an old recipe card hanging from a magnet on the fridge. *Rose shortbread cookies with rose water buttercream.* The same cookies Emily Kaffe planned to make the day of her death. It seems Vera had been the one to give her the idea. "I need to," Bel continued with a shudder of dread, and together they pushed into the house. The air changed the second they vacated the kitchen, a heavy oppression bearing down on their shoulders as the two watched the techs catalog the scene. And what a scene it was.

Bel's face was plastered everywhere, a dark shrine of sorts built below her photos, some of which dated back to her accident. Eamon had left every sign of magic in her home, and Bel was thankful he did. Only they knew just how real her power was, but the officers assumed the shrines confirmed Alcina's mental instability.

"Oh, my god." The Sheriff froze, his hand instinctively going to her elbow as if to protect her. "She's been following you since New York, doing all of this because she was obsessed with you? Was she the one who…" he trailed off, and Bel recoiled at the sight of her unaware self taped in an endless array across the wall. Her walking Cerberus, reading at her kitchen table, exiting her bathroom in nothing but a towel. She flinched, knowing Eamon hadn't planted these intrusive photos. No, these had hung next door for months, and she hadn't known. She had trusted this woman, ate in her home, spoke of her love life, and all the while, these violating photographs hovered mere feet away.

"Yes," Bel answered, struggling not to hyperventilate. "She was the one who tried to kill me in New York." It wasn't entirely a lie. "It appears she followed me to finish the job."

"And all the murders?" Griffin asked.

"To torture me. To draw me close. To remind me of my own near death."

"Emerson," his voice was disgusted. "I'm so sorry. I put you on the case. I threw you into this woman's crosshairs."

"She did that long before I ever met you, Sir."

"I hate that so much death is on our hands, but I'm glad she didn't kill you too. Thank goodness for that dog… and Stone. What are the chances he was running at the exact time she attacked you, but thank God for divine interventions, right?"

Bel swallowed, her skin burning at their deceptions. "He jogs here often, actually. I've seen him a few times."

Griffin studied her, eyes pinched as if he sensed something amiss, but then he turned back to the shrine, either dismissing the thought or choosing to ignore it. "Well, I'm glad he and that dog were there. We have to bury too many of our own already." He patted her shoulder with fatherly affection as a deputy approached them, an evidence bag firmly in his grip.

"Sheriff." He held the bag out for them to see, and Bel realized what Eamon meant when he said *precautions*. "We found prosthetics, wigs, and makeup in the bedroom. Seems this is how she posed as Vera without anyone noticing."

Bel held her breath, hoping the Sheriff would accept the evidence despite the holes in its reliability. Alcina had become Vera, assuming even her voice and mannerisms, and she worried the makeup wouldn't satisfy him. But after a few seconds, Griffin nodded.

"She was stalking her victims," he said, gesturing to photos hanging further down the hall. Some were of Lumen, Kaffe, and Legat, along with a few of Garrett and others she didn't recognize. "She must have watched Vera closely before assuming her identity."

"You knew her longer than I did," Bel said. "Did you notice a change in her? Perhaps we can pinpoint when Alcina took over her life."

"Honestly?" Griffin shrugged. "I couldn't tell you. Vera was elderly. Forgetfulness was nothing out of the ordinary." He shook his head. "How did this happen right under my nose?"

Bel didn't answer. How could she? She had slept only a grassy yard away from this monster, and her profile of the killer suddenly made sense. Someone who wanted attention, who wanted the glory. Bel had predicted the killer would revisit the scene, and Vera had been at each one, pretending to comfort the town with her motherly hugs and fresh cookies. She had Bel over for tea, letting a detective sit a single wall away from this web of insanity taped to the wallpaper. Bel was wrong about so many things on this case, but this one thing she had predicted correctly. Alcina had wanted a show, and as Vera she had claimed a front row seat to the madness.

"Sheriff?" a male voice called from the basement. "You need to see this."

Griffin and Bel exchanged a look before heading down the stairs. The sight that met them stilled their hearts for a second, and if the photos upstairs were proof of Alcina's guilt, the basement was the nail in her metaphorical coffin.

Tools littered the workspace along with wooden structures, metal carvings, screws, bleach, tarps, pulleys, and every other manner of damning evidence. Bel noticed immediately which object Eamon graciously left for them to discover. The larger mechanisms were his that he cleaned and planted to explain lifting the bodies, but the small leaf carvings, the wood shavings, and the metal wires? Those were undeniable testimony that Alcina had been posing as a caring grandmother to gain access to her victims. Whether the witch had used magic to help design the murder scenes or her eternal years gave her skills that rivaled Lumen's, it didn't matter. This basement had been transformed into a workshop, months of design work evident in the blueprints and the discarded failures. The officers photographed and cataloged the basement, but they wouldn't find traces of Eamon, not even on the pieces he planted. She felt guilty about asking him to fake evidence, but all he gave the police were real-world explanations for what magic had accomplished. Everything else? The true testament to her guilt had already been here. Been right below Bel's feet, inches from where she sat as she ate dinner with the woman she believed was her friend.

BEL EVENTUALLY DRIFTED BACK OUTSIDE, giving the Sheriff and the others space to work, but as she walked to where Eamon waited with her dog, a splash of color froze her in her tracks. She had always seen Vera's garden from her cabin, the tall bushes blocking its inner design, but this new angle, as she escaped the house, offered a full view of the red blooms. As if drawn close by an unseen cord, Bel moved for the roses, their crimson petals vibrant and delicate, but it was the snipped branches that captured her attention. Harsh cuts wilted where flowers had been severed. Branches died from where roses were pealed apart and assembled into beautiful hearts.

Bel wasn't sure how long she stood staring at the bushes, but then suddenly she was moving, yelling for help. She knew. Deep down she knew, and within minutes, deputies crowded around her, Lina Thum hovering in wait. Bel felt Eamon's eyes on her as they dug, and as the shovels fractured roots and displaced dirt, Vera came into view. The real Vera, buried beneath her roses, her heart ripped out and missing.

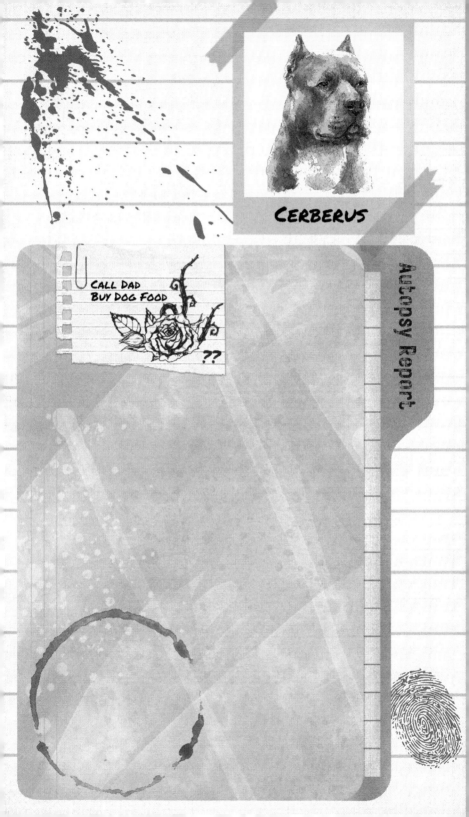

CERBERUS

CALL DAD
BUY DOG FOOD

??

Autopsy Report

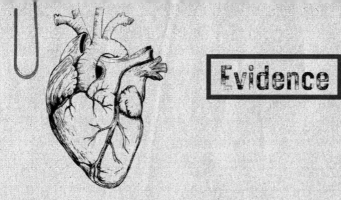

Chapter Thirty

THEY DID NOT LAY ROSES ON GARRETT'S GRAVE AS THE TOWN said goodbye to their public servant and friend, as the force said goodbye to their detective, as Bel said goodbye to the man she cared for. The man she hoped she might one day love.

When the time came, she stepped to his coffin and placed her tulip atop the shining wood, tears spilling from her eyes. There had been too many funerals, too much heartbreak, and Bel lifted her fingers to her lips and pressed a kiss to his coffin. She prayed that wherever he was, it was a place of peace.

The funeral ended, and Bel stayed at the reception to pay her respects, but the pain in her bruised chest and her broken heart begged her to go home and lay down. Eamon's foresight helped sell the self-defense narrative, but every inch of her torso screamed for relief. She couldn't consume any more of the healing potion since a miraculous recovery would raise too many questions, and so she was forced to endure the aftermath of her assault. She should be thankful his quick thinking had kept her from bleeding out, but every time her mind traveled down that path, she pictured Garrett laid to rest. No one had come to his rescue. He had bled out, and Bel wanted to hate Stone for visiting the station that night but missing Alcina's attack. It wasn't his fault as much as it wasn't hers, but in her sorrow, it was simpler to condemn the beast in their midst. It was easier to be angry at him than to admit that despite the trauma he had inflicted, she couldn't bring herself to hate the stranger infiltrating her life. She had experienced the impossibly strong magic. She had been helpless to fight it, and that Eamon defied the curse for her was a magnitude she was currently unwilling to unpack. So, she cried and hugged the funeral attendees, and then she left, letting Eamon's absence at the funeral bear the weight of her blame. Somehow, she knew he would accept and carry it for her even if he was there.

Cerberus seemed to sense her need for oblivion when she arrived home, and he curled his muscled body around her as she fell asleep still wearing her black dress, and for the first time in months, the nightmares abandoned her. There were no teeth. There was no terror. Only a deep sorrow that lulled her into the peaceful sleep she so desperately needed.

Cerberus let her rest, but hours later, he woke her with a tap dance of nails against the wood floors. Bel sat up, surprised by her dreamless nap, and smirked at her dog. She'd been so emotionally drained when she got home that she forgot to take him outside, and his pacing spoke volumes about how badly he needed a walk. She considered changing out of the black dress, but she didn't have the energy, so she shoved her feet into her sneakers and clipped on his harness.

The minute she opened the front door, Cerberus bolted for the woods, and Bel hesitated as she stared at the encroaching trees. She hadn't set foot near the forest since the attack. Alcina was gone, the sensation of being watched vanishing with her, but the pain and helplessness of that night were seared into Bel's brain. Cerberus, though, possessed no such qualms about his favorite hiking spot, and as he dragged her enthusiastically for the tree line, she chose to confront her anxiety, thankful for the dog to guide her through the stress. He'd proven himself her worthy defender, and Bel knew adopting him hadn't been an accident. No one at that shelter had wanted the black pitbull with the cropped ears and the meaty face. She used to pity him for his abandonment, but now she realized her pity had been misguided. He hadn't been abandoned. He had simply been waiting for her.

After doing his business, Cerberus found a stick and shoved it into her hand. With a smile, Bel launched it into the trees, and the dog tore after it. She waited for him to return, but after a few minutes, his black fur still hadn't re-emerged from the leaves.

"Cerberus?" she called, picking up her pace, that familiar fear bubbling in her chest. "Come here, baby beast."

"Hello, Detective." The seductive gravel crackled over her skin, electrocuting her heart with its deep perfection.

Bel's blue eyes followed the sound, unable to resist its call, and Eamon stepped into the open, Cerberus glued to his side as he waited for his new friend to throw the stick.

"Are you following me?" Bel asked as Eamon tossed the makeshift toy, and Cerberus leaped after it. Her voice sounded accusatory and harsh, but after the emotions of the funeral, she didn't trust herself around the perfection captured in this man's skin.

"Would it bother you if I was, Detective?" He stepped closer, as if to force her to acknowledge her awareness of him.

"I could arrest you for stalking a police officer."

"But you won't, my little Detective. You like my eyes on you." He gently captured her jaw and tilted her head up. She hated how her skin burned to life at his touch, how his words rang true as she stared up at his looming height.

"Was that you? Those nights I felt someone watching me?" She despised the way her voice sounded as she both feared and hoped it had been his black eyes hunting her.

"Sometimes." Cerberus returned, bumping Eamon's leg with the stick. He took it from the dog, who tap danced in place until

Eamon launched it down the path. "Other times it was Alcina stalking you as Vera since your neighbor's was the only scent I detected. I'm sure you knew the difference in our gazes."

Bel opened her mouth, but her words were unnecessary. He recognized the realization in her eyes. The times when terror licked like hungry flames at her skin, that had been Alcina. Her memory flickered to that morning when she spoke to her father. She hadn't even realized Eamon was watching her until she caught sight of him. His watchful gaze felt different. Safe, protective, possessive.

Eamon smiled a wicked grin as he leaned forward and breathed her in, his eyes closing for a second as he savored her scent. The action surprised Bel, and when his eyes opened, they found hers harsh and confused.

"I thought..." she cleared her voice. "I thought with Alcina dead, the curse would be broken."

"It is."

"But..." she trailed off, unsure how to put his hunger into words.

"I still crave you," he answered for her, stepping so close, his chest almost brushed hers. "The undeniable urge to kill you was lifted with her death, but I've tasted you, my little Detective. Every part of me wants every part of you. Your scent is intoxicating."

She should move. She should step back.

"She's dead. I'm safe now. You don't need to watch me." Bel whispered, stepping forward so her dress brushed against his shirt. "You can leave."

"Isobel." He lifted a hand and tucked her hair behind her ear, the way he said her name enough to light the world on fire. "You're a part of me now, and I will always be able to sense you. I can no more leave you than I could stop the sun from rising. No matter how far you flee, I will feel you. I cannot abandon you to suffer this life's dangers. You are mine to protect."

"I don't need you to protect me." She tried to deny the way his declaration settled in her chest and fused to her bones.

"I know, Isobel." He stepped back, and she gasped for breath at his sudden absence. "But I will protect you all the same."

"Will you protect me from yourself?"

"I am evil, but not the evil you hunt," he repeated his sentiment from the other day. "I am a killer, but your life is one I will not allow to end."

"You shouldn't admit that to a detective."

"You're one of the few people in this world to see me for who I am. I won't hide from you, Isobel Emerson."

Bel gasped slightly at the way her name left his tongue. Who was this man, this beast, that both terrified and comforted her? "If you ever so much as step one foot out of line, I will offer you no mercy."

"I would expect nothing less."

"And there's no way for me to convince you to leave Bajka and me alone?"

"None."

Bel captured her dog's leash and pulled him back toward the cabin for dinner. "Then I guess I'll be seeing you, Eamon Stone."

"It's been a pleasure, Detective, as always." His whiskey-smooth voice wrapped around her like sunlight and smoke, and she waved her hand over her head at him without a backward glance as she and Cerberus left the forest.

EAMON WATCHED Bel and her dog walk home, but he stayed rooted to the spot she left him standing on. Isobel Emerson. His little Detective. He told her the truth, mostly, but there was one fact he kept hidden. If he told her what he tasted in her blood, the truth about why he could never leave her side, she would have been alarmed, and he had already caused his beautiful woman enough fear. He would fight an endless war to earn her forgiveness. He would sacrifice himself to save her life, but this? It wasn't the time for her to know, so he kept that knowledge to himself, content knowing that she hadn't cast him out. He could be patient. He was older than he cared to remember and had endured those years before her. He could endure a while longer.

He stood in the woods until the sun set and her scent disappeared. Even at this distance, he could see her clearly through her cabin window. She was making the first proper meal he'd seen her cook, complete with a steak for her dog, and he could tell by the way she spoke on the phone, it was her father. He couldn't stop a smile from gracing his face. His detective was eating, healing, sleeping. He was proud of his beautiful Isobel.

The moon rose, and finally, Eamon turned to go home, when he froze, his skin pricking with awareness. He rarely felt fear, his strength a monster even among the beasts, but the scent that wafted on the breeze was foreign. A scent of danger, of a threat. Eamon Stone took a deep breath, but there was no mistaking that smell. Another predator had entered Bajka. A predator he did not recognize.

THANK YOU FOR READING AUTOPSY OF A FAIRYTALE. BEL, EAMON, & CERBERUS WILL BE BACK FOR ANOTHER FAIRYTALE INSPIRE CRIME SOON. YOU MAY FOLLOW THEM ON KINDLE VELLA OR WAIT FOR THE BOOK TWO TO COME OUT, BUT FOR NOW, IF YOU ENJOYED THIS BOOK AND FEEL COMFORTABLE LEAVING A REVIEW, I WOULD GREATLY APPRECIATE IT. REVIEWS GO A LONG WAY IN HELPING AUTHORS LIKE ME.

Also by Nicole Scarano

About the Author

Nicole writes fantasy, sci-fi, mystery, & romance as Nicole Scarano & steamy fantasy & sci-fi romance as N.R. Scarano. She doesn't like to box herself into one genre, but no matter the book, they all have action, true love, a dog if she can fit it into the plot, swoon-worthy men & absolutely feral females.

In her free time, Nicole is a dog mom to her rescued pitbull, a movie/tv show enthusiast, a film score lover, and sunshine obsessive. She loves to write outside, and she adores pole dancing fitness classes.

For all links & to sign up for her newsletter visit:
linktr.ee/NicoleScarano

 instagram.com/nicolescarano_author
 tiktok.com/@nicolescarano_author
 twitter.com/nicolerscarano
 facebook.com/nicolescaranoauthor

Printed in Great Britain
by Amazon